The Double Cross

The Double Cross

Anna J

www.urbanbooks.net

Urban Books, LLC
300 Farmingdale Road, N.Y.-Route 109
Farmingdale, NY 11735

ISBN 13: 978-1-64556-011-1
ISBN 10: 1-64556-011-2

First Trade Paperback Printing March 2020
Printed in the United States of America

10 9 8 7 6 5 4 3 2

Distributed by Kensington Publishing Corp.
Submit Orders to:
Customer Service
400 Hahn Road
Westminster, MD 21157-4627
Phone: 1-800-733-3000
Fax: 1-800-659-2436

Also by Anna J

Novels

Anthologies

Independent Projects

Acknowledgments

Father God, I thank you for this opportunity. Sometimes when we are blessed with so many talents, we have no idea what to do with it. Oftentimes we take advantage of it, thinking it will always be here. They say if you don't use it, you lose it. I'm witness that you can use it and still lose it. I don't deserve it, but you just keep giving me chances to shine. You keep preparing this table before my enemies. You keep giving me one creative idea after the next to execute without trouble. I am a firm believer that no matter how many weapons are formed against me, they can't touch me because of you.

Carl Weber, thanks for holding a seat for me in the Urban Books family. You asked me years ago why I stopped writing, and what I was waiting on, but I didn't have a real reason. . . . Still don't. Just know that I'm back like I never left, and I'm grateful for the opportunity to do what I love again. Not many people get signed to a major publishing house, walk away, and get to go back. Thanks for the blessing. I had a lot of false starts, but being able to go back home was well worth the effort.

N'Tyse . . . girl! When I say you showing all the way out in these streets! When I first contacted Diane Rembert about a short story opportunity she posted on FB, she asked me was I interested in representation instead. I was nervous because of things that happened in the past, and my trust wasn't all the way there because of those experiences, but I decided to just do it. Y'all are phenomenal! I really can't thank you enough for orchestrating my come back. You, Diane, and the entire team are lit! You listened to my intent, heard my concerns, and fulfilled our vision flawlessly. I look forward to all the BGM we will create together.

Who has the best wife in the world? I do! Dynita, I have no clue how you put up with me. I'm either writing, baking, crafting, working, in school, working some more . . . and you are supportive through all of it. My mind NEVER rests, and you never hesitate to get me whatever I need to see my vision through. I'm happy you were chosen for me. I don't think anyone else would be able to do it so effortlessly.

I also have the best sister in the world! Tiff, you been rocking with me since book one and before that. I appreciate you, but you already know this. I always tell everyone how dope you are. Thanks for always supporting my whims, even though it takes me forever to make my mind up sometimes.

Marlaka and Tanya . . . got this book done, y'all! You both listened to me ramble about the story line and gave me ideas on what should happen along the way. I just met y'all a year ago and had no idea I would love y'all like I do. Thanks for everything. Y'all are stuck with me for eight hours a day, five days a week, and even after work and on the weekends periodically. You deserve all the blessings you have coming for dealing with my craziness!

Readers, you ever just have to sit down for a minute and get your life together? At one point in my writing career, I thought I would always have a story to tell. Who knew a seven-year hiatus would come into play? (Last novel, *Exposed: When Good Wives Go Bad*, dropped in 2013.) I'm thankful to be back. Y'all never gave up on me, always asking me when my next book was coming out. Even when "they" tried to dog me out. It was so

Acknowledgments

many hurdles, and for a while, I thought it would never happen, but the way that prayer is set up . . . just saying. It hit different when you let HIM work his magic. I hope this read is up to your standards. I thank you for your continued support. And as always, be sure to spread the word!

~Anna J

The Double Cross

Friendship is designed to test your patience and gives you the super power to detect bullshit. . . .

Get ready for the ride.

Selah Gordon

When Digging A Ditch

"Dig just a little more. We don't want the body to sur-face for any reason. I don't feel like sitting in jail because of this man's foolishness." I instructed my friends to dig deep as we worked on our makeshift grave for my boyfriend's body. We didn't need any mishaps.

I never thought the day would come when I would really have to body this dude. I'd threatened to kill him many times, but for it to come to fruition was mind blowing. We loved each other. I mean really *loved* each other. That Jada Pinkett and Will Smith kind of love. That Aja and Fatin/*Surrender to Love* kind of love. That no-matter-what-you-do-I'll-never-leave-you love. I still loved him, and I would always love him, even though I had to let him go. Wait . . . that last line was a complete lie. You definitely couldn't do whatever you wanted to me and expect to get away with it. I still loved him, but that wouldn't last much longer. I felt like when I met Chase, I had finally found the one I was going to spend the rest of my days with. We were going to have beautiful babies, the crib with the picket fence, matching cars, pool out back . . . all that and more like a Philly Offset and Cardi B. Why did he have to go and mess up a good thing? Why did he betray me?

Our story was right out of a fairy tale. Girl meets thug, thug sees she's the shit, girl puts it on him, thug wifes her up, the end. We were like glue, the two of us. When people saw him, they knew I wasn't far behind, and vice versa. A couple that partied together stayed together, and we were always on the scene as a unit. Everybody knew he was my man and I was his girl, but you always have one person who thinks they're a damn superhero and wants to mess up a good thing. Sometimes it's the closest person to you, and they have to get dealt with accordingly no matter the relation—the one who knows all your secrets because you have to tell somebody some of the shit you did. It's not right, keeping all that mess bottled up inside. It causes constipation. Sometimes they're right on the scene when the tea spills, and hopefully, you can trust them enough to wipe that shit up and keep it moving without telling all that missed it how it really went down. Adjust your sister's crown without telling everyone on Facebook it was crooked. When they're close, it makes it a little harder, but not impossible. All is fair in love, and having me fucked up about my man, no one is off limits.

Now, I'll just go ahead and admit it to clear the air before we go any further because I need you to know how serious this shit is. Killing Chase was not an accident. Not in the slightest, and definitely on purpose. That was a straight shot to the dome at point blank range that landed square in the center of his forehead. I warned him numerous times that I would kill him before seeing him with another bitch. I guess he thought I was playing. Sharing my dick unknowingly and unwillingly was not a joking matter, and not to be taken lightly. Some shit just ain't funny.

The bitch had hers coming, too. Let's not get that fact fucked up. She was currently tied up unconscious in a basement not too far from where we were located. I was still trying to decide what I was going to do with her, and if I was going to spare her life. *If* I should spare her life. I wasn't convinced at the moment that she deserved to live, but I was open to discussing it with her if she could make some sort of sense of this mess. She was one of the close ones that blindsided me with deceit. The least I could do was hear her out, right? I'd leave it up to her on whether she lived to tell the story or died trying to convince me to believe a lie. Ultimately, the choice was hers.

That was a rare occurrence, sparing one's life in a life or death situation. It was not something that happened on a day-to-day basis. You could run the risk of them eventually spilling the beans, and we simply couldn't have that. People can't hold water without having to piss, so holding a secret was out of the question. Guilt made you do strange things. This one was close to my heart, though, and it hurt me what I might have to do to her. I was okay with living with guilt, though. I'd been doing it for years, but that's a story for another time. I wore guilt like a great pair of Spanx under a skintight dress. I kept shit tucked nice and tight. Right now, the most important thing was finishing the task at hand. We were losing darkness, and this type of matter definitely didn't need to see the light of day.

"I think we're good now. He won't be found for a while. You wiped him down good, right?" Skye, my home girl since pre-K, questioned as she climbed out of the hole, then reached back to pull me up. This was true friendship with us. She rode harder for me than I did for myself when it came to my well-being, and I knew for sure when things started looking crazy to me that she had been peeped it long before I had, but was giving me time to see for myself before we busted a move. Hell, initially this crazy fool was ready to go dig a hole in the cemetery to ensure he was never found. That's how you know the love is real. That's how I knew she would never be one to betray me in any fashion. That's how I knew that I would need her support until the very end, and there was no question in my mind that I had it hands down, one hundred percent.

Mount Moriah Cemetery had been closed to the public for years. The only time people went there was to visit loved ones previously buried on the grounds prior to closing and to upkeep the land, which was mostly done by prisoners or people serving some type of community service order. There wasn't a chance that someone would catch us digging at night, but the police rotation was heavy on Cobb's Creek, especially on a Friday, and I didn't want to chance it. I also had to remind her that it was against the law. I mean, so was burying a body in the back yard of an abandoned house in the bottom of West Philly, but we were less likely to get caught this way. Hood shit gets done in the hood where even if someone saw it, they didn't see it. They weren't about to say a damn thing out of fear of being next on the hit list. We were good right where we were.

"He's clean as a whistle," Vice answered as I reached back to get her out of the same hole. We were ride or die as a clique and known to not be the ones to play with on any occasion—a truth we'd had to prove on more than one occasion, unfortunately. It was a shame some had to learn the hard way. "My hands are going to smell like bleach for a week," she complained as she inspected her manicure. She was the extra prissy one of the group, but she wasn't afraid to get her hands dirty when the time came for it. No pun intended. I could dig it, though. A gel fill-in with the works cost upwards of $150 at Luxxe Nail Salon and Spa, so I already knew if anything as little as a rhinestone was missing, her next shop trip was on me—and thanks to Chase, I definitely had the money to cover it.

No more words were needed. We simultaneously gloved our hands, turned, and went for the body first wrapped in a sheet, and then in industrial sized black trash bags (to prevent leakage) to deposit into the earth. You'd be surprised how quickly a body starts to break down and decompose in the heat of the summer, and his body was already starting to smell because we had to hide him for a few days before coming to dig. I tried not to think about his rotting body sitting in my trunk, probably filling with worms as we speak. It didn't have to be this way.

Damn it, Chase! Why did you do this to us?

We respectfully handled his carcass as we half pulled, half carried him from the trunk to the hole, gently lowering him in enough so that it wouldn't be too far of a drop, and then letting him go on the count of three. He hit the soft dirt with a small thud, and a tear dropped from my eye as we dropped in three black roses. It didn't have to be this way, but he really made me do it. Just thinking about it made me want to jump in behind him and stomp him down two more feet. We were set up to live the best life ever, and now this.

Now wasn't the time to show weakness, though, so I wiped my tears, smudging dirt on my face in the process, and grabbed a shovel to help cover the body quickly before someone caught our black asses back there. Each pile of dirt that hit his body sounded like it echoed throughout the entire neighborhood, and I started to sweat a little as paranoia set in. There was no way to explain away a pile of dirt, a dead body, and shovels at this time of night. This would surely have us locked in the clink if we got caught, and no one had time for that. Once we were done, we packed the dirt down as neatly as possible, spreading the over-spill carefully across the rest of the yard so that it lay flat, and removed all physical evidence that we brought with us. As we walked out from behind the house, Skye used a broom to sweep away our footprints until we got to the concrete. We didn't want any trace of our ever stepping foot on this property, and we surely weren't waiting for rain or some other element to hide it for us. Clearly, this wasn't our first time at the rodeo, and we knew how to cover our tracks. I'd watched way too much Crime TV to get caught on an amateur move. The first thing they looked for was boot tracks.

We removed our shoes and jumpsuits when we got to the car parked at the end of the alleyway, depositing them into a trash bag that would be burned in the furnace once we got back to the projects later in the day. Tasker Homes was a popular dumping ground to hide your filth, and no one would say a word. It was also important to not have all the evidence in one place. If you're hiding a body down the bottom, you get rid of the shovels in Germantown, the clothing in South Philly, and the shoes in Clifton Heights. The cops would have to go on a wild goose chase for real to connect our shit that easily. Everything was burned to a crisp, and the ashes were let loose in the wind. Catch me if you can; I'm faster than the gingerbread man.

I had been casing this house for a minute once I realized Chase had to be dealt with accordingly. It was located in the bottom of West Philly (around that 38th and Haverford area near Olive Street, or what others may know as The Evil O), so Chase's body probably wasn't the only one rotting there. This neighborhood was known for never finding the missing that were plastered on the news and telephone poles daily. There were always people outside 24/7/365, but if asked any questions, they were all like Stevie Wonder to the bullshit. Nobody saw a damn thing.

When folks around these parts got rid of a body, they really got rid of it. It wasn't uncommon for a body to be crushed with a few cars at a dump on Essington Ave. or dumped in the river by Bartram's Garden. Just as long as you did your dirt in silence, no one questioned it. Ever. Unless, of course, they wanted to be next on a milk carton. If, by chance, your body was found, that wasn't a mistake. That was a clear warning for the family to back the fuck off. Ten times out of ten they listened. Besides, all they really wanted was closure, right? That's all any of us ever wants, and even then that's not enough.

We rode back to the spot in silence, my heart getting heavier each block we got closer to the bitch. I was torn on what to do with her. She of all people knew what the deal was when it came to my man. She was there from the beginning when I met Chase. What happened to our bond? She had me questioning my loyalty and shit, and it did not sit well with me. Was it jealousy? Was it boredom? Was she lied to? Was he lied to? They definitely both lied to me, and that was the most fucked up part about the situation. Lord knows I didn't want to put it all on him. Bitches are just as scandalous as men most times.

I was so confused about how they even had time to link up, but I was not naive to the fact that folks made time for what they wanted. When Chase and I weren't together, we were forever on Face Time. If we couldn't talk, we were texting. He never missed a beat, but come to find out, the slick ones never did. They knew how to play the game all too well—until they met me. You couldn't out-slick a slickster. I invented the game, honey. All who played, played by my rules.

"Selah, I know this one really hit home for you. It's hitting all of us equally as hard. Know whatever you decide, we rocking with you without a doubt. You're not

alone in this, sis. We promise." Skye always had a way of
making all the dirt we did seem not as bad.

Vice hugged me from around the back seat, and for
the first time since this entire mess took place, I really
allowed myself to cry and get it out. A good, ugly cry that
I wasn't even expecting. I was too shocked when I first
found out to feel anything other than rage, and for the
first time in weeks, I realized that my best friend was
gone. No amount of missing persons flyers or Facebook
posts would bring him back, and I had to walk through
the rest of my life knowing that I was the reason he was
now a hashtag.

I let Chase invade my space, something I rarely ever
did. I let him into my space in more ways than I'd
ever let anyone else in, and he did me the dirtiest. I
would miss him, but I'd never forgive him; and if I did
eventually forgive him, I'd never forget how he made me
feel in this moment. The wall was back up, and it would
take someone with super human strength to knock it
down again. My trust level was at zero, unfortunately,
and I just couldn't deal right now.

We pulled up to the spot after stopping quickly to get
beverages and some wings for Skye's greedy ass. Come
to find out, burying a body left you a little thirsty, and
for some of us, hungry. I couldn't believe how nervous I
was getting. My girls must have sensed it because Skye
reached over and grabbed my hand, and Vice put her
hand on my shoulder. We came to handle business, and
whatever happened, it was what it was going to be.

I felt like my bowels were about to betray me and I
was going to shit all over the place if I didn't move fast.
Clenching my butt cheeks, I removed myself from the
vehicle and made my way into the house where Chase
and his crew used to bust traps. They had to move the
operation after word got in the wind that the feds were on
to them, so now his old-ass aunt just lived there.

She had to be like eighty years old, but she didn't take care of herself during her lifetime, so she could pass for a smooth hundred-year-old without a doubt. Years of hard liquor and drug use (weed, sometimes coke) had her barely hanging on, but she was no trouble. She mainly stayed in her room, sometimes coming down to eat because we always made sure she had what she liked. You might catch her on the stoop on a summer night catching a cool breeze, but honestly, she was no trouble. Everyone in the neighborhood knew her and respected her, so they never allowed anyone to bring harm her way and were always ready to help her in need. She turned her hearing aid off when she didn't want to be bothered, and she never answered the phone or the door. Even though I killed her nephew, I felt like I had a duty to take care of her until she passed. I just hoped we wouldn't walk in one day and find her dead on the toilet or some shit, but so far, we'd been good. She never heard us bring in the bodies, and when I went to check on her, she said she was turning in for the night. That just meant we were cool to handle our business without being bothered. That was three days ago.

When we got to the basement, the bitch was wide awake, looking scared as hell with a tear-streaked face. A lump had started to form on her forehead and get dark from Skye knocking her unconscious two days in a row. She refused to stay asleep, and I couldn't make up my mind about what I wanted to do with her. We could tell that she must have been trying to get loose, but we had her bound and gagged so tight there was no way she was getting out on her own. If I learned nothing else from the Girl Scouts, I learned how to tie a good knot.

My anger returned instantly, but I was known for keeping my cool, even in the most stressful situations. Skye and Vice, not so much. It was a very rare occurrence

that I acted on pure emotion, and putting a bullet in
Chaos was one of those moments. I wasn't sure if I
regretted it yet. I could tell they wanted to pounce on her,
especially Skye, but because of the delicate nature of the
situation, they too remained as cool as they could, letting
me get this one off on my own.

I helped them sit her up in a chair, her sobs bouncing
off the damp walls and echoing throughout the space,
sounding like we were in a haunted house and she was
hired to do sound effects. I didn't have an ounce of
sympathy for her. She didn't have any for me when she
broke up my home. I was sure she was remorseful for
what she did, or at the very least, sorry she got caught. I
hadn't given her the chance to explain herself because, in
all honesty, it didn't really matter. Once you bit the hand
that feeds you, it didn't matter what happened afterward.
The hand was already bit, and there was no taking it
back. There was no explaining this one away. There was
no taking back what was done. No rewind button. No do
over. Now was the time for payback.

I grabbed a chair and took a seat across from her,
crossing my legs at the thighs. The smell of urine, feces,
and sweat was wafting around her body like stank off a
dead fish. My leg bounced heavily, a true sign that I was
pissed way the fuck off. I was sure my sister recognized
it because she reacted the same way when she was upset.
Guess we were more alike than we thought. Staring into
her eyes, I saw they were identical to mine. Nose, lips,
eyebrows . . . everything an identical twin sister would
possess. We shared a sac together in our mother's womb.
She was my first best friend. *Through thick and thin,
could never bend*: That was our motto from the time
we could communicate. I was not sure what changed
with us, but I couldn't help but feel as we got older, she
became jealous of me. I was always the fun twin, the

outspoken and rebellious one. The life of the party. Everybody wanted to be squad. Even her, but she had a shoo-in because she was blood. Come to find out blood was not always thicker than friendship, and sometimes ran thinner than water.

She had her own fair share of friends, though, all completely opposite from my friends, just like she was the exact opposite of me. More reserved. Bookworm. Grades always more important than being popular. Shy. All we had that matched were looks. Everything else belonged to two different people. It killed me to have to do this. I didn't want to, and as much as she begged and pleaded for me to hear her out, all I could see was her riding my man's dick and loving it. Both of them looked like they couldn't be in a better place than where they were right in that moment. Neither one of them gave a fuck about me at the time, and now it was my turn to return those same sentiments.

He was balls deep in the pussy, holding her body as she rode him in reverse cowgirl. Her back was arched so tight she was damn near bent perfectly backward, and the sopping sound that came from her pussy assured us all that she was wetter than an umbrella during a downpour. I was standing there in shock for at least sixty seconds before they realized I was in the room, smelling the sex in the air, making it hard for me to breathe. The sounds that came out of his mouth were like nothing I'd ever heard when he and I made love; and my dear sister . . . her eyes were shut so tight she was probably pushing her eyeballs out the back of her skull. That shit felt amazing to both of them. I could see it all over their faces.

I briefly wondered what she was thinking as her facial expression changed from being near orgasm to seeing her twin standing there watching it all. Was her pussy tighter than mine? Juicer? Felt better?

He tried to explain himself as he pushed her off him, and all ten inches of his meaty dick glistened from her juices, no sign of a condom in sight. His seed spilled out uncontrollably from both of them, making his legs weak as he tried to stand. I was deaf to him at that point and disposed of him quickly. She wanted to scream, but the sound was stuck in her throat. One shot from the door square in the middle of his head. I had to before I changed my mind. For him, I hoped it was worth the betrayal. For her, I hoped it was worth destroying our bond.

When it came to my dear sister, this shit was hard as fuck, and I just couldn't make up my mind. Neither Skye nor Vice had an opinion because they learned from the past that once I made up my mind, that was what it was going to be. I stared at her—eyes that matched mine, tears that were identical to the ones I'd been shedding for weeks. I looked her dead in the eyes to see what I missed, and I wondered how I was going to tell our mother her daughter was dead.

Selah

365 Days Ago

There was no doubt in my mind that I had chosen the right one this time. After going through quite a few of the bullshit men that Philly had to offer, I really wasn't beat or easily impressed by these dudes. They were corny, for lack of a better description. Everybody label-chasing and label-crossing, but nobody really had shit of their own. Walking around mixing labels and shit, looking ridiculous. Gucci shoes. Hermes belt. True Religion jeans. Designer everything, all courtesy of the Premium Outlets and 52nd Street stands, but all that shit was stacked neatly in their momma's house in the dresser they been using since they were three, or in a Rubbermaid tote stored behind their bedroom door. I was not about to be having quiet sex because your mom was in the next room or your little brother a bed over. I needed more to my man than a good shot, and when I met Chase, it was like a breath of fresh air.

His swag was incredible. A quiet confidence, a very humbled soul that Philly dudes knew nothing about. He knew he had the juice but wasn't in your face with the shit. He had a silent power that had chicks all over the city flocking to be in his presence, and out of all the bad bitches he had to pick from, he chose me, Selah Gordon from Lansdowne, a long-haired, thick, redbone (sung in my Lil' Wayne voice) with a light splash of freckles across the bridge of my nose and hazel eyes that changed depending on what type of mood I was in. Pretty beyond comparison, most would say, but I also knew my strength, so I wasn't cocky about it. I was a good catch, not to be thought of as average. I had the juice, too.

He knew it, and that's why he wanted me so bad. Oh, I brushed him off for a long time, but Mr. Chase Warren was very persistent. He could have easily had my gullible-ass twin, but he knew I was the one that had the spark. He knew my fire was brighter than anyone he'd ever met. He had to have me, so I made him hunt me down. I made him sweat. I made him beg for it. He was going to have to work for it. Victory would not come easy for him, and because of that, he would appreciate me more (or so I thought). He didn't shy away from the chase, and his determination sealed the deal.

The New York accent was what you first noticed about him. Well, maybe not the first thing. He was gorgeous . . . in a Rip the Runway kind of way. Had a heavy Brooklyn accent that always put me in mind of Ghost from *Power*, but only if Ghost was dark chocolate and a little taller. He was smooth, standing maybe six feet even, caramel, curly top, with the whitest teeth ever. He wasn't stocky, but he wasn't skinny. He had a nice build on him, and any woman would instantly start to undress him in her mind, fantasizing what he was capable of in private. I, for one, couldn't wait for him to fuck me up against a wall and talk shit to me in that deep-ass voice of his, but it wouldn't be that easy. This pussy was priceless and not just freely given to anyone. At this point, he would have to work harder than any of his predecessors because I'd been disappointed so many times before.

My sissy and I were not your average around the way girls. Our parents taught us values, and we handled ourselves accordingly. We were not easy get-overs. That was to be understood from the very beginning.

Rule number one: never play mind tricks with the weak. Yeah, it was every man's fantasy to bed twins, but we didn't get down like that. Never did. Never would. Our shit was separate, and that was considered incest as far as I was concerned. Sisters should not be licking on each other. We spent most of our teenage life trying to prove how different we were because although we looked alike, we were not the same person by any means. In our younger years, we did the switch-a-roo sometimes because even standing next to each other, unless you really knew us or were our parents, it was hard to tell us apart. We were truly identical. It was even spooky to us sometimes.

We hung with different crowds, but occasionally I could talk my favorite girl into rolling with us to a hot party if she wasn't eyebrow deep in textbooks. She knew how to turn up with the best of us, but her focus was well beyond the party scene, and I had to commend her for that. At the now tender age of twenty-three, I was all the way over the college life. I got my associate's degree right quick, landed a gig for the City of Philadelphia and kept that shit, taking a class here and there toward my bachelor's degree to appease my parents. I did not plan to spend any more time in the classroom than was required. School was not for me, and I knew that early on.

Sajdah, however, was all the way there for it. She graduated a year early at the top of her class and was year two into her bachelor of science in engineering. She was fittin' to make all kinds of crazy money, having early on gotten the opportunity to design several buildings right in the downtown Philadelphia area. Little Sister (a nickname I sometimes called her because she was born four minutes after me) was well on her way to the top. She wanted me there with her, but I didn't want all that. I was cool right where I was, at least for now. Hell, I wasn't at the bottom, but floating somewhere in the middle. That was cool with me. Whatever I decided as a career couldn't be rushed because I needed to love it. That was my story, and I was sticking to it.

She never liked Skye and Vicerean (we called her Vice for short because that name was dumb as hell). She felt like once they came into the picture, she got pushed to the side. I tried on so many occasions to explain to my sister that no one could take her place, but for some reason, she just couldn't warm up to these two, even though she never had a problem with any of my other associates. That may have been where the true separation began if I think hard enough about it. She was never outright obvious with her jealousy, but you could see it brewing. I should have paid more attention back then, and just maybe we wouldn't be where we were now. Hindsight is a bitch in red bottom heels, I swear. She wanted me all to herself. I just never thought she would be so destructive in trying to keep me. Given the opportunity, we could have taken another route and talked this out.

So, Chase was a charmer. I was not sure how he found out so much about me. I knew he was a trap boy, so why was I seeing this man in Starbucks every morning like he had to be downtown? I didn't work near the courts, so it was not like he had to report to my area for probation. I was not even sure if he was on probation. I just assumed all drug boys were. It was cute that my coffee was paid for when I got to the counter. The fact that he was even up and out the hood at that time of day showed he had drive. I had to be at the gig by 7 a.m., which meant I was at Starbucks around 6:30. That's early as shit to rise for a maybe, but I guess he felt like if he wanted to secure the bag, he had to do what he had to do. The effort was definitely noticed and noted. I still ignored his ass, though. Seven-dollar coffee was nice, but it would take more than that to impress me. I was sure he knew that already, though. Chase was very smart and very calculating. He knew how to set the trap, and it was so smooth you wouldn't even know you were caught until you were already in it and struggling to be set free.

"Have you ever seen the guy Chase?" I asked my sister one night while I was practicing my look for the next day. I loved makeup! But not because I needed it. Both my sister and I had flawless skin. However, I did love a smoky eye and a pouty red lip from time to time. It was impossible to resist any pallet coming from The Crayon Case, and M.A.C. had my card on lock indefinitely. I was a slave to Fenty as well, and not ashamed to admit it. She would just sit and watch, always telling me I was prettier without it. Of course, I ignored her. I knew I was pretty. Makeup was just an enhancement.

"Yeah, I've seen him," she replied nonchalantly. That meant one of two things: she liked him but didn't know how to approach him, or she was now irked that I mentioned him because, in her head, that meant she was out of the picking. The thing is, she never once said she was interested in him, or else I would have never entertained him. My sister and I were not in competition. The minute she said she had dibs, I would've backed off, and vice versa. I wonder what happened to her confidence. We were clearly two of a kind—she had no need to second guess herself ever.

Rule number two: Thou shall not step on thy sister's toes. I knew how to remove myself from drama, and I definitely didn't want any ill feelings toward the only person in the world that knew me better than anyone. The only one in the world that meant the world to me. I'd never let dick come between us no matter how good it was. She of all people should have known that. It was one of those things that didn't need an explanation. I thought we were on the same page.

"He's been low key stalking me lately," I replied with a short laugh to gauge her emotional state.

"All the girls drool over him. I don't see it, though. He's not ugly, just not my cup of tea," she tossed out, never looking up from her textbook. "I've never seen him with anyone, so I guess he's free for the taking."

That was music to my ears . . . kind of. Just because no one had seen anyone didn't mean there wasn't someone. Men were very slick and could hide the biggest chick on the block in the smallest space ever. I did like that there was maybe an option with him, though.

I watched my sister through the mirror while I worked my magic, and she just didn't seem fazed. I was always pretty good at reading her, and maybe this time, I missed the mark. Maybe this time I didn't want to see what was really behind that nonchalant facial expression. Maybe because I was so damn selfish I was willing to push my sister dead in front of the bus to have what I wanted. Maybe I pushed her into his arms. All of this shit just might be my damn fault.

Satisfied with my look, I got up to wash my face so that I could get ready for bed. I was already late to work once that week and didn't want to fall into a pattern. By the time I got back, my sissy was already gone and locked in her room for the night. I wanted to knock and ask her one more time to be sure, but I didn't want to beat a dead horse, so I just let it go. By the time I got into bed, I had convinced myself that I would give Chase a chance. Who knew what would come of us if we tried to make it work? A small smile crept up on my face as I fantasized about him before falling asleep. Hopefully he wasn't all looks and no stroke. That would truly be disappointing and a definite deal breaker.

The next morning, I woke up a little later than expected, so I had to skip Starbucks so that I could get to work on time. I was truly not a person that needed to be anywhere in the world without first having my coffee. They were about to be all the way irked with me in the office that day, but I tried to keep my head in check. Maybe once I clocked in, I could talk my boss into letting me sneak out and get a cup. She had the same habit I had, so she would surely understand, especially if it was my treat.

Rushing to get ready, I ran out of the house, having to beat my face on the express train to Center City, and arrived at the office with exactly one minute to spare. Heading to my desk, I almost dropped all of my belongings as I got closer. On my desk sat a large coffee, a Cinnabon cinnamon bun, and a dozen yellow roses in a beautiful vase. I was speechless.

"Someone delivered these maybe ten minutes ago." My team partner leaned her head out of her space and looked at me with a curious eye.

"Did he say who he was?" I asked, assuming it was Chase as I moved closer to examine my gifts.

"Nope. Just asked where you sat and placed everything there. Tall guy, kind of caramel, I guess, accent from somewhere. Sounded like New York, but what do I know?" she rambled. I loved Cici. She didn't miss a damn thing that went on around these parts and knew all too well that I would want all the details.

Chase was definitely resourceful, and it made me wonder who was feeding him info about me. He knew too much for someone I didn't know at all. Maybe I needed to knock some of the ice off and let him warm me up a little bit.

"Well, thanks, love. This came right on time! I was running crazy late this morning and didn't have time to stop."

She gave me a knowing smile and went back to the task in front of her.

My mind was racing all over the place, trying to figure out how I was going to get close to Chase. I needed to see what it was really hitting for with him. He certainly knew how to wow a lady, but what else did he have to offer? I had been blowing him off for a while but decided it was time to start letting him in. I had a heart of ice, mostly from getting played more times than I liked to admit. Every time I thought I had found the one, he turned out to be a damn dud. Shit, being pretty was half the battle. To get what you really wanted, you had to get down and dirty with the rest of them.

I was not the chick that was going to kill myself working a million hours to take care of some dude that refused to rise and grind as early as I did. Ideally, he would hold a corporate job, but I was not afraid of the block. In fact, I preferred the block. I needed excitement in my life, and a dude that did the same thing I did was not in the running. I'd be damned if I would be stuck with someone who only talked office politics all day. That type of man was more my sister's speed.

I liked them in the trap. Some of the most brilliant mindsets came from down the way. If he were smart, he'd know how to stack so that he could step away and let the up-and-comings run the game. I got that vibe from Chase, and it was time I let him know I was crushing on him too. I wasn't just going to fall into his arms like a damsel in distress, though. I wasn't that chick, but I would let him know he was working on me a little.

As I waited for my computer to power up, I sent a text out to my girls Skye and Vice.

We have to TALK a.s.a.p.!

It looked like their girl was about to be off the market soon, and I needed their ears and eyes to the street to see who this Chase Warren really was. He wasn't about to catch me slipping out there, no matter how hard he made me smile.

Chase

Get It, Got It, Gone

She woke up late. You need to get breakfast to her desk asap.

I got the text at like six in the damn morning from my connect, but I was not ready to be making moves at that time of day. Sis was making me work harder than I was used to, and I just prayed that her pussy didn't end up to be trash at the end of it all. I was used to chicks just dropping the drawers and busting it open, but this one had the nerve to have values.

I didn't respond to the text. Waking shorty up next to me, I pulled her leg up and banged her from the side once more before I put her ass out.

Rarely did they get the chance to stay until the sun came up. I didn't want anyone thinking we were a fucking couple. And no matter what I said, chicks always went with their own thoughts. You've seen it before. All y'all did was fuck—no date nights, no birthday gifts, no phone conversation. All you got was a text, a dick down, and the occasional wing platter from the Chinese store. If you were nice, maybe I'd let you get a drink other than tap water to wash it all down before I put my dick down your throat. I wasn't spending no bread on the chicks. Bed them and then boot them. See ya next time.

In these chicks' minds, y'all was in love out this bitch. She was telling her homegirls future plans for y'all and everything. Even though I always made it crystal-ass clear that this wasn't shit but sex. I swear, it just be too much of a hassle, which was why I had to stop bringing them to the crib for a while. I'd had two motorcycles and the paint scratched up on my Benz lost in the struggle, and I just couldn't afford to keep going through the hassle. Listen, my Benz looked like a pack of wild wolves was practicing salsa dancing on the hood of my car. I was pissed and thought about getting her ass dragged by one of my young chickens, but I just let it go. It hurt them more not to get the dick. Trust me. They'd be out there looking like fucking crack heads, feigning to bust just one last nut and sorry they wrecked my shit. I be skipping right past they ass every time. I liked to live my life drama free at all costs. None of these hoes were worth my sanity.

This one, though. Dudes were falling over her left and right, and she acted like she was immune to the shit. Like she had no clue what was going on around her. That was how you knew she knew she was a bad bitch. I saw her out and about on a few occasions, ass looking perfect every time, lips looking kissable as fuck, and those damn eyes could see right through to your soul. She had me hypnotized, but I wasn't about to let her know that shit. She was going to work just as hard to get me as I did to get her. I was worth it, I promise. Just hoped she was, too.

By the time I got done smashing, and ol' girl taking her sweet-ass time getting ready, I didn't have time to make it down to shorty gig, so I had to send one of my boys over there again. He held a regular gig in the same building she worked in but held down the block for me at night whenever I needed him. He knew to follow directions specifically once I texted him what to pick up and where to take it. He never veered from the plan, and that was why whenever he needed me, he got it without question.

It was a good thing, though. Just as I went to spin the block, I received an urgent call from another crew member. These Philly cats had no loyalty! Every time I turned around, I had to dead one of these fools, and there was no doubt in my mind this situation would be exactly the same. By this time, it was seven in the morning, and I was just receiving a text from Selah thanking me for her breakfast and flowers. I made a mental note to pay my guy a little more for following directions as I made my way through the Dunkin' Donuts drive thru to grab a coffee and croissant before heading down the bottom. There was no way I was going to make it through this bullshit this morning without it.

I slammed my breakfast as I made my way over to the spot. It looked like any other house down the bottom of West Philly—row home, leaky porch when it rained, broken shades in the windows. It looked very deceiving to the naked eye, but a lot of money was made in those walls. Thousands on a daily basis. Every so often, we had to take someone to the basement, but it had been happening more often than not lately. To me, that was a sign that some of these dudes thought I was soft. Someone had to be made an example of. Fortunately, I didn't mind teaching anyone not to fuck with me.

When I pulled up on the block, I double-checked to make sure no one was following me before getting out of the car. Don't get me wrong, I was mad respected on these streets, but it was always someone who thought they were smarter than the average bear out this bitch. I trusted a lot of people, but no one fully. Desperate times would make someone kill they own mother for money. I was no different. I bled the same as everyone else. The key was to get the drop on them before they got it on you.

I punched in the lock code on the door, and as I entered, the smell of blood rushed right to my head. Seemed they started without me. In cases like these, my goons did not always wait for me to make a sound decision. They handled whatever needed to be handled until I arrived. I trusted these guys with my life for the most part, so I trusted their decision to the fullest.

Going upstairs first, I said hey to my auntie and made sure she was kosher before handling business. She lost her sense of smell to a cocaine habit years ago, so I wasn't concerned that the smell of rotting flesh would be upsetting to her. She knew to utilize the entire house except for the basement. That door had a lock code on it as well that she didn't know and didn't need to know. There was nothing down there for her anyway. Everything she needed to utilize was right where it needed to be. She was sweet and really just a front so that people thought someone actually lived there and it wasn't just a bunch of drug activity. She wasn't involved in any way. I promised my mom before I came to Philly that I wouldn't get her mixed up in any shit. I just made sure she had everything she needed and that she stayed out of the way.

My mom hated that I ended up a thug, but what could she do? Sometimes the streets got ahold of you and refused to let go. No amount of prayers could keep me from getting this fast money, but I stayed prayed up so that I wouldn't burn in the hell fire. I wondered how many sins I had to commit before God stopped hearing me. I thought about this often. The fact that I was killing people, be it through drug or slug, all of this shit had an expiration date on it. I just had to ensure I was good before my time was up.

WHACK!

Checking the fridge and cabinets to make sure everything was stocked up for my aunt, I made a mental note to pick her up another loaf of Stroehmann's potato bread. If nothing else, she loved a good sandwich.

Upon entering, I could hear them roughing up the culprit, and I was almost sad to find out who it would be this time. I was not originally from Philly, but the flavor I brought to the city was undeniable. Some of these dudes could not get with the fact that I wasn't locally born and raised, but that sounded to me like a personal problem. I'd been there too long for them to keep taking me through the motions. If I had to kill they asses off one by one until I found loyalty in an entirely new crew, then so be it. I was trying to at least keep it respectful and not bring my entire NY squad down there, but they were really testing my patience. Why couldn't folks just chill?

"Chance, listen. I can explain. . . ."

I had to adjust my eyesight to see in the semi-dark room. There wasn't a lot of available light in the basement. We didn't need it. If you were down there, you were either counting money in the back room (which was well lit), or you were about to die. It didn't matter if you could see us or not if you weren't going to make it to see the next day. He probably didn't want to see the disappointment on my face anyway. It was getting harder to hide and making me angrier by the minute.

"Cecil, tell me what's going on." Honestly, I didn't care. He was a done deal. I did like to give people a chance to speak their peace, though. Let them get whatever they had off their chest. It made me feel like they had a chance to earn forgiveness before I offed they ass. I always said a prayer for their soul to make it to heaven afterward. No one wanted to burn in hell.

"My daughter, man. My baby mom started using again, and my mom been taking care of her. My peoples is charging me out the ass, yo." He droned on and on, telling me his family issues. It was weird that he mentioned it because I thought I saw his baby mom copping from one of my boys not too long ago. My question was, why

didn't she just get it from him? He could have found a
way to keep us both satisfied. That's why it was important
to have a backup plan.

"She stole the last pack I got. I was trying to come up
with the money, but it was just too much to try to flip
without enough product. I'm in a jam, man. I don't know
what to do."

That's what I was waiting to hear. The truth about what
was really happening. He wasn't in here crying because
his girl was a drug addict. He was in tears because she
just possibly got him killed. Did I care about his baby
being left without parents? Not in the least. It wasn't my
concern. His job was to protect the bag by any means
necessary. The Notorious B.I.G. gave us the game in the
Ten Crack Commandments. He already knew how
the game was played.

His sobs bounced around us, but all of us were unfazed.
I took my time rolling a blunt, allowing him to cry in
peace. There was really nothing for me to say. I heard
this story so many times before—either the drug dealer
becomes the drug user, or someone close to them.

"Tell me why I should give you another chance."

Everyone in the room stopped and looked at me. I'd
never in my life given a second chance to anyone, but
every so often, you need to be spared. We all need a pass
sometimes. The older I got, the more I understood that
point. There were some people I wished I had given this
opportunity to. Maybe we'd just look at this situation
as me giving back to the community. His answer had to
be good, though, and he needed to understand that an
opportunity like this would probably never happen again.

"I fucked up. I should have let her go when she first
started using. If you give me the opportunity, I promise
you won't be disappointed."

So basically, he didn't answer my question, but that day, I was feeling generous. Well, that and I didn't feel like trying to hide another body right now. I decided to spare him just this once. For his sake, he better not make me regret it.

"That wasn't the answer I was expecting, but this is what we're going to do . . ."

I ran down to him the breakdown on each brick he would move, and how much off the top he would pay me in addition to what the brick was worth. I slightly threatened to put him in the ground if this deal went wrong or he just so happened to disappear.

"The entire house would be sprayed. Mom, daughter, everybody gonna feel the heat."

He shook his head profusely and thanked me for giving him a chance. I gave the cue to my head man in charge, and they swooped in on him once more as I left the room. He was gonna get that money beat out of his ass if it was the last thing they did. The next time I'd see him would be to collect.

Hopping back in my car, I took a spin around the city to see what the flow looked like for everyone else just in case the chop shop had to stay open a little while longer. As I made the left to head down South Philly, I got a text from my connect. Sighing loudly, I pointed my car in the direction of my home. I had to find a way to get rid of this little problem, too, if it was the last thing I did.

Selah

The Thrill of the Chase

"So, I hear he'll be at Dame's party tonight. We should definitely go now," Skye advised.

You absolutely didn't want to miss a Daddy Dame party. He was our local DJ that knew how to turn all the way up. Trust, if you weren't there, you were certainly square and would forever be salty you missed out. He pulled out all the stops, especially for his birthday. Last year was epic, and each year got better than the one before. I swear he had to take an entire year to plan this shit. It was too extravagant to just be thrown together and fall into place the way it did. You had to be red carpet ready for these events, and I was ready to shine like I was nominated for an Oscar.

I was sitting having lunch outside with Skye a few days later, discussing Chase. She worked in the same office building as me, but for a different company a few floors down. She'd been #TeamChase since he dropped on the scene a few years ago. She was the one that pointed him out while at a hotel pool party last summer, and it appeared that he was riding solo. There were plenty of scantily clad women present, but none seemed to be *the* girl that he was with. He showed the same love to everyone in his section, buying bottles and rotating tightly packed weed-filled blunts that he never puffed from. He didn't seem fazed at all by all the chicks that were

grinning up in his face and twerking him up against the
wall as we kept catching eyes from across the pool. My
metallic gold-and-leopard two-piece was giving them all
life, but I kept batting them all away like flies, captivated
by the new guy that I had been seeing around.

Surprisingly, my sister was at the party too, her bath-
ing suit just as stunning in navy-and-silver zebra. Unlike
me, she was really there for the music and scenery. She refused to let any man distract her from her goals. She never
really got over the heartbreak from the last boyfriend, so
her factory was shut all the way down. We offered to "handle" him for her, but she respectfully declined, so we kept
it moving.

We were looking like a pack of Doublemint gum while
sitting poolside. Most of the people present grew up
with us, but we still kept getting the double take every
time they walked by. We were cute kids, but these grown
woman bodies we now had were everything. Curves in all
the right places, and a pretty smile to top it all off. They
all fantasized about us, trust me. Too bad we weren't beat
for the bullshit.

We were sitting side by side, so maybe all that time, he
was really looking at her and not me, but since I was the
aggressor, he chose me out of default. So many scenarios
raced through my head in hindsight, but at that moment,
I was simply living in the moment. When our song came
on, we hopped out of the pool and found a space on the
side to dance with some of the other partygoers. We
really enjoyed ourselves that night, and before we left, I
made sure to put my number in his cell phone when we
saw him waiting by the exit. He just gave me a knowing
smile, and we kept it at that.

It took him a few days to call me, as it should have. He
knew that had he called too soon, it would have shown
desperation, and I would have been completely turned

off. Waiting too long would have had him dismissed, so he played his cards well with the morning coffee and random flowers until he was ready to make his first move. He was definitely playing chess, and I was just as ready to claim the crown.

"Oh, we in there! I got the perfect dress for tonight, too," I responded, excited as we made plans to secure my future with Chase. I was actually looking forward to getting to know him, and I was secretly hoping that he ain't have some big bitch hidden somewhere claiming to be his baby's mom. Chicks came up from a thousand years ago as soon as they smelled they ex happy with someone else. She didn't want him, but she didn't want anyone else to have him.

By the time we were done with lunch, we had convinced Vice to come also and was ready to really turn up.

I could barely concentrate when I got back from my break, my mind frequently slipping into daydreams of Chase and me. I wondered what kind of man he really was, and was he really worth my while. He seemed chill every time I saw him out, not rowdy like the clique he ran with. I could clearly see that he was the H.N.I.C because of the level of respect he received from the people around him. They didn't fear him, they respected him, and that was more important. I swear I couldn't keep the smile off my face, and Cici kept teasing me, calling me Mrs. Flowers in reference to the roses I had gotten earlier in the week.

I was packed and ready to go that day, unlike most days where I was dragging, barely making the clock out by the grace period. I had to make sure I was on point for real this time. I was on a mission, and step one was to make myself look irresistible.

I texted Skye when I got back to my desk and was so hype she was able to squeeze me in before the party.

There was no way I was showing up on the scene with week-old curls. I knew she would get me right, and I had spare time to get home and take my time with my face. That way, Vice would be able to do both of ours and not rush. I didn't need a pound of makeup; I just needed to make sure these eyes were poppin'. There was no doubt in my mind that everyone in the hood was busting out their Sunday best, so I had to ensure I was amongst the best dressed. The way pics would be flying around on the internet the next day, there was no way I was not coming prepared to slay.

When we got to the party, it was definitely lit. Everyone from around the way was there, representing properly. The scene looked straight out of that movie *Paid in Full* as one exotic car after the next pulled in front of the building. Women draped in jewels and men alike showed up to show out. Just standing in line was turned up, and I was happy that we decided to come out.

I definitely came to slay, baby. I looked like someone dipped me in red and stood me up in the perfect pair of heels. I went with a form-fitting body suit that hugged me flawlessly and matched the red bottom of my shoe perfectly. Skye worked the hell out of these wand curls, and Vice had me beat to the *gawdz*. I stepped up in there like they were all waiting on me and not the birthday guy.

The DJ for the night was killing the ones and twos, and even though I tried hard, I couldn't keep myself from dropping it low on the dance floor. He was playing one jam after the next, and I hadn't even had my first drink yet. The party was all the way live with a good mix of 90s rap and current music. When I say we were all tearing the dance floor up—not one wall flower to be seen.

I was in the groove with the music, but it wasn't lost on me that Chase hadn't shown his face yet. At first, I was getting concerned, but then I had to check myself.

I didn't want to seem desperate at a time like this. Nope, at this time, I had to make sure I wasn't looking thirsty in these streets. It could ruin everything.

I had to make myself go to the bar and hydrate myself. If I didn't, I was sure to pass out soon. As Skye and I approached the bar with Vice and my sister in tow, I was greeted immediately with a drink.

"From the gentleman at the end," the bartender responded as he moved on to fulfill other requests.

I found my guy looking extremely handsome at the other end of the bar with a smile on his face. There was a girl dancing in front of him, but he wasn't giving her any rhythm as he looked past her and stared at me. I held my glass up in thanks and turned to sip before he could see me blush. This man was trying to have me open, but I wasn't giving him the satisfaction that easily.

By the time I finished my drink, I was pulled back out to the dance floor as another of my favorite songs blared throughout the building. I was extra sexy with my dance this time around because I knew I had a certain person watching me. My twerk game was vicious as I threw my ass in a perfect circle on the beat.

This went on the entire night, with us going back and forth from the bar to the dance floor. I yelled in Skye's ear that I was going to take a quick bathroom break, and that's when I bumped into Chase again.

Even up close, he was the shit. I felt my thong becoming soaked as I got lost in his eyes, and those naughty thoughts that I had been having about him raced through my mind again. I briefly fantasized about him pinning me to the wall in front of everybody and taking me right there. I was tipsy enough to let him do it, but I settled for basking in his dimpled smile instead.

"You gonna make me keep chasing you, or you letting me in?" he questioned as he cornered me a little.

My heart started to race with a little fright and a little excitement because he had never been this close. This man had me turned on in a serious way. His cologne wrapped around me like a snake and squeezed me a little, making my clit jump and pulse like a heartbeat. I had to pull myself together because this man was making me unravel fast, and I didn't want to blow it.

"You've been chasing me? I hadn't noticed," I flirted back. I was a little lit from the drinks, so I hoped it didn't have me looking crazy.

"I have, and I'm done. You're mine now. Are we clear?"

He leaned down so that we were at eye level, and I could see the seriousness in his face. I nodded my head up and down, suddenly losing my voice. Why did this man have me open like this? He leaned in and kissed my forehead, and I swear I almost slid down the damn wall.

I pulled myself together enough to go to the bathroom before my bladder exploded and embarrassed me. I took a second to dab a cool paper towel over my eyes before rushing out to tell my girls what happened. I quickly scanned the room for him but couldn't see him anywhere. Did that shit just really happen? Was I really Chase's girl? I could hardly contain myself as I got back out on the dance floor and gave it up for the crowd one more time. I was really feeling myself and couldn't wait to see where this thing would go.

The next morning, I woke up to my sister bringing me another bouquet to my room. This man was really showing off! I took the flowers and inhaled, taking in their floral scent. I completely missed the look of disdain on her face as I basked in these fresh feelings I was having for a man I barely knew—yet another moment in hindsight that I wish I had paid attention to.

As I got up to prepare for my day, I knew if nothing else, I had to give him a call. Even if it were to simply thank him for the flowers. I was on cloud nine right now, seeing through rose colored glasses . . . all of the above. This man had me open, and now we all know what being open gets you. For now, I would just relish in this moment, because men like him didn't come around often, and that's how he caught me slipping.

Vicerean Gray

That's My Best Friend

Pause for a second. This is what I need you to know before we get any further into this bullshit romance you think you're about to indulge in. I never fucking trusted Sajdah. Ever. Not since we were kids. She tried to play the innocent, naive twin, but I always saw through the bullshit. *Off with her head!* I'd been saying that shit from the gate. She had always been jealous of Selah, always a damn sabotager, always in this silent-ass competition. *Why won't she just die already?*

Don't get me wrong. Sajdah may have very well had the qualities that she partially exhibited. Shy. Naïve. Quiet. Focused. Yep, all of the above. But you know what else she was? Sneaky as shit. Like a fucking cat that wouldn't stay on the damn floor, and you always caught it on your dining room table when you walked in the room. I didn't like that bitch, but I gave her respect because her sister just happened to be a dear and true friend of mine. I tried to love Sajdah the same way I loved Selah, but she made it so hard for no real reason. I'd been banging my head against the wall for years trying to figure out what this bitch beef was with me, and for the life of me, I just couldn't call it. Clearly, I was missing something.

I even tried to put myself in her shoes for a second. Maybe, just maybe, Chase took a shot at her. Fuck, he was a nigga. That's what they did. Her only job as

Selah's sister was to cut that shit completely short and let her sister know the deal so that it could be dealt with accordingly. We all knew Selah would have never chosen dick over the love of her life. She adored Sajdah and oftentimes told us how much she looked up to her even though they were the same age. Sajdah did this shit on purpose. Point. Blank. Period. No one could convince me otherwise. What shit? Oh, we getting to that, so don't worry your pretty little head about it. Just know that trust is a hot commodity. You can't trust a damn soul breathing. Don't say I didn't warn you.

Because I knew how crafty men could be, I almost felt sorry for Selah, but some shit you just needed to find out on your own so that you could move forward appropriately. He was too squeaky clean for me anyway. We couldn't find shit on this dude, and trust me, every damn body had some shit they were trying to hide like a taco in a purse belonging to a fat bitch on *My 600-lb Life*. I didn't even trust myself around myself because I knew what I was capable of. I had some shit I couldn't say to nobody but Jesus H. Christ, and even then, I may not be able to voice it. I couldn't find a damn thing on homeboy, but that didn't mean I would stop looking. Not until every damn stone was accounted for. That's the type of loyalty I had for Selah. That's the type of loyalty she had for me.

Mr. Warren . . . he was a damn magician. Skye and I searched hard, but nothing came up. I even contacted my people in Queens to see if his name struck a bell. Not saying he was from Queens, but New York was just like Philly. It didn't take much to hold a reputation. If you made some noise in South Philly, trust we heard about it in Mt. Airy. My connect had nothing for me. He was either a really good dude, or people just weren't talking or too scared to. However, no matter how you painted a zebra, they always showed their stripes. Sometimes you just had to sit and wait patiently for what you needed to come to you, like UPS on a Saturday.

I decided to let Selah be great and have her love story. Shit, we all wanted it for her, especially after what happened with Kev, but we won't speak on that right now. Just know that the kind of heartbreak she felt from that definitely had us on his ass. They still can't find the body, and now they won't be able to find Chase either. Sucks to be both of their dumb ass.

It was weird how I got the scoop on Chase and Sajdah. I was just on the stoop chillin' on a nice fall night. You know how it is when the weather is warmer than it should be for the season. It brings the hood outside. I decided it was a good time for some Lincoln fried chicken with a side of mac and a buttered roll, and the closest one was located on 40th and Lancaster Avenue. It didn't take much convincing to get one of the guys out there to drive me, especially since I was treating. Since I was the only single one in the crew, I was really just hanging with the hood that night. Skye and Selah were boo'd up, or so I thought.

I was enjoying the night breeze while shooting the breeze with my ride, contemplating if I was gonna let this lame give me some head or not. He was really feeling the kid, and honestly, I ain't have shit else to do. He had a tongue. That's all that was required for this mission. While we were talking, it looked like I saw Chase's car pull up across the street in front of the chicken spot. Nobody in Philly had the same car as Chase. He had some custom type paint shit on it that changed color in the rain or some shit, but when it was dry, it was like an electric blue that seemed to glow at night. I was a hundred percent sure once I saw the black-and-yellow license plate. I didn't want it to seem like I was spying, so I entertained my guest as I peeped the scene at the store.

At first glance, it looked like Selah getting out of the car after Chase came around to open the door. She got out and kissed him before he leaned in and grabbed her ass as they walked into the store. I smiled at the happiness my friend had found, but something just didn't sit right with me. Selah told me she was under the weather, and chicken was not enough to get my friend out of the bed, no matter how good it was. If anything, she just would have sent Chase to get it for her while she rested. This shit was looking fishy, and I had to focus.

Totally tuning out dude I was with, I waited for Chase to come back out of the store. I took them a while, but just as I thought, that was not my lovely friend with her man. It was her twin sister instead. If you didn't know them, you would think she was Selah, but I could clearly tell them apart, and that was not appropriate behavior for the way those two were acting with each other. I tried to grab my phone so that I could zoom in and snap a pic right quick, but I was only quick enough to get a half-ass blurry pic of him getting in his car on the other side. I was steaming on the inside. How dare both they asses try to play my fucking bestie.

I knew with Selah I would need rock solid proof before I went to her, and this blurry-ass pic wasn't it. I needed a definite action pic. The shot I got wouldn't be enough for Selah, but it was unquestionably enough for Skye. I sent her a text, letting her know it was an emergency and to meet me on the stoop in fifteen minutes. My ride and I gathered our food, but him pounding my pussy that night would have to wait. I had a more pressing issue that needed my immediate attention. I promised him we would reconvene, though. I would definitely need a good nut after this shit.

"So, what the hell happened?" Skye questioned when I got back to my house. I was so mad I was turning red. I wanted to call Selah immediately, but this was a delicate subject that could possibly ruin our friendship if not played correctly. Selah loved us, but her love for Sajdah would have you six feet under if you weren't careful.

"This motherfucker was at Lincoln hugged up on Sajdah. He kissed her in the mouth and grabbed her ass and everything," I explained to Skye as I paced back and forth, wearing my carpet out. My head was pounding so bad from the frustration I was feeling at the time. I was ready to go hunt this dude down and body his ass that night. I had to pump my damn brakes and remember this wasn't my situation directly; I was just involved because I saw this shit.

"When did they start hanging out?" she asked as she stared at the pic on my phone.

"Bitch, I don't know. I thought maybe they were there to get Selah some food, but they were too damn intimate for my liking. They fucking, bitch. I put my life on that shit."

Skye looked like she was ready to snap. We took Selah personal. We'd been ride or die with her A-1 since day one. We also learned from experience with her that we had to come correct, or at least lead her in the direction she needed to go to see what she needed to see. That one was a ticking time bomb waiting to explode, and it didn't matter if you were family or not. Once that gun started smoking, it was only right for it to shoot. Sajdah knew this, and it confused us as to why in hell she would stab her sister in the back like she did. She would definitely pay for this; we just had to get a plan in action.

I had been waiting to get her ass for years! Now it looked like I might be getting my chance finally. Yeah, I knew it was horrible to want to kill my best friend's sister, but she was as slimy as they came. People like that needed to be disposed of properly. Fuck every last one of them walking the earth.

"Let's not say anything to Selah right now until we have something more concrete. Now we have to put a plan in action for her to catch their stupid asses. You know how Selah is. This shit has to be solid. She won't just take our word for it." Skye spoke as she set my phone on the table.

This was some horrible shit indeed, but it had to be done. After making sure she was safely in her car, I checked to see if my little honey dip was still on the stoop. I needed a distraction before I spilled the damn beans.

Chancing a peek out the window, I saw him out there in some other bitch face, but I wasn't fazed by that shit. I was getting that dick that night, whether she knew it or not. Checking my stash to make sure I had some condoms, I made sure the crib was tight before walking Skye out to her car. I leaned over in her passenger-side window, rocking my ass back and forth like a python hypnotizing him and ready to strike. He couldn't even concentrate on the wack-ass conversation he was having with old girl. It took everything not to laugh in her damn face. I was about to get that nut tonight. *Sorry, sis.*

"I love you, Vice," Skye said as she made herself comfortable in her car. "Please don't say anything until we figure this out."

"Skye, my lips are sealed until they're not. We need to move on this asap."

"Indeed," she agreed as she put her car in drive. "Now let me go before my honey dip start wondering what's taking me so long. It looks like you got some dick to get as well," she said with a sly smile as she looked past me. When I turned around, I saw my little friend at this point was all the way tuned out of his current conversation and needed me to save him. I smiled to myself and made my move.

"Text me when you get home." I leaned up out of the car and made a show of waving my girl off, knowing it would make my ass jiggle in my tights. Turning to my boo thang for the night, I sauntered up to him and stepped right in between him and old dust bucket like she wasn't even standing there. Gently grabbing him by the neck, I pulled him into a semi-sloppy kiss and then walked away. They both had a look of shock on their faces that I completely ignored. When I got to the steps, I turned around to see them both staring at me.

"You coming to bust it down, or nah?"

Without hesitation, he two-stepped his way to me, leaving old girl just hanging in the wind. I shot her my brightest smile as I led him into the house and locked the door. I had some dick to get, and I was really not in the mood to argue with anyone about it. He could explain whatever he needed to her at a later date. That wasn't any of my concern.

Any-who, I'll let Selah finish telling you this bullshit-ass love story she was convinced was happening. Trust and believe that when the time came to swoop in, we'd be like hawks out this bitch. Just wait on it.

Sajdah

Get In Where You Fit In

I had to do everything for him. I swear I could send the simplest directions, and he would still mess it all up. So damn frustrating. Most times, I had to treat him like he was a five-year-old. I texted him the night before when Selah got in the shower to let him know she was in on the transition. His alarm was to stay set for 6 a.m. until otherwise discussed. That way, he had time to get on that 6:13 train that would have him downtown in enough time to see her in the morning. He could order her breakfast using the Starbucks app, so that wasn't a big deal.

No, she didn't know, per se, that I was sending him to her in a roundabout way, but I was a tad bit instrumental in orchestrating their meeting. Chance wanted me; I didn't want him. I didn't have time to entertain these dudes when I was too busy building an empire, and he was too yummy of a distraction to get caught up right now. The next best thing for both of us was my body double. He would basically get to enjoy the same body type, but a less smart one. I mean, Selah was smart . . . I guess, but I was a genius. Real live beauty and brains. I didn't trust any other chick he had in mind, and this way, I could keep an eye on him. At first he tried to buck against me on this, but I wasn't trying to hear him.

"Why can't I have you? Why do I have to have her? Am I not good enough for you?" He asked me these questions one night while he had me pinned down and was balls deep in my pussy. He had my legs locked at my ankles and was pumping into me so slow it was killing me.

Chase had a long and meaty dick. It would definitely stretch you to the point where it was almost painful, but it felt so good you never wanted him to stop. I called it The Damager. If he wasn't careful, your entire uterus would fuck around and be lying on the bed next to you when he was done. I really wanted to keep him all to myself, but I didn't have time for him. The next best thing was my sister. That way, I wouldn't be worried about diseases and shit. I typically didn't share my dick, but his shit was so good I wanted Selah to have some too. She deserved it after what lame-ass Kevin put her through. This was sort of like a gift that would keep both of us satisfied. She didn't know it, but I was looking out for her. As twisted as it looks, it was the truth.

Chase approached me so long ago I couldn't clearly remember when we first started talking. I would see him all the time when I was transitioning from the regional rail to my car every day. Trust me, there was nowhere to park in Center City unless you wanted to pay a million dollars to do so. I, for one, wasn't interested in spending my hard-earned coins on parking my car, so I decided it was smarter to at least drive halfway and ride halfway.

I noticed the funky-colored blue car driving by every morning, but the windows where tinted so dark I couldn't see inside. I noticed the New York license plate, too, and automatically put him in the trap boy category. That took him out of the running immediately. I wasn't even sure of his race, but I knew whoever owned that vehicle had to have a ton of money. One thing I didn't mix was drug dealers and my residence. You wouldn't have the police kicking my door in looking for your stupid ass, and I would not be spending time behind bars because I was

was concerned because I never call out. I assured him everything was okay and that I would be there tomorrow.

As I circled the car to get in, I could smell the lemon pound cake and coffee he had resting on the dash. I didn't even ask; I just snatched out the items and began to indulge as he pulled out of the station. I briefly thought about the possibility of being kidnapped, but at this point, it was too late. I was already in the car. Whatever was going to happen was going to happen regardless. I just hoped I didn't end up chained to a pole in the basement after this.

We rode for a while out of the city limits, but for some reason, I wasn't nervous. He made me so comfortable. The inside of this car was plush and custom to the max. Heated seats, chrome-on-black detail, and a screen big enough for me to watch movies while he drove. He also had smaller screens in the headrests. This man definitely had a coin or two. I'd never seen a car like this, and I was around money all the time.

Eventually, we ended up on this winding driveway that had a beautiful condo-style house sitting at the end of the driveway. The neighbor wasn't too close, aside from the unit attached to his, but far enough away that they both had privacy. I made sure to peep my surroundings, just in case I needed to run for help.

He was a true gentleman, getting out to open the door for me and escorting me into his home. It was absolutely stunning—very modern and very masculine, but not overly boyish. You could tell a man lived there. It smelled like coconut and vanilla, and everything had its place.

I took the liberty of looking around downstairs, low key searching for a bobby pin, stray thong, or anything that indicated a woman was there. He took a seat and let me do me, a slight smile on his face as he watched my ass bounce with each step under my skirt. I was definitely

guilty by association. That was the type of shit Selah got into. He was more her speed.

One morning as I was crossing the lot, Mr. Blue Car was already there, parked right near where I had to enter to get on the train. As I approached, I could see his window sliding down. I was immediately in love when I saw him. My pussy literally did a happy dance in my panties, and I had to squeeze my legs together to keep from walking funny. Model-type looks with a hint of thug . . . just how I liked them. He just came along at the wrong time.

"Good morning, gorgeous," came this deep baritone from the car that made my nipples rock hard.

"Good morning," I shot back, never breaking stride as I moved toward the platform. My train came in exactly six minutes. Whatever he wanted to say, he had better make it quick.

"Let me take you to work. I know you don't really want to ride with all those people," he responded, giving me a smile that made the pulse in my clit race even faster. I was not ready for him that morning.

"I'm okay. My dad told me not to ride with strangers." That was the truth. He had been telling us that since we were kids. I picked a fine time to pay attention.

"I'm not a stranger. We been making eye contact with each other for weeks now."

I laughed a little. He was cute. I entertained the thought for a second. I mean, would he really kill me, and all these people saw me get in his car? Of course he would. Killers didn't care about that type of shit. Once I was in the car and it was moving, it was really his call on where he took me. I thought about it, but then I saw my train pulling up.

"Maybe next time," I responded as I stepped up on the platform and boarded the train. I could see him pulling off as the train left the station, and for a second, I regretted not taking him up on his offer, but I was sure he would pop up again. He seemed like the persistent type, and he definitely put a smile on my face that morning.

I didn't even get his name, but I made a mental note to properly introduce myself the next morning. He was sure to be out there. For now, I had to concentrate on the presentation I had that morning. This was a project I worked extremely hard on, and I was finally seeing the fruits of my labor. I smiled a little as we rode along. I was definitely going to give him some time, but it would be on my terms.

The next morning, I was shocked to not see the blue car sitting at the train station. He was out there religiously. Maybe me shooting him down the day before scared him off. I was a little sad about it, but then figured he might have just woken up late.

Little did I know I wouldn't see him for almost six weeks. Surprisingly, I went from being concerned to worried about his wellbeing, to being pissed clean the fuck off. Who was he to just fall off the face of the earth? I was literally distraught one day, wondering what happened to him, and decided for my peace of mind that someone killed him, and that's why I wouldn't see him anymore. It made it easier for me to sleep at night.

One day, I woke up late. That never happens. I promise you I'm the person that gets up extra early just in case I need to iron my shirt. I hated being late anywhere and showed up to work at least forty-five minutes early to prepare for my day. When Selah peeked her head in my room to make sure I was okay, I knew for sure my ass was late. She ran late on a daily basis, so for her to wake me up was something new. I hopped in the shower and barely lotioned as I threw on some clothes and hustled out the door.

I was tearing the road up, still trying to make the train on time, and I pulled up just in time to see it ride by. I wanted to cry. The next train wouldn't come for another half hour, and I was trying to decide if I felt like sitting through traffic or just waiting. Getting out of my car, I decided to go into the little train station store to grab a piece of fruit when I saw Mr. Blue Car sitting there. I was ready to climb on the hood and kick his window out. How dare he show up here after all this time. I was livid!

I prepared myself to walk right by him—until that window rolled down and I saw that smile. The heartbeat in my pants was pounding like crazy, and I was so mad he made me weak like this. I wanted to punch him and fuck him at the same time.

"Just missed that train, huh?" he said in a slightly sarcastic tone. "Take the day off, love. You look like you need me today."

"How you figure? I don't even know you." I tried to sound nasty but wasn't a hundred percent sure it came out that way. This man made me so weak. He had me thinking, and it had been a while since I had a day off. I rocked my presentation a few weeks ago, and at this stage, it was just cleanup work. They wouldn't miss me for one day, would they? I never called out. I thought that day just might be the day.

I couldn't let him think he had me that easy, though. Whatever he had planned, he was going to work for it. It had been a while since I had some good dick, too. I was turning into a dog in heat right before his eyes, and I could tell by the look on his face that he knew he had me. I wanted to decline, but I couldn't. I didn't know when I would see him again. I couldn't miss this opportunity.

Pulling my phone out of my pocket, I sent my director a text, letting him know I wouldn't make it into the office that day. I didn't give him any details, and of course,

prancing like a show pony. He needed to see what he was missing out on all that time he was gone.

I walked the entire living space on the first level but did not go upstairs. That, I would need an invite to, but first, we had some rules to discuss.

"Who else you giving that dick to?" I asked as I came back and straddled him. I knew my crotch felt warm as shit against his. My pussy had been pulsating from the moment I saw him, and it was nice and juicy if he wanted it, but he would have to act right first.

"It's yours if you want it. All yours," he replied, cool as a cucumber. The look on his face held it all together, but the lump in his sweats that was pressing against my clit said otherwise.

"Here's the deal. I can't be with you, but we can do this sometimes if you behave."

"I'll change your mind about that shortly," he responded with a smile as he held me around my waist and stood up.

I locked my legs and arms around him and let him carry me up the steps. That shit had better be good. For his sake, he better hit the mark. He knew he had one chance to get me on board. I just hoped he took advantage.

Chase

Double the Pleasure

Motherfucking twins! Man, how did your boy luck up on that? Sajdah was bad, but come to find out there was an identical twin sister? Oh, the things I would do with both of them in my bed. I got brick hard every time I thought about it. Sajdah was dead set against that shit, though. No matter how much I tried to convince her, she just was not with it.

"That's not what we get into. That's incest," would be her response every time. It was annoying. I bet a stack the other twin was with that shit, though. Sajdah was freaky as fuck, so I could only imagine what that wild one was capable of. I called her the wild one because, unlike Sajdah, she was more blunt and straightforward, from what I could see. I asked around about her, and every dude I knew told me she was a tough nut to crack. I had time, though, and my approach was different. I knew there was a way I could get and keep both of them. I just wasn't sure how at the moment. Just the thought of having both of their tongues on my dick at the same time was all the motivation I needed.

We need to talk.

The text came through at like seven in the morning. I jumped up out of bed, but as soon as I saw what time it was, I just laid my ass back down. I overslept, and she was already on the train. I had been smashing at this point for a few months now. We still weren't exclusive, but she wanted me all to herself. The fire that came out of her the last time she came here and someone else was already here almost ended in death. I didn't think she had it in her to be so violent. The girl that was here ended up having to walk until her Lyft showed up. I felt bad for her, but what was I supposed to do? Sajdah came to slay, and she had an offer I couldn't refuse.

I didn't bother to respond to the text. I learned from past experience that her texting me was just to inform me of what was to come. It was not an invitation to converse. A few thoughts went through my head as I wondered what it could be about, but I decided to just lay it to rest until it was time. I had too much on my plate to be getting caught up in some shit I probably couldn't control.

Checking up on the block, I could see the effects of my new product, especially in Kensington. Fiends were barely alive as they nodded out on just about every corner near Allegheny Ave. At this point in the game, I had no fucks left for people like this. Some would question why I was feeding drugs to my own people. I always countered that it was better to get them from your own than the white man. They were going to be drugged out regardless. Why not capitalize? I had no picks. Eight to eighty, blind, cripple, and crazy—if you had all my money, you got what you needed. If you were a loyal customer, I looked out for the cookout. I wasn't Nino Brown out here giving out turkeys and shit at Christmas, but I always made sure everyone was good until I couldn't anymore. No second chances. You fucked up, you disappeared. End of story.

Satisfied that everything in this part of the city was kosher, I made my way down South Philly, then to Center City to make sure my high-end clients had their fix. I had so many lawyers and politicians in my pocket it should have been a crime. Well, it was a crime, but you get what

I mean. That was part of the reason why even though we played it safe, a lot of the activity my boys did was overlooked. From the Philadelphia Police to Governor Kenney and everyone in between, I was covered. Judges in some of the highest courts, too. No one with a high status wanted to be associated with being on drugs, and trust me, the amount of drugs they had at these parties were crazy. Coke, pills, weed, anything you can handle—and I always made sure they were good.

I played around with some of their wives as well, unbeknownst to their husbands, of course. A lot of these judges and lawyers were married to younger women who they couldn't fuck well, and they just stuck around for the money. They were smart, making sure to get married and birth kids to secure the bag. All they wanted was a good dick down, and for the right amount, I was on it. I even put a few of my team members on because I wasn't greedy, and they paid well. Hell, I couldn't fuck everybody. I mean, I could, but I really didn't have time. I had a business to run. We would rotate so that they didn't get attached and derail the whole shit. We had to keep a level head about this, for the benefit of everyone involved. No slip-ups allowed. Ever.

Sajdah could never know that much about me, though. No woman would understand that kind of grind, no matter how much it paid. She said she wanted me to herself, and if that meant that every low-level chicken head I bedded was off limits, then so be it, but I was going to continue to collect on them rich bitches. That was nonnegotiable. The best way to keep that rolling was to just not bring it up. Plain and simple.

By the time I got done making runs, meeting with the connect, and making sure no one was being grimy, I was back at the train station, waiting for Sajdah to pull up. I missed her that morning, so there was no way I was going to let the shit happen twicc. I was there an entire hour early, running in to grab her favorite snacks from the train station ten minutes before she was due to get off.

I could see her when she got off the train, and she looked good enough to eat. I wanted to put her in the back seat right there at the train station. From head to toe, she was all the way together, but her face showed a little attitude. I was hoping this was going to be a light conversation, but it looked like this shit may get heavy on me. What was bothering her that bad?

I got out and around the car in enough time to open the door for her. She gave me a slight smile as she got in, and I didn't close the door until she made herself comfortable. By the time I got back in the car, she was enjoying her snacks. I leaned over to give her a kiss, and we made our way back to my home. I knew not to ask her about her text that morning. She would tell me what I wanted to know when she was ready.

Upon pulling up, she waited for me to let her out of the car as instructed, and I grabbed her bags for her so that she could get up the steps. Watching her ass as she walked was hypnotizing, and I was almost ready to really let go of everyone else. I swear I could watch her walk all day. I mentally went through my morning to make sure the chick I had over the other day didn't leave anything. I did not want to feel her wrath anymore after the last time.

"So, I want you to date my sister."

My head exploded. Was she serious? This had to be a damn setup. Any time I inquired about her sister, she snapped off at me. Now she was basically handing her to me on a gold-lined platter. Why was she playing with me like this?

"Why can't I just date you?"

"Because I don't want you," she said with an exasperated eye roll like she was tired of me questioning her. I couldn't care less, though I needed clarification. "She's the next best thing to me, Chase. You will date her and no one else."

"And what does that mean for me and you?" I asked, feeling like I was getting pimped out. I couldn't believe I was about to agree to this shit.

"It means I still get that dick whenever I want it. The two of us will be your only source of satisfaction from here on out. So, whomever you're hanging on to, it will be beneficial for you to let them go."

I was speechless. Did she just demand that I give up chasing down any cat I want just to have theirs? I've never had a female shut me down like that before. I was impressed by her boldness. I just wasn't sure that's what I wanted to do. What was really in it for me? What made them so special that I had to let everyone else go? I wasn't ready to just give in like that, though. I wasn't sure what made her think she was running the show, but li'l mama had another thing coming.

"So, what if I said no?"

"I wasn't asking you, love. This is what it is. Did you pick up the wine I asked you to get? I've had a long day."

The queen had spoken—in a very dismissive tone, I might add. I just chuckled on the inside and let her think she had it her way. *You want me to fuck your sister? Cool, I can do that.* I planned on wearing both they asses out until I couldn't anymore.

Something on my spirit told me this wasn't going to end well, but at the end of it all, she couldn't say I didn't do what she asked me to do.

Getting up to grab her a glass and some wine, I made sure to put my phone on Do Not Disturb. I didn't need anyone unexpectedly calling while she was there. It was easier to just block the rest out.

When I got back to the sofa, I removed her shoes and proceeded to give her a foot rub. Sajdah liked to take the lead, so I knew not to make a move until she was ready. She leaned back on the sofa to get comfortable as my massage went from her feet to her ankles and calves. I could still smell the perfume she sprayed this morning as her body began to heat up. I took my time with her, though. This one was very temperamental and flighty. It wasn't worth the stress later on down the line.

It didn't take long for things to escalate, and before we knew it, her legs were stretched out, and I was enjoying my meal. I had to hold her down to keep her from running away. The more I worked on her body, the more I began to think about her proposal. Why did I have to share with her sister? What if I just wanted her? She really gave me no option or out. I wasn't cool with it. I even surprised myself with that one.

"Why can't I have you?"

"Just do what I say, Chase," she responded, gasping as I swiftly slid into her.

Normally, I took my time with her, but I was heated for some reason. Who did she think she was exactly? We hadn't even discussed us being exclusive, and she decided to willingly share me with the person of her choice? That shit had me tight.

"Why can't I have just you?" I asked her again, this time grinding into her a little deeper and a little rougher. That shit took her breath away for a second, and she had to grab on to me to get herself together. I grabbed her hands and locked her arms over her head, taking all control from her. She was going to really have to sell me on that shit there because I really felt like later on, this would all turn out to be my fault if it didn't work out.

"I don't want you, Chase. I have to stay focused."

I immediately began to work the shit out of her. She wanted me to have her sister? She was going to wish she had stayed on board. I was not about to do some foul-ass shit behind her sister's back and she catch feelings, not knowing what was really going on. That shit wasn't fair to her, and what type of person would set up they family like that? It reminded me of the shit fiends did to get high. They would sell the drawers off their kid's ass for their next hit.

This idea only benefited her. I didn't want to lose her, either. Was I stuck doing this shit? I had to think, and the easiest way to do that would be to get her out the crib as quickly as possible. I knocked her ass out the frame for a little while longer before letting her know we had to go. I faked like I had to check up on my people, but on the real, I wasn't sure how I felt about her anymore.

"Just think about it, Chase. I don't want to lose you, either, but I know I can't put in the time right now. Everything will be fine. Just trust me."

I trusted no one, and I just hoped she was right on this one. I lay in the dark, staring at the ceiling, tossing back and forth about what I should do. I mean, they were twins. No, I couldn't have them together, but I guess one at a time wasn't bad. After a few hours, I decided to just give it a try. If I didn't like it, I could always just cut one of them off.

Reaching over to grab my phone, I sent a simple text. Now, it was time to play my part. I didn't bother to read the response. I meant every word I said.

It's a deal. For your sake, you better not play me.

Selah

Almost Mrs. Warren

What can I say about Chase? He was truly amazing. I'd never had anyone like him before, and I was starting to wonder why I had waited so long to let him in. At this point, we were around three months into our relationship, and I was loving every day that we spent together. You know how most guys go all the way out to get you, but once they got you, all of that shit stops? I was truly waiting for the other shoe to drop, but to my surprise, he got better than he originally was. Like, he was still getting up and buying me coffee every morning, even though I told him repeatedly that he didn't have to.

Life with Chase was truly out of a fairy tale, and the squad was riding this thing out with me like true soldiers. No one complained to me when I spent time with him, and he didn't feel any type of way about me making time for my girls. For once in my life, there was a perfect balance between love and life. Even my parents liked him, and my dad didn't like anyone we brought home. Little sister seemed to be on board, too, or maybe I just wanted to see that through these apparent rose-colored shades that I had been wearing around her. I was actually smiling all the time, and it didn't feel forced for once. Life was good. No, actually, life was great.

I was spending a lot of time with Chase, regularly spending nights in this gorgeous condo he called home just off of City Avenue. I woke up to the smell of maple bacon cooking, and I couldn't wait to dig in.

Chase tossed me around the room all night, literally. Sex with him was like running a triathlon. It wasn't some regular you on top, then me on top kind of thing. He had me in all kinds of compromising positions that had me wondering how flexible I really was. I didn't know my legs could stretch that wide without snapping at the hip. Since he deemed me light enough to pick up, he took full advantage of that by pinning me to the wall, making sure to go in deep, or literally dangling me from the chandelier in his dining room while he ate the box. I'd been his meal plenty of nights as he spread me out on his table and served himself.

Open like the damn freeway at three in the morning is how he had me, and I had lost my head weeks ago, totally surrendering to him. I'd never let anyone in like I let him in, and I hoped on a daily basis that I didn't regret it. He was good to me—too good, sometimes—but I let him do what he did best, which was spoil me rotten.

He was the boss in this relationship, but he didn't make me feel like I didn't have a choice. Although he was very authoritative, I still felt like his equal. We were on an even playing field, no one more important than the other. I liked being there with Chase, but low key, I missed having my sister right across the hall. Even though we were both now grownups, our parents weren't in a rush for us to leave the nest, and we weren't eager to get out. They let us come and go as we pleased and wouldn't take our offering to help with bills even though we both made good money at our jobs. We still stayed up a lot of nights just talking, but I noticed that once Chase became a permanent fixture, all of that stopped. I had no clue why, though.

I felt so damn bad right now. I was supposed to be laying there enjoying the aftermath of great sex with the best man I'd ever met and anticipating the amazing breakfast that he was currently whipping up. I was supposed to be happy, but all of a sudden, all I felt was guilt. Did I abandon my sister? For some dick, no less? Did I allow Chase to push her out of the way? Was I being selfish at the moment? Wait, didn't I deserve a selfish moment? Gosh, I was such a horrible sister, and I needed to make things right.

Grabbing my phone, I held it, trying to think of what to say to her. Maybe I was all upset over nothing and she was perfectly fine. What if I was tripping for nothing? I figured if I sent the text, at least she would know I was thinking about her.

Before I could formulate any words, Chase came back into the room. All he had on was an apron while holding a tray full of food. I didn't know which one I wanted to devour first. This man made me feel like electricity was shooting through my body with just eye contact. Where had he been all my life?

Setting the tray down, he took a seat next to me and began to feed me breakfast. All thoughts of my lonely sister briefly flew right out of the window as I swallowed strawberries dipped in whipped cream, then eventually him because he was just too much to pass up. Gently setting the tray on the floor because I was always so nervous about ruining his white carpet, I leaned in from the side of him to take him into my mouth.

He loved when I circled the head first, and I always took my time with him because he was more than a mouthful. A moan found its way out of my full mouth as his fingers found their way inside of me in a slow stroke that took my breath away momentarily. His fingers played my clit like a flute, causing me to explode prematurely, and we hadn't even gotten to the good part yet. My legs gave out, and I felt weak, but I knew with Chase I had to be ready to go. He did not give in easily, no matter how much I begged.

I made sure my hair was out of the way so that he could see me in action. He loved to watch, and I certainly didn't mind the attention. As he began to grow, I took him in deeper, trying but failing to swallow him whole. It was just too much. His deep moans were like music to my ears as I crawled in between his legs, freeing myself from the delicious torture that he was causing, and licked him like a lollipop from the base all the way to the tip, his pre-cum a pleasant surprise when I reached the top. I slurped at his honey greedily, hoping he would give me more.

"Babe, let me in," he spoke in a low tone as he began to pulsate on my tongue. Chase had miraculous control of his eruptions, and even if he fed me a nut, it was nothing for him to get it back up quickly so that we could keep rollin'.

I didn't respond. I just kept doing what I was doing. I could feel his toes curling next to me, and his grip on the back of my neck got a little tighter. Having him like this was the only moment when I could really be in total control of him. I loved the feeling. It let me know that I had what it took to please my man fully. I had no fear of anyone else. I always took care of him.

"Babe . . . let me in, please."

He was starting to beg a little, and that shit had me ready to pop my damn self. Pleasing him truly pleased me, and I just knew I was in for a serious treat. I took that moment to gently lift his balls and slide my tongue into that space underneath, slurping and lapping at it just a little, while simultaneously stroking him with long, firm strokes. He was pulsing like crazy, and I knew the cream was slowly starting to rise to the top. He tasted sweet, and I definitely didn't want to waste it, so I kept it going until I was sure he would cum for me.

I took his testicles into my mouth one at a time, then made my way up the underside of his length until I was at the top, where a nice puddle of pre-cum waited for me. I took him into my mouth, softly humming as I tried to stuff all of him in without scratching him with my teeth. I couldn't wait to feel him inside of me, but I wanted to swallow him first.

One thing I was not was a prude in the bedroom. I was willing to try almost anything that was in reason. My man would not use the excuse of not being able to bust in my face to be fucking with some other bitch. I was down for whatever he was down for.

Mentally, I was preparing myself, but when he finally did let go, it was just too much to take in at one time. I swallowed what I could and used the rest to jerk him back into an erection. There was no way I was about to let him out of me getting this last ride in before I left.

Once he got himself together, he pulled me up from him, lifting my body up so that I was positioned over his dick. In a squatting position, I slowly started taking him in, holding on to the headboard for support. Damn, he felt good. I almost lost my footing when the pad of his thumb found my clit, causing me to scream out loud. That shit got me every time, and he knew it.

"Don't lose your balance, babe. Stay up there," he coaxed me as he leaned up and took my nipples into his mouth one at a time.

I didn't think the piercings made a difference. I honestly just thought it was something cute to do, but once healed, they were overly sensitive and drove me crazy any time they were touched. I swear even a cold breeze had me standing at attention. Most times, I was thankful I had them done, and this was one of those moments.

"Chase, wait. I can't take it," I pleaded with him. I was about to explode. My damn legs were starting to feel like wet noodles, and I was gushing out all over him. I could barely breathe as my entire body got hot, feeling like I was on fire.

"Come on, ma. Let that shit out."

He grabbed me by my waist and held me still as he fed me his dick in long but powerful strokes. My damn brain was scrambled at this point, and I didn't know whether I was coming or going. I felt like my damn head was spinning in a 360 on my shoulders, and I couldn't control the sounds coming out of my mouth.

"Cum on this dick. You can do it," he cajoled me in a voice barely above a whisper, but I heard him loud and clear. That shit sent me into overdrive, and before I knew it, I was holding on to him for dear life as my orgasm drained me of everything I had left.

He wasn't done with me, though. He kept stroking me like he had something to prove. I was trying to get loose, but he had me locked down. I was straight losing control of everything, and I was loving it.

He pulled out long enough to flip me over. I was half on the bed, half off, as he got right back in like he never left. He had my ass cheeks in a firm grip, spread apart so that he could get all the way in. He had me pinned to the bed, and all I could do was lay there and take that shit as I used my pussy muscles to milk and squeeze him as he pushed in and pulled out. Lord have mercy, this man was the shit.

I was all the way in it until something caught my eye. I saw my phone lying on the floor with my sister's number on display. I must have accidently dialed her when we got started, but why hadn't she hung up? Was she listening the entire time? I didn't want to bring notice of it to Chase because that shit was weird. Why the hell would she be listening to me and my man having sex? Maybe she didn't notice her phone had rung and it was in her purse or something.

This man was giving me life and taking it back, and I couldn't do shit but enjoy the moment. Just as he was flipping me over, I reached for the phone and pushed it under the bed so that he wouldn't see the screen. It would have been too obvious for me to try to turn it off or disconnect the call, and I could only hope that she didn't hear a damn thing and I was just losing my mind.

What if that shit was on her voicemail? All kinds of thoughts went through my mind, but I had to get back in the game so that I didn't throw him off. I didn't want to ruin the moment.

Chase slowed it down and really took his time with me. As I stared into his eyes, I wondered if this was truly a forever thing. Would he ever betray me? What would our kids look like? Would he stay good to me?

By the time we were done, he had cracked a hard nut that was so deep inside of me, it probably wasn't a far trip to reach my damn ovaries. He laid on me for a while, kissing me deeply and professing his love to me. This man was a keeper for real, and I was glad I took a chance on him. Now, to figure out this shit with my sister.

When he got up to use the restroom, I was finally able to grab my phone from under the bed. To my dismay, the phone still had her number displayed as if we were talking. I put the phone to my ear to see if I could hear breathing and heard nothing. Her phone must have picked up on voicemail and recorded the entire thing. Damn near 45 minutes of me and Chase getting that shit in. The upside was she didn't actually hear us doing it. Now how was I going to keep her from listening to the message?

I disconnected the call and shot her a text, letting her know that we had to talk and the voicemail was an accident. I set the phone on the nightstand and cuddled up under Chase when he got back to the room. I thought we were going to take a nap, but he was rising back up for the occasion. I did what I had to do to put him to sleep this time, but this thing with Sajdah had me worried. I had to go back home so that I could see where we were in our friendship. I loved Chase, but I loved my sister more than life itself. I needed both things to work so that mentally, I could be good either way.

Sajdah

Ready, Set, Go

I had the phone on mute the entire time. Chase was really the man out there, I saw. I'll admit that I was very jealous to hear him with my sister like that. I knew I told him to go ahead and make her think she was his, but maybe I spoke too soon. I knew what sex was like with Chase. She was living her best life right now.

At first, I didn't know what I was hearing. I said hello a few times, but once I stopped to listen and then really paid attention to who was calling, I couldn't hang up. I could only imagine how he had her twisted like a damn pretzel because he definitely had me looking like a professional contortionist plenty of mornings. I was so mad! What the fuck was I thinking letting him go? Why didn't I think this would happen? Hell, he was just doing what I basically begged him to do—fuck my sister. Good, I might add. Yes, I could go get him whenever, but that shit sat differently in your spirit when you knew for sure what was going down. I was thoroughly irritated.

Putting the phone on mute and placing it between my ear and my shoulder, I reached into my stash and pulled out one of my favorite dildos. I had plenty to choose from, but this one reminded me of Chase, girth and all. Chase had some weight on him, and I just closed my eyes and put myself right in my sister's place. I made sure my door was locked because sometimes my parents had a habit of peeking their head in to see if we were up, and I didn't need either one of them to see me busting it open for a fantasy in my head. Also, I didn't want anyone to know I was listening to my sister get nailed to the wall by the man of my dreams. That alone was disappointing all by itself.

Getting myself comfortable, I closed my eyes and pretended that whatever he was doing to her to make her sound like a cat in heat, he was there doing to me. By the time I was done, my hand was going to be all kinds of tired, but I was not about to stop until they did. I was slippery wet, and I just pretended that Chase just gave me some bomb-ass head and was ready to go in.

My sister's moaning turned me on as well, which shocked and appalled me at the same time. Did I sound like that when we were together? That shit was getting to be too much, but I had to hang in there until the end.

Sliding just the head in, I pulled my knees up to my chest and slowly tip-drilled myself just like he would have. Chase never liked to just push himself all the way in at once. He preferred to tease you with the dick and make you beg for it. He would have you feeling like you were going to die if he didn't hurry up and take his time with you. I wanted to feel that stretch as I would try to adjust to how big he was. He could really hurt someone if he wasn't careful. I slowly worked my toy in, and I listened to Selah give one hell of a performance. Envy started to set in pretty quickly at this point, but I pressed on.

"Who else you giving this pussy to?" he asked. I think at this point, he had her from the back because before she had a chance to respond, I could hear his hand connecting with flesh. My clit jumped and pulsed like crazy as I wished it was me. I had to squeeze my legs shut and cover my face with the pillow to keep my parents from hearing me.

"It's all yours," she replied, barely able to catch her breath.

"It better be."

The sounds that came from her next took me over the edge. I wanted to hang up so bad, but I just couldn't press that END CALL button. I was too far in to let go now. I finally got as much as the toy in as I could, and I was working it in and out like my life depended on it. I was sloppy wet, and a warm puddle was beginning to form under my ass. My entire body started to shake, and I was losing control of my rising eruption. So was my sister as she began to beg Chase to let her cum. I was hoping he didn't listen and he would punish her like he did me, but he actually gave her permission to let go. I took the liberty as well, and it felt like every ounce of fluid I had in my body came out though my pussy. I had a hard time breathing for a second, and I finally had to just let the phone go.

If nothing else, I knew I had to backtrack on what I told him. I wasn't willing to give this shit up, even to my sister. I didn't care how he did it, but he was going to have to let Selah go. She would get over it, just like she got over the others. We would just have to keep it extra low key for a while until she was able to live again. After this, she would surely be devastated. I really didn't care if she was or not.

It took me a while, but I gathered myself. When I looked back down, the phone screen was black with a little green light flashing in the corner, indicating that she finally hung up. Just as I was reaching for the phone, a text came through from Selah saying she wanted to talk. When I checked my call log, I saw that we were on the phone for forty-five whole minutes. I hoped she enjoyed herself because I was about to stop all this shit in its tracks. I was kicking myself for even suggesting it, but it was cool. I made a mistake, and now I had to correct it.

I finally got up to get in the shower. Thoughts of Chase had me back in heat as I used the shower head to bust off one more time before I started my day. This man made me weak. I didn't want to be, and it pissed me off.

As I got dressed, I was thinking maybe derailing them wasn't a good idea. I didn't want Chase forever. He was a drug boy and not necessarily the marrying type. There was no future with him. I didn't want that for my sister either, honestly. She deserved better than Chase. She deserved happiness. She deserved a forever that was secure. Chase definitely couldn't provide that. What I needed to do was just pull him away from both of us. Neither one of us was good for him. I wasn't sure what I was going to do, but I knew something needed to happen.

"Hey, sweets, are you up? Your mother is making brunch."

My dad's deep voice seeped through the door, and I immediately smelled bacon cooking. My mom put it down in the kitchen, and I certainly worked up an appetite that morning.

"I'm up, Dad! I'll be down in a second."

By the time I got downstairs, my mother had a beautiful spread of waffles, bacon, eggs, fish, grits, biscuits, and fresh fruit. You would have thought she was feeding a party. I took my usual seat and waited as she first served my dad, then me, and finally herself. She was selfless like that, always making sure everyone else was good before she was. She taught us that quality. That's what I felt like I was doing for Selah. I was making sure she was good while we both enjoyed the benefits. I was sure she wouldn't see it that way at first, but eventually, it would sink in, and she would see where I was going with this.

"Where's your sister?" my mom asked as she prepared her plate.

"She didn't come in last night, I actually need to return her call, but I'm sure she will be in before the weekend is out. No one misses your Sunday dinner," I responded, followed with the fakest smile known to man. I couldn't tell our mom that her daughter wasn't here because she was across town swallowing a dick. Selah would definitely show up if for nothing but the food.

I chatted with my parents a little longer before heading out. I typically didn't work on Saturdays, but because I was spending so many nights with Chase, I actually got a little bit behind at work. He made it hard to focus, which made me start to think that maybe I needed to let Selah chill with him a little longer. She kept him out of my face and occupied for the most part. The only time I really thought about him was in the morning when he wasn't at the train station. I kind of got used to seeing him there, and up until that morning, I was okay with him being gone, until I heard him and my sister together. Decisions, decisions. Did I let them continue, or did I break that shit up early on?

When I got into work, I ran into one of the project managers that I was working with on my current project. I wasn't shocked to see him there, being that we were all overachievers. Our name was on this building. We all absolutely did whatever it took to guarantee success. This dude was funny, though. He'd been practically begging to eat my pussy for months. I really didn't like to mix business with pleasure, and I wasn't a hundred percent sure that he would keep it between us. He was very handsome, and he knew it. Just about every woman in the building was willing to let him bend her over a dirty toilet in the bathroom stall, but he didn't bite. He always declined gracefully and never made them feel stupid for pursuing him. That's how he remained likeable. I don't know what it was about me that he couldn't leave alone, but he was persistent.

"Look what the cat drug in." He greeted me with a smile that would have had me bent over, too, if I were any other person. He was trying to wear me down, playing a patient game of cat and mouse that some days had my body tingling, but I would never admit it. I must admit I was wearing the hell out of these Fashion Nova high-waisted jeans and cropped sweatshirt, complete with a cute kitten ankle boot. I was smelling scrumptious to boot, and I could see it all in his eyes that he wanted to strip me naked on the spot.

"Let's get caught up. I don't want to be here late."

He simply smiled as I shot him down, and he followed behind me like a puppy to my office. This man was really making it difficult to remain professional, but I had to keep my head in the game. I said I would never date someone I worked with, and I meant it.

We barely managed to get through the workday, and by the end, I had to practically run out of my office. He was smelling and looking good, but I couldn't do it. I wanted Chase and was not willing to take on a substitute.

On the way home, I sent him a text, but he never responded. I figured he was maybe still entertaining Selah, but when a few hours had gone by and he hadn't gotten back, I was starting to get irritated. They were doing too much, and he was supposed to just be keeping it simple.

When I got in, Selah still wasn't there, and I refused to call her back. Me and him were going to have a talk. He needed to move the way I told him, or else he would be very upset that he didn't.

I stayed up until I couldn't anymore, but I definitely took note that Selah still wasn't home yet. He definitely had some explaining to do.

Selah

Sister, Sister

I finally made it home Sunday night just in time for my mom's world famous lasagna and garlic bread, and my dad's equally famous peach iced tea. It was good seeing my family after being holed up with Chase since Thursday. Not that being with him was bad, but I loved my family, and spending time with them was important to me. I typically let them know when I wouldn't be home, but it still felt kind of funny.

How did Sajdah do while I wasn't there? She still hadn't returned my text or call from the other day, and I was getting concerned. We'd never gone this long without talking, and I missed my sister.

Chase dropped me off. I invited him in, but he said he had some business that needed his attention. I kissed my man goodbye, promising to call him later in the day before I went to bed. Our conversation got a little deep before we left his house, and I had some thinking to do. As much as I enjoyed Chase, I felt that it was a little soon for us to be officially living together. It had only been three months, for goodness' sake. We still needed time to get to know each other.

"You can be with a person forever and never truly know them." He argued his point as we showered, and he took me doggy style under the water. I could dig that, but we still needed to know more than what we knew now.

Yes, he was charming. Yes, he fucked me good. Yes, he spared no expense to make me happy. Yes, he always put me first, but so did Ike before he started whooping Tina's ass. I just needed to know that he wasn't going to have me chained up to a bed in his condo, unable to move, or locked in a room, pissing in a bucket like R. Kelly allegedly did those chicks on the documentary. Did he have a fetish for little kids? Was he allergic to cats? Where would all of my things go? How many bitches lived there before me? I had questions, and I'd learned that it's sometimes better to just let shit play out as opposed to asking for answers. People would tell you what they thought you wanted to hear, but their actions would tell you what you needed to really know about them. Eyes and pictures never lied. Chase was good and all, but I really needed to see him, and not just when he was naked and dicking me down all crazy.

"I love you more than you know," he said to me as he held my face in his hands.

I had to pinch myself. This shit was just too good to be true.

"I love you, baby," I said to him, kissing him once more before he was able to convince me to go back to his condo for one more ride. My pussy needed a break. He had been in me since I got to his house, and I was sore from all the action. He could do without me for a few nights. I just needed some time to gather my thoughts.

When I got inside, my parents were finishing up dinner. I hugged them and kissed them both on the cheek, immediately conscious of what I had been doing with my mouth since the last time I saw them. The thought made me blush as I hurried to my room to put my stuff down, then to Sajdah's to chat with her before dinner. My room just looked so small now compared to all the space I had at Chase's place. I would have more room there, but I still needed to think things through.

Dashing across the hall, I knocked then twisted the knob to my sister's room, only to find it empty. Where was she on a Sunday evening? A little put off by her absence, I went to the restroom quickly, and then made my way to the kitchen with a puzzled look on my face.

"Where's Sajdah?" I asked my parents as I sat down behind a nice square of lasagna and cheesy garlic bread. My sister never missed lasagna. Where the hell could she be? Was she avoiding me?

"She got picked to work on the new Comcast building project at her job. She should be here shortly," my dad tossed out as he served my mom, then himself.

We held hands as he blessed the food, then began to feast. I felt horrible all over again. How could I miss one of the biggest projects of her career? Why didn't she call me? I was definitely bothered, and I was sure my face showed it. My parents usually knew when something was going on with us, but they pretty much let us handle our own beef until they felt like they had to step in. My sister and I never argued or didn't get along for too long, so I was optimistic once we were able to talk, this too would pass.

It was good talking to my mom and dad. Those two were so in love with each other. They flirted continuously while we ate dinner, my dad tapping her on her butt when she got up to get him more food. They kissed often—not like a tongue-down, sloppy kiss, but a quick peck on the lips or kiss on the cheek while we conversed. They laughed and joked a lot, and you could see the love just oozing out all over them. That was the kind of relationship I wanted with Chase eventually. I couldn't remember a time ever where my parents argued in front of us or anything of that nature. If times got hard for them, we damn sure never knew about it. They didn't miss a beat. We stayed fly, in the best school and best neighborhood. We'd never

missed a meal or gone without utilities. We always had
two things that matched. As far as we knew, they were
always stable, and they genuinely cared about each other.
You can't fake that kind of happiness. Seeing them happy
made me happy.

Our conversation was lit as we caught up talking about
our week and what we had planned for the family for
the summer. We took trips every year, and my parents
had property in Aspen that we frequented. I was a
little shocked that my dad asked if Chase was going to
accompany us on our annual trip to Turks and Caicos in
the spring. He must have really been feeling him.

I was concerned at first about them meeting, but after
the third time with Chase coming in to chat with my dad
when he dropped me off, I felt more at ease. I wanted to
introduce him to Sajdah, but she was never around. This
made it easy because if I had to choose, I would choose
my family every time and drop Chase like a bad habit. I
loved him, but my love for family was unconditional.

Just as we were laughing at some show my dad was
trying to convince us to watch, Sajdah walked in. She
kissed my mom and dad on the cheek and threw me a
quick "hey" before heading toward her room. My parents
didn't seem to notice, but the tension was definitely
there. Usually, we exchanged a hug or something when
we hadn't seen each other, but she straight slid past the
kid like I wasn't family, avoiding eye contact and all. That
shit hurt my feelings. I started to get up and go after her,
but what would I say? Maybe she was acting like that
because she heard the damn message.

I didn't want to cause a scene in front of our parents,
so I grabbed my phone and scrolled through to see if I
had missed a text from anyone important. I put my ring-
er on mute as a rule so that we wouldn't be interrupted
during dinner. Just when I thought I couldn't take wait-

ing for her anymore, she came out and joined us at the table, scooting her chair closer to my dad so that she wasn't right next to me. Our mom had made her a plate of food and began serving our dad and me slices of lemon cake and chocolate ice cream.

She jumped into the conversation, sounding extra excited about her venture with Comcast. She didn't speak directly to me at any given moment, just kind of keeping the conversation mutual amongst everyone. I wanted to share in her excitement, but she wasn't letting me in. There was no way I would be able to sleep that night if we didn't talk.

While they were finishing up, I excused myself from the table and went to grab a quick shower. I put all the clothes I had dirtied in my bins for washing, and I began going through my closet to see what I had for the next day. I tried to rock out, but I was truly bothered by my sister's behavior. Was I overreacting?

I hopped in the shower right quick, and by the time I got out, I heard her moving around in her room. I took that moment to go in there and see how we could make amends for whatever was coming between us.

When I reached for her door handle to turn it, it didn't budge. She locked me out! This was more serious than I thought. Tears shot to my eyes immediately, and I had to blink them back before knocking. It had been years since we'd been in this space. Why wouldn't she talk to me about whatever issue she was having? This behavior was so unlike her.

"Who is it?" she answered from the other side.

"Selah."

It got quiet for a while. She actually made me stand at the door for damn near a minute before opening it. At this point, I was just getting irked. There was no way my having a boyfriend was causing this much anxiety in her life. Chase was not my first man.

"Yes?" she asked, sticking her head out of a crack in the door.

I was steaming. "Hey, love, can we talk?"

She looked hesitant at first, but I guess once she got done spinning it around in her head, she decided to let me in. I came in and took a seat on her bed and looked around. She was so anal about everything. There wasn't a thing out of place in the entire room. Shoes lined up perfectly, clothing color coded in her closet, accessories stacked nice and neat—her room looked the complete opposite of mine, even on my best day.

"So, I got your message," she said with a look of disgust on her face. I was immediately embarrassed. "As soon as I realized what I was hearing, I deleted the message."

"Sajdah, I didn't know. I thought I had hung up . . ."

"Listen, adults have sex. It's no big deal. Is that all you wanted to discuss?" she asked before turning back to her closet to rummage through her clothing.

Wow! She straight dismissed the fuck out of me. It took everything in me not to get a running start from the end of the hall and drop kick her simple ass. This was just too much to deal with.

"Well, actually, I wanted to know why your attitude has been so fucked up lately. Why are you avoiding me?" I didn't hold any of the punches I had planned to. I was thinking of a subtle approach, but she was succeeding at bringing the bitch out of me. I didn't deserve the way she was treating me, and we both knew it.

"Right now we are in two different places," she began with a sigh. "You have love right now, and that's great. I'm happy for you. Right now, I'm loving the direction my career is taking me in, so I'm focused. We won't be joined at the hip forever, Selah. We're not growing apart; we're growing up."

I was crushed. We were definitely growing apart, and I wasn't ready. Before I lost control of my emotions, I just stayed quiet. Shit, I really didn't know what to say because I wasn't expecting that response. Normally, we talked out our differences, then kissed and made up. This time around, it wasn't working out like that.

"So, did you need anything else?" she asked, finally facing me. She still wouldn't make eye contact with me. Was this shit really that deep?

"I guess not," I replied as I got up and moved toward the door.

She turned back around, now searching through her shoe collection. I closed her door quietly as I left, and by the time I got to my room, I was a mess. I buried my face in my pillow so that no one would hear me cry. This was horrible.

Gathering myself enough to grab my phone, I texted my girls to let them know we had to talk. My heart was broken, and I wasn't sure it could be easily fixed.

Calling Chase, I spoke to him for a little while before taking it down for the night after promising him that I would come and stay with him a few nights that week. I was sad, but I was sure by the time I saw him, I would be ready for what he had to bring.

Saying a quick prayer before sleep, I asked God to show me what I needed to see to get my relationship back on track with my sister. I wasn't used to us being in such a negative space, and I wasn't about to allow it to drag out.

Chase

It's What You Asked For

Basically, I had to start ignoring her calls and texts. What you was not gonna do was tell me I couldn't fuck no other bitch but your identical twin sister because you didn't want me like that, and then turn around and get mad because I started to feel some type of way about her. What did she think was going to happen? Clearly, she didn't think that shit through, and I didn't want to switch shit up now on her terms.

I didn't get into this to like Selah. Hell, I was really just in it for the pussy. I was well prepared to hit that shit until I couldn't, but she had your boy in his bag. I genuinely started to like her. I'd even put it on the record that I loved her. She was really cool people, come to find out. We laughed a lot, we talked about some deep shit, and in all honesty, I was ready to wife her up. She literally had me out there thinking that I could pass this drug game on to one of my strongest soldiers, maybe open a storefront or something. I don't know, but I did know that I was really digging old girl, and Sajdah just had to get over it. Contrary to popular belief, she really had no choice in the matter.

I tried to play it cool at first, but shorty was getting too demanding. It was easier to let her think she was running shit, but what I didn't tolerate was disrespect. She'd fuck around and find herself at the bottom of the

Schuylkill fucking with me. She had the chance for me to care about her, but she passed it on to her sister. It wasn't fair to Selah, and it was time for me to let her know how we were moving forward. I was trying to let it just play itself out, hoping maybe she would just get tired of me avoiding her, but this one was persistent, and it was working my last nerve.

We need to talk.

I read the text and started not to respond. I used to think her being demanding was cute. Now, not so much. Maybe it was time that we did talk so that the boundaries could be understood. I didn't argue with women, and I wasn't about to start with her.

We sure do.

I texted back right as this little honey dip I had walked into the room. I had to stop this shit, and I knew it, especially if I was going to take shit with Selah to the next level. I kept these hoes around to keep from catching feelings, but that wasn't working anymore, and lately, all I'd been feeling was guilt. I didn't see it coming, but when those feelings got there, it hit me like a ton of bricks. In my Kevin Hart voice, *I wasn't ready.*

Shorty was bad, too. Honey-colored complexion, wide hips with a fat ass, a slight trace of stretch marks from a previous pregnancy that only added to the sexiness of her body, nice breasts that could go braless, and cute honey-colored curls cut close to her head. She was amazing to look at, and a part of me couldn't wait to see what her mouth felt like. She had nice full lips that I wanted to kiss, but I deemed it too personal. The only person I kissed was Selah. Those were my rules. She smelled like cocoa butter, and her skin was so soft. I wanted to bust her guts open so bad, but for some reason, I couldn't do it. I mean, I wanted to do it, but my dick wouldn't cooperate. This entire situation was frustrating.

"When did you start getting so nervous around me?" she asked, a slight smile on her face as she crawled up my body on the bed and lay on top of me. She was tall for a girl, standing almost 5 feet 11 inches flat, in heels over six feet. She was thick, Lord knows, and the warmth of her body on mine had my senses in overdrive. This wasn't our first time at this rodeo, and she was damn good from what I remembered. I just couldn't do it and quickly came to the conclusion that it was best for her to leave.

"I'm not nervous, love," I assured her, gently lifting her body and placing her next to me. The pout on her face was adorable, but I had to get her out of there. "Now is just not a good time. Can I get a raincheck?"

Reluctantly, she got up and began to get dressed. She was never one to argue. That's what I liked about her. She knew how to keep this adult, no matter how much she wanted me. I slid her a stack on the way out to compensate for her time, and I stood in the door until she was out of the lot. This shit was crazy. I'd never had a female put me in my feelings like this. Maybe it was time I settled down. I wasn't even sure that settling was what Selah wanted to do. We never really talked about it, and we talked about a lot of stuff. Current events, work shit for her, street shit for me, but never any past stuff. That alone scared the hell out of me because I wasn't completely sure she could handle all of these bodies I had on me. The luggage I carried wasn't for the weak. I wanted to tell her, but I had to wait on it. What I had to say wasn't casual conversation. All of this would be a life changer, and once she knew my secrets, she was in for life, or I had to kill her. No pun intended at all.

Deciding to get in the shower and get my life together, I went and turned the water on so that the bathroom could get steamy. I turned the radio to Pandora and queued up Carl Thomas because ya boy was definitely emotional right now. I wanted Selah to come over then, but I knew she had to spend time with her family. They were very important to her, and I liked that about her. I couldn't wait to introduce her to my people, the same as she did with me. As far as she knew, I hadn't met her sister yet, although I'd seen them out plenty of times, and all I knew was that she was a twin. If only she knew how far from the truth that was.

When I stepped into the shower, I stood directly under the force, allowing the extra hot water to relax my tense muscles. Immediately, I began to fantasize about the last time I had Selah in there with me. At first, I had her pinned to the wall with a firm grip on her hair right at the scalp, just how she liked it. She had a deep arch in her back as she took that shit like a true champ, all with water spraying in her face. It wasn't long before I had my dick in my hand, using the soap as a lubricant as I stroked myself into an erection so hard it was almost painful. Visualizing her now hanging on by the curtain rod as I pounded up into her was getting me right where I needed to be. I had a firm grip on her soft ass as I bounced her up and down, and she started screaming out that she was about to explode. I stepped out of the shower as carefully as I could so that we wouldn't both end up on the floor, and planted her on the sink, never missing a beat until we both were satisfied. That last playback took me over the edge, and I splattered all over the wall in front of me. I was literally shaking afterward and knew I would have to convince her to get there before midweek. She needed to be there every night.

It took me a minute or two, but I finally gathered enough strength to get washed and out of the shower. When I got back to my room and looked at my phone, I had seventeen messages from Sajdah. She was really working my nerves, and I didn't have the energy to give her at the moment. I wanted to just chill that day, but old girl was making it impossible. I decided to get some clothes on my body before dealing with her. I barely got my boxers on good before I heard someone outside, acting like a damn maniac and banging on my door. This was a peaceful neighborhood.

I didn't need my neighbors hearing or seeing her out there acting a ratchet mess. Sprinting to the door, I opened in just enough time to catch her preparing to throw stones at my window. Needless to say, I was turned off by her actions.

"What the fuck is wrong with you?" I asked as I snatched her simple ass in the house and then looked to be sure no one saw this bullshit before closing the door. I had drugs in the crib. I didn't need the damn cops to come and be on some extra shit because I was black in this type of environment. She was doing way too much at this time of day. Why wasn't she at work? That's what was more important, right?

"I've been calling and texting your phone for over an hour." She had the nerve to really be upset.

I just looked at her like she was a strange piece of fruit. When I saw her, I saw Selah, and I had to keep in mind who I was talking to.

"I was in the shower, Sajdah. I do that sometimes."

I turned and walked away from her, heading up to my bedroom to finish getting dressed. My plan was to hit the block that day and make sure everything was kosher, then later hit the mall to see what Zales had in the case. Yeah, it was a little early on, and I wasn't necessarily buying the ring today. I just wanted to be prepared to move forward when it was time. Selah deserved all of me. I was ready to give it to her.

"I don't want you seeing my sister anymore."

"What?" Pause. Was she psycho? There was no way I was walking away from possibly the best thing I'd had ever. Bye, girl.

"I don't want you with Selah anymore."

"So, you plan on putting the time in? I thought work was more important."

Her entire demeanor changed, and so did mine. Smug look on full blast, I turned and continued my journey up the stairs and to my room. She was out of her damn mind, and the right thing to do would be to let her ass go. That way, she could move on, and Selah and I could just move forward. I could hear her finally coming up the steps behind me, and I began to get dressed as quickly as possible so that we could both get out the house. She had me weak in that atmosphere.

When she got to the room, she was only wearing heels. How in hell she got naked that fast was beyond me. I stood at attention immediately, and it was starting to be more of a struggle to maintain my composure. Why was she doing this to me?

"I know what I said," she said, walking toward me. She looked damn good, and I responded to her unwillingly. These two just had me like that. "And you're right. I don't have the time, but hearing y'all on the phone the other morning made me so jealous."

What in the hell was she talking about? My face said everything as she went on to give me the explanation. By this time, she was right in my face, completely waxed pussy in kissing distance, clitoral hood piercing begging for my attention. The temptation was just too much, and I broke out in a sweat. She could see that she had control at this point, and it made me nervous.

"She dialed me by accident on Saturday morning, and I heard everything. You were really putting in work. I couldn't get my dildo out fast enough." She smiled as she bent down in front of me and pushed me back so that she could pull down my sweats. She stopped briefly to take off the one shoe I had on, and when she pulled my pants down, my dick jumped out like a damn jack-in-the-box and swayed back and forth like the king cobra he was, begging her to taste him. I didn't want this to happen again, but she had me, and she knew it.

"I can wait for you, though, and I guess we can just move forward as planned. Just keep in mind who set this all up for you."

Before I could respond, the head of my dick was touching her tonsils, and my toes were gripping the carpet for dear life. This shit wasn't right, but at this moment in time, there was nothing I could do. By the time she started her slow ride, that sealed the deal, and I was at least able to get her to agree to fall back just a little. Her sister didn't need to know all of this, and I needed more time to plan on getting away from her indefinitely. She was playing this game like a boss, and it was time for me to level up.

Selah

Getting Fed Up

By the morning, I was more so irritated than hurt. I tossed and turned all night, trying to figure this shit out. When I saw her in the hall as she was coming out of the bathroom, she avoided eye contact as she practically sprinted to her room, no good morning or anything. I wanted to dog-walk her ass, but I had to remember she was my sister. Maybe what she was going through had nothing to do with me, and I was out there feeling all guilty and shit for no damn reason. I knew my girls would make better sense of it, so I just held my thoughts in. They would know what to do.

By the time I got to work, of course, my coffee and muffin were already paid for. That definitely put a smile on my face. Chase had me covered whether he was there or not. I felt secure with him, and that was a great feeling. By the time I got to my desk, I had a text from him that made me smile even harder.

Good morning, beautiful. Enjoy breakfast. Missing you over here.

This man really knew how to wrap me around his damn finger. At first, I was blushing from reading his message, then I was blushing because Cici caught me blushing. I had to laugh at myself.

"Somebody is glowing," she instigated as her fingers flew across her keyboard at a mile a minute. "You must have had a spectacular weekend."

"It's always good with that man of mine," I responded with this crazy-wide smile on my face. Chase really made me happy, and it momentarily made me forget my issues with my sister.

Sitting down and booting up my computer, I texted with Chase a little more before officially starting to work. In the midst of that, I also confirmed my meetup with Skye and Vice for lunch. I needed them to talk some sense into me before I straight snapped on Sajdah. We'd had beef before, and shit got bad, but not like this. Hell, we were all entitled to our emotions, but when it was directly affecting the flow, something had to give. There was nothing I could think of that was so deep that it would have her gunning for my jugular like this.

Thankfully, lunchtime came around quickly. I grabbed a salad from the cafeteria and met Skye and Vice in the garden behind the building. We embraced like we hadn't seen each other in years. I was so happy to see them I almost cried. You ever have someone that no matter how embarrassing a situation, you could just tell them and not feel judged? I had that with both Skye and Vice. We'd always kept it a bean with each other, and if I were wrong about something, they would surely tell me.

"So, I don't know what the hell is going on with Sajdah," I tossed out as I looked down and began to slice up my salad. Had I been looking up, I would've seen the knowing glance that these two shared, but they knew me enough to know that some shit, I had to find out on my own. It wasn't until they felt it absolutely necessary that they would step in.

"What's going on with y'all?" Skye asked as she devoured her turkey burger. She was the only girl I knew that could eat any damn thing under the sun and never gained a pound out of place. She was curvy and thick, but definitely not fat. All that horrible food went right where it needed to be. Meanwhile, I was running off of coffee and good dick to keep me stable. I had to do better.

"I really don't know. I know I've been spending a lot of time with Chase, but I've been giving y'all time too. It's been a while since I've had any man, let alone one like him, so you would think she would be happy for me."

"Man, fuck her," Vice said between bites of her burger and shoving fries in her mouth. She did not like my sister for some reason. Like, they really did not get along. Vice always gave her respect, though, and, as far as I could see, never tried to purposely make Sajdah feel any type of way. I just didn't entertain the shit with either one of them because I refused to choose between them. We would have to learn to coexist.

"Be nice, Vicerean." Skye laughed as she enjoyed her food.

I had a piece of lasagna from the night before, but I was saving it for later when I went to see Chase. He loved my mom's lasagna. These two already had me feeling better.

"Maybe she's jealous. She won't let anybody close enough to that pussy to loosen her tight ass up. She needs a good dicking."

We looked at Vice and fell the hell out. This girl thought dick would solve all the world's problems. It would be pretty dope if it did, though. As much as I hated to, I kind of agreed with Vice. If Sajdah had a man, she wouldn't be so worried about what I had going on. She needed a distraction. All the hell she had was work and school. I didn't even think she hung out with the few friends she did have.

I wondered if Chase had siblings. He didn't mention anyone, and that realization just made it to the list of reasons why we weren't ready to live together. I really didn't know much about him, even after all this time. I made a mental note to talk to him about that when I saw him again. If I were eventually going to be Mrs. Warren, I needed to know that I wasn't marrying into the Mob against my will.

"Well, what do you think may be happening?" Skye asked.

"I don't know. She should be happy right now. She just landed a development account with Comcast through her firm. This is maybe her third one in the last six months. She's a good worker and a very innovative thinker. They pick her for a lot of projects, so her bank account has to be sick as hell right now," I replied while sharing her good news in the process.

"The damn flu! I know she got 1 . . . 2 . . . 3 . . . 4 . . . 5 . . . 6 . . . 7 . . . 8 . . . *M*s in her bank account," both girls sang in unison.

We were out there cracking up. I promise they always made me feel better. I lost it when Vice jumped up from the table and started twerking. Good thing we were in the yard by ourselves!

"Well, don't stress yourself. You know how she gets sometimes. I'll definitely keep a lookout to see if some shit popping off that she ain't telling. You know I be Inch High Private Eye out this bitch," Vice assured me as she tore into her fully loaded cheese fries.

Vice got the scoop on every damn thing, and always only accurate information. I hated to put the team on my sister, but I needed solid facts so that I could handle her properly. She wasn't making it easy to figure her out, so I had to do what I had to do for my own sanity.

We finished up our lunch while discussing what we had planned for the week. Skye was currently boo'd up too, so her week was pretty much centered around her man. My crazy ass signed up for another semester, so I had homework on the agenda.

"I'm digging in pockets and riding on dicks for the next four days," Vice said with a straight face. We busted out in laughter again. She was dead-ass serious, but it was humorous, something we all needed.

Going back to work, I set thoughts of my sister to the side and decided to concentrate on what made me happy, and at the moment, Chase was it.

Hey, love, how is your day going?

Better when I see you, I responded, smiling hard as shit in the process. Do you have time to stop by my job when I get off? I got a piece of my mom's lasagna for you, but I have to go home. I have homework to do.

While waiting for him to respond, I worked on my project for school a little so that I wouldn't have a ton of work to do when it was time for me to turn it in. I was only taking two classes, but I swear the amount of work they gave me was enough for, like, ten people. These classes were supposed to cater to working adults. How did they think we had time for all of this stuff they wanted us to do?

"You can come feed me the lasagna and do your home-work here."

Now, he knew that was a damn lie. Chase didn't know how to be in my presence and not touch me. Vice versa for me as well. This man turned me on in any way you could possibly imagine. If I were going to focus, I couldn't be around him. I wouldn't get a damn thing accomplished at his house but multiple orgasms.

I'll come by Thursday. You know I can't focus around you, I texted back as my mind began to wander. I had to stay focused before he had me twisted like a pretzel. Again. Standing firm, I decided I was going home.

Okay, I'll stop by and get it. See you shortly.

I hurried through my work for the rest of the afternoon, begging the clock to keep up. I kept saying to myself that I was going straight home and not letting him persuade me to do anything else. I really lucked up with Chase. He knew what he had in me. Too bad my ex, Kevin, couldn't see it. I hated that thoughts of him even popped in my head, but at least I didn't have to worry about him anymore.

Skye Moore

Just Can't Act Right

"So, how we gonna tell this bitch about this snake-ass nigga?"

It took everything in me to keep it together during lunch with Selah the other day. I could have died when she asked what was up with Sajdah, and I was hoping Vice's crazy ass didn't just spit that shit out. It was going to take more than a blurry picture of his car in front of a chicken joint at night to convince Selah that Chase wasn't all he pretended to be. We still didn't even know why they were together. We had to at least figure that part out first. He had my girl floating on cloud nine, and if we were going to yank that cloud from under her, we had to make sure that she could at least land on her feet. This shit could get real messy, so we had to be extra on point this time around. There was no room for mistakes. We didn't want another Kevin type situation to arise. It was hard to bounce back from that one.

I was ready to body that fool. How dare he have my sister/friend looking crazy in these streets. I was the chick that would be out in the street with your picture on a T-shirt, hashtagging everything and passing out flyers to find you, knowing the entire time you were clocked in my trunk, bleeding to death, but couldn't scream because I done cut your damn voice box out. I was the one hugging your momma at the wake like Bishop in *Juice,* promising to find the one that killed you, knowing I was the one responsible for your demise. I didn't give a fuck about no nigga when it came to my girls. I was an only child, so these bitches were like my true sisters.

I didn't play around when it came to them, and they didn't play when it came to me. Everyone thought Vice was the loose cannon because she was the loudest, but the quiet ones were always the ones that got shit done for real. Don't sleep on me, or you'd be sleep for real. Don't sleep on Vice, either. She was more than willing to back up every loud-ass word that came out of her mouth. Trust me on this one. If you valued your life, you let us be great. Please and thank you.

"Girl, I'm not sure. I need to really see what's up with them, though, before we move with that, because this shit is about to be devastating for her."

"Tell me about it," I replied, shaking my damn head. "Well, it's time we start making moves before it gets too out of hand. Hopefully, it's not what we are thinking and we can just get past this shit."

"Girl, you know it's exactly what we think it is. We just gotta prove it. I'll hit you as soon as I know something more."

Damn. I was really hoping that Chase was one of the good ones and just maybe we were finally wrong about some shit. This was not going to end well, and I hated that we couldn't prevent it from happening, whatever "it" may be. Looking at my guy while he slept beside me, I knew I wouldn't hesitate to put a bullet right between his eyes if I found out he was playing me. I didn't take my heart getting tampered with at all, especially since it took so much for me to let people in. Selah was the same way, so if it were some shady shit going on, it wouldn't end well for those involved.

Foster care makes you a different person. I'm not going to say I had to fight my way through the system. My struggle wasn't that hard because I was not weak, but I had to knock a few niggas in they face that thought they were just going to slide up in my bed. I would not be taken advantage of by anyone. I sounded like Sofia in *The Color Purple* because I swear all my life I had to fight to some degree or the next. I was fighting cousins, uncles, and friends of the family off of me to keep from getting raped and molested. I had to fight my own mom for trying to steal from me to feed a drug habit. I fought bitches in school because I didn't have a lot and they thought they were going to tease me and play in my face. Ask the last guy that tried to play me. Oh, you can't because we got rid of his ass. Sorry, not sorry. It never really felt like my struggle was any harder than anyone else. People like me did what we had to do to survive.

Looking over at my man, my heart fluttered a little. He was the first in a very long time to show me that he cherished me and did not just say whatever to pacify me. He actually got me, who I was, what I stood for, and what I would not tolerate. I gave him that same respect, and I prayed over him and for him daily. Some shit was just too good to believe it was real, and on so many occasions, I had to check myself to keep from self-sabotaging what we had. He was the real deal. I had to give him his props where they were due.

Deciding that he had slept long enough, I pulled the covers back to get a clear view of what he was working with. Even flaccid, it looked heavy and veiny. I started salivating just thinking about the taste of him. I had just put him to sleep about an hour ago and figured that was enough time for him to rest up. The call I had with Vice took a little longer than expected, but it was required for us to move forward.

Going down, I lifted him gently and took him into my mouth. I loved how I tasted on him as well, and that shit had me turned all the way on. Slow and steady always won the race with him, so I knew just what to do to get him back ready to go.

He slowly began to wake up, his hips moving in an up and down motion, letting me know that he liked what he felt. Pretty soon, he began to rub my back, periodically grabbing me by the back of my neck to stop me from making him explode. I took in as much of him as I could, partially gagging. Tears sprang to my eyes as I tried to swallow him whole. That kind of shit turned him on beyond belief.

Moving my hair out of the way so that he could see me in action, I made sure to make it real sloppy and wet as I sucked him up and down like a lollipop. Every time he closed his eyes, I stopped, only starting again when he looked at me. His fingers found their way to my clit, moving in a slow, circular motion that had me humming up against him as I greedily stuffed his balls into my mouth one at a time.

"Baby girl, what you tryna to do me?"

My mouth was too full to answer. I needed him to understand that I was willing to do anything that needed to be done. There was no need for him to search for anything outside of this home. He was the man on these streets, and it was always some bitch in his face trying to link up. He shot they asses down without hesitation because he knew there was nothing out there worth losing what he had here.

The only people that knew about us were my girls and a few of his friends. We didn't feel the need to broadcast our shit. It was our business what we had going on. No one else's opinion really mattered.

He begged for it, and I finally complied. Lying down next to him, I opened my legs so that he could get in. He crawled up to me on his knees and inserted just the head. We could feel each other pulse as I greedily contracted my walls, trying to pull him in more. I got extra wet for him every time, and that shit drove him crazy.

I must admit sex with him was pretty damn good. It wasn't the most mind-blowing sex I'd ever had, but it was close. He brought so much more to the relationship than just good dick, so it was easy to enjoy times like this with him. He actually courted me in the beginning, often saying that we had plenty of time for sex, and he wanted to know me aside from being able to suck his dick good. Not many dudes like that in the street, ya heard? Every man out there was out to bed as many bitches as possible, and then you'd find that one that was the bomb. Lucky me.

I was a little leery of that shit at first. Who doesn't want free pussy? I even said something to my girls about it, and of course, Vice had all kinds of answers. He had a small dick, his stroke game was fucked up, he had a girlfriend already, he had a disease—this girl came up with everything under the sun. I was curious, though, so I decided to take a chance on it. It was the best decision I'd ever made.

By the time he got done spoiling me to death and showing me what it really meant to have someone genuinely care about your well-being, I was begging him to take the pussy. Baby, let me tell you how he killed that shit. He was the silent but deadly type. You never knew what he was going to do, and the mystery surrounding him just added to his appeal.

Immediately, I was impressed with the size. He wasn't super long, but he had enough, and it was thick and meaty. That shit made me salivate every time I thought about it. There was nothing like too much dick when the man attached to it had no idea how to use it. That was a super annoying situation and a waste of time for everyone involved. His dick, though . . . lawd! It was pretty to look at, if a dick could be pretty, I mean. I swear I could just stare at it all day as if it were a statue in a museum. More importantly, he knew how to work with what he had. He wasn't a pound-me-to-death type dude. He knew when to give me just some of it, and when I wanted it all. He knew just when to speed it up or slow down so much I was ready to pull my hair out. He wasn't afraid to let me be in control sometimes, and when shit felt good to him, I knew it. He wasn't all loud and dumb, but he was very expressive.

I fell in love with him long before we were intimate, so I knew he was going to be it for the long haul. I was ready to propose to this nigga, but I wasn't that bitch. It'd never happen if he were waiting on me.

I knew he had me when I didn't have the urge to hit anyone else up. I was a bit of a ho and always kept a heavy rotation just in case someone wasn't available. He had my undivided attention, and I didn't need the attention of anyone else. I felt safe with him. I knew he would protect me, and he never disappointed me.

Selah felt the same way with Chase, so if it were some shit going on, she would be distraught. Hopefully, Vice was just overreacting. Maybe he was still one of the good ones and it wasn't what we thought it was.

As I surrendered my body to my man, I just sent a quick prayer up that Chase wasn't as stupid as he appeared to be. He would not like the outcome if he were.

Selah

Flash Back Friday

I lived and breathed Kevin. He was my first real *boy-friend* boyfriend, and I loved everything about him. He made me feel so special, and I never would have guessed that the amount of hurt and betrayal I received from him would change me the way it did. Because of him, my trust moving forward was at an all-time low with anyone I dealt with, and if you wanted me, you really had to prove yourself to me like you were trying to get into the pearly gates and I had control of the golden book.

I caught my first body with him. I hoped he would be the last. I quickly found out I would have to do it again. These dudes knew nothing about loyalty nowadays, and sometimes you just had to do them dirtier than they could have ever done you. Men couldn't handle that kind of shit, though, so when you got they ass, you had to be prepared to body them if necessary.

It was weird how we met. I thought he worked in my building because he was always there. At the time, I was friends with this girl name Shanna. She was the fourth member of our crew, kind of, and I loved her the same way I loved Vice and Skye. She had her own group of friends that were from her neighborhood in Bartram Village, and I had my girls, but sometimes we hung out together. Like, we weren't best friends, but we were cool as fuck. She was a little instrumental in helping Kevin and I get together, but come to find out snakes sometimes roll in packs. Unfortunately, I had to get her ass too. Vice never liked her. Skye was always neutral about her being around. I just let the chips fall where they may.

Back to the situation at hand . . .

There were hundreds of offices and different practices in our location, so all kinds of people came in and out. We weren't all dressed in suits, etc., so you were liable to see a young man looking like he just stepped right off of Beard Gang, dressed in the signature gray sweats and white tee. I learned a long time ago that clothes don't make the person. Even millionaires had dress-down days.

He was nice and dark—that smooth black with a full goatee and juicy lips. I knew for sure he had a million bitches on his ass, but I didn't care. I wanted to dip into that fountain with everyone else. During those days, I wasn't looking to give my heart to anyone, I just kept my pussy waxed so that they could put the entire thing in their mouth and not choke on a hairball. I got my nut and bounced on they ass every single time, not calling or returning correspondence until I was ready to. I was a free spirit and definitely not ready to be tied down. In my mind, I had plenty of time for that, and at that moment, the world was my carnival game, and these dudes were all the prizes I had to choose from.

Typically, I didn't play with dudes at the gig, but this one for a split second seemed worth the risk. At the moment, it was a risk I was willing to take.

He always smelled amazing, too. Not like stale blunt guts and Chinese store platters. He always had that fresh-out-the-shower smell that I was sure drove every woman in his life bananas. And let's get into this body. He definitely worked out a few days a week, but he wasn't overly muscular. He had enough strength to carry you around the room, but he wasn't so toned that his arms couldn't touch his sides. He had a pretty white smile that was a stark contrast to his dark chocolate complexion. Definite model material.

He had me open very early on, but I refused to clue him in on that tidbit of info until I was ready. I'd be damned if he thought he was going to treat me like the rest of the chickens around there running and clucking behind him. I knew my worth then, and I know it now. I just had to clue his ass in to what the deal really was. I was able to submit and let a man lead if he showed himself capable. If he were not, he was treated like a thot.

So, I ignored him for a while. I wasn't about to let this dude know he had me masturbating every night like a damn dog in heat. I wanted him, but he wouldn't get me that easy like he got the rest of those hoes. I wasn't above a quick fuck in the bathroom stall at work, but he wouldn't know that right away. I'd have to see how he acted first before divulging that little secret. I was a real freak for my man and was ready to drop that shit at the drop of a dime. I was the bitch giving him head while he did a hundred on the freeway at 3 a.m. Hopefully, he would be fortunate enough to experience that with me. He had work to do. He would get to chase me just like everyone else did.

I would see him in the building, and come to find out he worked in the mailroom there. He flirted with all the ladies in the building like most of the mail guys did, and we blushed and gushed over him like idiots. I noticed that his conversations got a little longer over time with me. We went from offering me a hello to small hugs and coffee over a few months. My cat twitched every time he got near me, but I held it down, determined that he was surely getting enough head and tail from everyone else around there. He didn't need to add me to the mix.

"I want to take you out," he announced one day while dropping off mail. It wasn't a request; it was more like a demand.

I was stunned. What did he see in me that he skipped everyone else? Or was I just next on the list of lunch dates? He had me smiling but questioning him at the same time. I wasn't about to let him have me out there looking crazy, but I wasn't about to pass up a free meal with my greedy ass. He had me turned on a little bit, but not enough to not hold my ground.

"What did you have in mind?" I inquired while already deciding what I had a taste for. If nothing else, I never passed up a plate.

"DMX is going to be at the TLA. We should go. You look like you like to turn up."

Oh, did I! This man was really trying to get some yams! I was just looking at the lineup on Facebook earlier in the week and was trying to decide if I wanted to go. The Theater of Living Arts honestly was like a death trap, literally one way in and one way out. So, if some shit went down in there, you were liable to get trampled. However, it wasn't a huge venue, so the amount of people was limited, unlike the Wells Fargo Center, where thousands would show up. I was really trying to decide if seeing The Lox, Lil' Kim, Foxy Brown, and DMX was worth risking my life. I quickly decided it was.

"We should go. Let's talk details later," I replied, afterward storing my number in his phone. I didn't know at the time that this would end in such devastation. This wasn't supposed to get serious. We were just, you know, kicking it. Folks had a way of sneaking into your heart that caught you completely off guard, and then the next thing you knew, you were digging a hole to hide the body because they thought you were the one to play with. Dating was too damn exhausting and frustrating for no good reason. Why couldn't people just act right?

Your boy asked me out, I texted to Shanna jokingly. She had a thing for him low key but kept saying it wasn't that serious. We were on some ho shit that summer—no serious relationship, just getting the dick and scramming on they asses. Neither one of us wanted a serious relationship with anyone. At least that was my truth.

Say word, she replied back.

I could only imagine her face. We both geeked over him, but it wasn't a competition. She worked in the building as well, two floors down in one of the law offices. We always rode in on the regional rail in the morning, and one day we just started chatting it up. Come to find out we had a lot in common. Vice and Skye were not beat for her ass, though, even though I tried to make us all friends.

Word.

Yaaassss, bitch! Get that shit! she replied, causing me to bust out laughing.

I'll let you know for certain before the day is out. Meet me at the crib just in case it's some real shit happening.

Later in the day, I got a text to confirm he was serious about our date. The show was in a few weeks, so I guessed he wanted to make sure he should purchase the tickets. Shortly after confirming, I got a text showing paid tickets. I immediately started mentally going through my wardrobe to see what I had to wear or if I needed to get something fresh. As mentioned, the TLA was not like the Wells Fargo, and it was a rap concert. I wasn't walking up in there in a short dress and stilettos, but even a pair of jeans and some cute sneakers had to make a statement. You never knew who you would run into while out, and I needed to always be on point. Deciding that I would raid my sister's closet before purchasing something new, I was satisfied with the options I thought I had.

Things with Kevin moved pretty quickly leading up to the concert. He still flirted with all the ladies in the building, but he paid extra special attention to me when he stopped in my department to deliver mail. Our conversation lingered a little longer each time, and my clit would always jump every time he showed up. If he pressed hard enough, he was bound to get to test this cat out, but I wasn't about to let him know that. I was battling with myself to keep this situation light, but my hormones were winning.

"Bitch, your pussy is worth more than a concert at the TLA. If he was taking you to The Garden and buying the outfit, that would be a different story."

Gotta love Vice. Whether I wanted to hear it or not, she always kept it a bean with both me and Skye, who at the moment was going through a crazy breakup with her dude. I saw his creep ass with some other bitch, but I didn't press the issue at first. Seeing is believing, but sometimes you still had to be a hundred percent sure that your eyes were really telling you what you needed to know. No room for mistakes, just straight facts. What was crazy was we caught him with one of her other friends and had to stomp this bitch out because she just wouldn't respect the girl code. If his girl told you he got a girl, just keep it pushing. Don't go trying to be a super hero and get your fronts knocked out. No dick was worth a set of veneers. It was too costly of a price tag to have to deal with.

I felt bad for my friend and didn't want to burden her with my shit. Kevin had me giddy as fuck, but I was respectful enough of her space and time to let her grieve in silence. Vice was always in ho stroll mode, so talking to her was the logical choice.

"Girl, I know that. He just makes me want to drop it low and sweep the floor, girl. Did I show you his pic?" I asked, grabbing my phone to bring up the pics he forwarded to me in our many text messages. They were tasteful, shirtless photos showing his reward from regular gym visits. I was impressed.

"Only a hundred times," she responded dryly while trying on outfits from my closet. I fell out laughing at her lack of enthusiasm because we both know when she really feeling someone, she did the same thing.

"Whatever, girl. Just help me find an outfit."

While we were looking through shoes and clothes, my door flew open, and Shanna came in all smiles. Her and Vice barely got along, but I wasn't really sure what the beef was about. Me, Vice, and Skye were thick as thieves, and they didn't have other friends. In Vice's world, it was the three of us. She didn't like Shanna, but she tolerated her for my sake. I just hated to choose, and luckily Vice and Skye never made me. They were firm believers in giving people enough rope to hang themselves, and being right there at the perfect time to kick the chair from under them. Vice mentioned it was something about her that she couldn't put her finger on, but she didn't beat that horse.

"Folks can tell you what you want to hear, but they always show you what you need to see. You just have to be patient," was Vice's only advice for me when it came to Shanna.

I heard her loud and clear, and I kept one ear to the ground when it came to her. She seemed regular to me, no shade at all, but you never knew what people saw on the outside looking in. So far, she had been a cool friend, but time always shows that other side.

"This is the one, girl!" Shanna squealed as she held up a cute pair of ripped jeans and a Marathon cropped hoodie. "Wear this with a wedge sneaker and some gold hoops and you'll be all the way in there. A DMX concert is not the time to pull out a ball gown," she said, laughing hard at herself afterward.

I was cracking up too, but Vice just sat there looking at her with the stank face. She was so annoying sometimes.

"I was just saying that to Vice. I want to be cute but not overly dressed," I responded as I held the outfit in front of my body while looking at it in my full-length mirror. She had a cute little style about her, and I actually agreed with her choice. I chose to ignore Vice's attitude for the time being. I would talk to her in private once Shanna was gone.

"I like this choice. I think I'm going to go with it. I was thinking of wearing my hair up in a sloppy pony. That way, my hoops could be seen, and I wouldn't get hot once the show started."

"Yep, that sounds like a plan!"

We chatted back and forth, Vice never once jumping in the conversation or breaking her stare from Shanna. Shanna was unbothered as fuck, though, as she moved around the room, helping me pick out shoes and jewelry, and eventually helping me practice my face with some new pallets I just got in from The Crayon Case. She was definitely more hype about the date than my best friend, and I almost couldn't wait for her to leave so that I could pick Vice's brain about it.

After about an hour or so, Shanna bid us good night after bragging about this guy's pockets she was digging in. She never gave us a name, but just said she was basically using him for money and sex.

"I'm on some eating-pineapples-and-tasting-like-candy-to-these-niggas-all-summer type shit," she said as she gathered herself up to go. "This one been sniffing around me for a while, and I'm thinking I might let him sample the pot."

"Okay, cool. See your way out." Vice finally spoke from the bed, not even bothering to look up from her phone. Best friend was really showing out that night, so it was probably best for Shanna to go now.

The look Shanna gave her would have definitely got her shit split had she been anyone else, but I could understand it. Vice was definitely being overly aggressive, and we hadn't the slightest clue why. She reached in and gave me a hug, afterward glancing at Vice once more. Vice was doing a great job pretending she was invisible.

"It'll be show time in no time. Get ready to show out!" she said real hype to me. "Have a great night, Vicerean," she threw toward Vice. Vice didn't even so much as grunt a reply. We made eye contact once more before she turned to leave, saying goodbye to my parents before closing the door behind her.

"Bitch, what's your problem?" I asked her as I began to pick up strewn clothing and putting them back where they belonged while I still had the energy.

"I don't trust no bitch from the Ville. Don't she hang with Mina and Karen? We all know those hoes ain't loyal," she said while rolling her eyes, the scowl on her face evident. "They always setting motherfuckers up. I'm good on them project-ass hoes."

"Bitch, you from the same projects!" I said, falling out laughing.

She eventually started laughing with me as the stereotype set in. "Yeah, I am, bitch, but they from 54th Street. They grimy on that end."

"I hear you, beloved," I said in my Aunt Yani (Iyanla Vanzant) voice. "You know I got my eye on everybody, but you need to chill. She was just trying to be nice."

"Man, fuck that bitch and that raggedy-ass outfit she picked out. We going to get you some fresh shit after work tomorrow."

We laughed some more, and then she eventually left too. I finally responded to Kevin's texts that he sent while we were in there messing around, and it seemed that he was really a sweet guy. I'd see how far he was willing to take it in the coming weeks, but for now, I decided to just live in the moment. Surely if some bullshit was in the midst, I was usually wise enough to see it a mile away. For now, I wasn't worried.

As we sent our last few texts, I got myself comfortable and fell asleep. I was hype about this concert, and I couldn't wait for it to get there.

Selah

Enough Is Enough

So I decided that enough was enough with Sajdah. I felt like I'd spent our entire lives trying to appease her. She had the sense of entitlement for some reason, and it was really damn irritating. She always had to be coddled, and right now, I just wasn't in the mood. She was making moving in with Chase look real appealing. I'd been home for a few days, trying to make amends with her, and she was acting real catty. I wasn't beat for the bullshit. Even my mom pulled me to the side to ask me what the deal was, and I didn't have an answer for her. My parents never really got in our shit, so for my mom to notice and say something confirmed that Sajdah was acting the fuck up.

"Baby, I know you love your sister," my mom said to me as we ate lunch together on our break. She worked in the building a few doors down from where I worked, and we often met up for lunch dates when weather permitted. "But sometimes you just have to let people be in their own space. You're not responsible for your sister's happiness."

That shit made me bust out in tears. I always protected Sajdah, and I had no idea what I was trying to protect her from now. It was all so confusing to me. I didn't really know how to let her do her own thing because we'd been doing our thing as a team for so long. I didn't want to let her go. I wasn't ready to ride solo.

"I'm just trying to figure out what I did to her," I explained as I wiped my face. I was hurt, and my mom could clearly see it. I could see it in her eyes— the same eyes that matched mine and Sajdah's. She was hurting for us.

"Stop trying. If she wants you to know, she'll tell you. If she never does, then don't stress about it. Growing apart hurts sometimes, but you'll always have us. Even your sister, although it doesn't look like it right now."

She leaned in and gave me a hug only a mother could possess. I needed someone other than Skye and Vice to help me through this, and without having to ask, my mom came right on time. I decided to just let Sajdah be great for now, and the chips would fall where they would. She wanted to act funky, cool. I'd always have her back. Right now, I just had to love her from a distance for a while. I had hope that she would eventually come around and at least talk to me. We never held grudges forever. Come to find out, there's a first time for every damn thing.

When I got back to the office, there was a bouquet of yellow roses on my desk. I smiled, but that didn't take away from the fact that I had been trying to reach Chase since the night before. He had never not answered my call or not returned a text. When I looked at my phone, he still hadn't texted back from when I first got to the office. I even tried hitting him on Face Time, but it kept saying he was unavailable. I was trying not to get worried. He didn't say he was going anywhere. Normally he let me know when he was going out of town or had to step away for a while. He didn't mention either.

I picked the card off of the roses, and it was from Chase, requesting my presence at his condo after work. This time, the roses didn't ease my frustration. Why wouldn't he answer my calls? I picked up my phone to try him again and got the same thing. No answer. I was pissed. I started to leave work early and go over there, but I had too much to get done to roll out early.

I could barely concentrate as I struggled through the rest of the day. I was definitely going to read his ass up one side and down the other. I would not be disrespected, and we were not about to start this disappearing shit so early in the relationship. Damn the jokes.

I was on time at the clock that day, hopping straight in a Lyft to go to Chase's house. The driver could not move his car fast enough for me. I was prepared to go in there swinging if necessary. This was not about to become a habit with him. What the hell got into him? He'd never done anything like this before, and by the time I got done, he would think twice about doing it again. I would not be treated like some rugrat-ass bitch.

When I finally got to his house, I typed the code into the keypad to let myself in. I stormed up the steps only to find an empty living room. It smelled like food had been cooked, but when I went to the kitchen, it was completely clean. My blood was boiling at this point. I grabbed my phone and dialed Chase again, thinking maybe I would hear it ring in the house, and it went straight to voicemail again. Livid at this point, I took the steps two at a time up to his master bedroom. It was completely quiet as I crept up to the door, hoping I would hear something on the other side.

When I opened the door, I was shocked as a million balloons rushed out of the door toward me. I didn't know what the hell was happening at first. Finally, as the onrush of pink started to subside, I was able to walk into the room, where I found Chase sitting at a table set up with dinner and candlelight. He was looking damn good in only a bathrobe and slippers. I almost forgot I was mad at him.

"Come in and have a seat, love. I've been waiting on you."

I hesitantly walked to the table, battling between punching him in his damn face or kissing all over him for what he had done. I removed my jacket as he helped me into my seat. Covered dishes sat in the middle of the table, and as he removed the lid off of each one, I could only smile that he had all of my favorite things to eat. The room was dimly lit, and there were roses strategically placed throughout. The gold candleholders were absolutely beautiful. The candles where pure white, but as they melted, the wax turned pink. He had the finest china set out, and I could see that he had put a lot of effort into pulling this off. I was proud of him, but he wasn't off the hook.

"I've been trying to—"

"Shhh." He hushed me up as he kissed my neck before taking his seat on the other side of the table.

"But I've been calling—"

"I know, baby, and I should have answered, but I was too busy getting all of this together for you. I'll make it up to you shortly."

"Since yesterday?"

He was so damn cocky. I wanted to hate him, but I couldn't. Not too many men knew how to go all out like this and pull it off. Who helped him do this? Or did he do it all himself? I thought something had happened to him, and with all the shit going on with Sajdah, my emotions were all over the place.

He moved his chair over next to mine and began making my plate. I was truly speechless as I watched him take control. Was this what I had to look forward to? He began to feed me a little bit of everything as he told me how much he loved me and how sorry he was for making me worry. He assured me that he would never hurt me on purpose and that I was all that mattered to him. I took it all in as I enjoyed lobster, seafood mac and cheese, garlic shrimp and mussels, grilled asparagus, and sweet white wine. This man had me open, and I wasn't sure how I felt about it. I was losing control, and it was pissing me off.

"So, I'm feeling like you should just spend the rest of your life with me." He set a box from Bailey Banks & Biddle down in front of me.

I was speechless yet again. We were moving too fast, too soon. He opened the box, and the most beautiful diamond I'd ever seen was inside. The clarity on that thing was ridiculous. VVSI quality. He'd spent a pretty penny on it definitely. Cushion cut, diamonds all the way around, three pieces that all connected to look like one . . . I was in love.

"So, what are you doing with the rest of your life?" Before I could answer, he slid the ring on my finger and kissed me deeply.

I had so many questions. Was I ready for this?

He carried me to the bathroom, where he had a bath drawn full of bubbles accompanied by rose petals and candles everywhere. As he undressed me, he kissed the parts of my body that became exposed as he went down. I didn't have it in me to protest, especially once his tongue found its way to my clit. He had me on the side of the tub, eating me out, with my legs up on his shoulders while I held on, trying not to slip inside the water headfirst.

He had his way with me all over the bathroom, fucking me from the back with a firm grip on my hair that made me look in the mirror while he was doing me. Every time I closed my eyes, he would stop until I looked at him again. His technique was sick, and as good as it was, I still couldn't help but wonder if I was making the right decision. He was practically a stranger, but not really. Like, I knew him, but I didn't know him. He was basically a damn stranger that I only knew on the surface.

By the time he finished having his way with me, I was weak from back to back orgasms. I just needed to know that it would always be this way, and if not, how would we get through the tough times? If we were even made for tough times. You'd be surprised how minute shit will tear a relationship to pieces, and I wasn't sure if I could get through life without him. I already lost my sister. I couldn't take another loss right now.

We sat in the tub, him between my legs, and let the water relax us as I stared at my ring. I loved Chase without a doubt. Why was I so hesitant with him? I knew it was mostly because this shit was just too good to be true. He didn't have any flaws, or at least none that I could see, just like the diamond he gave me. This shit made it hard for me to trust him, but at no fault of his own. Past niggas did this to me, had me out there all insecure and shit. I should have been able to just enjoy him fully, but that nagging thought in the back of my mind wouldn't allow it. What if he played me? The last one hurt me to the core, and it took me a long time to get over it. I couldn't go through that kind of pain again. I had more bodies than I wanted under my belt. I didn't want to add him to the list.

"Tell me what you're thinking," he requested as he massaged my legs lightly under the water.

I wasn't sure how much to reveal. Did I just keep that shit a bean and tell him what was on my mind for real, or did I just skirt around the issue a little to feel him out? He would want me to keep it a hundred, so I decided to just go with my gut. The worst he could do was end it with us.

"I need to know more about you," I spit out.

"What do you want to know?"

"Everything. I really don't know much about you at all. Where is your family? How did you end up here? Why did you choose me?" This dude was like Batman, living a secret life and shit. If we were going to get married, I needed to know what I was dealing with. What was I getting into with Chase?

He got quiet for a second, and I wondered if I had fucked up. Did I go too far? What if he refused to share? Then what did I do? I stayed quiet as I massaged his shoulders and continued to stare at my ring. It was gorgeous, but I'd give that bitch right back if he didn't shoot straight. I wouldn't be entertaining a liar.

"I hope you're ready. You might not like me much after this," he warned, kissing my palm.

"As long as you keep it truthful, I'll always love you. Me liking you is a bonus," I replied, trying to make light of the situation to hopefully put him at ease.

He sighed deeply and took a deep breath. I was beginning to think maybe I wasn't ready, but I done already opened the damn box. It was too late to turn back now, so I embraced him, letting him know I was ready for whatever he wanted to share. I was preparing myself to feel the same way about him when he was done. Hopefully, it wouldn't be too heinous a story, and I could handle it. I felt like I was Alice falling down the rabbit hole, and it made me just a little uneasy. Hopefully, it would be worth it.

Chase Antoine Warren II

"Are you sure this is a good idea?"

Sajdah had me meet her downtown, but she never said what we were doing. I really didn't want to be seen in public with her, because I didn't want to mess anything up with Selah. She hated to hear it, but I was really digging her sister. I was finding all types of ways to avoid being alone with her, but today she threatened to tell Selah everything if I didn't show up on time. I was smart enough to take the threat seriously and was in Center City early. Whatever this was, we needed to make it quick.

She walked ahead of me, and I stayed a few steps back so that it didn't look like we were together. When she went into a store, I gave her a few minutes, and then I went in. When I got inside, she was looking at rings. I damn sure wasn't about to buy her one, so I had no clue what she had in mind.

"This is the one," she said, pointing at a pretty nice ring. "You need to get this for Selah and get ready to level up."

I had the blankest look in the world on my face. She wanted me to propose to her sister? What kind of freak shit was she into? Now, I knew I told her that I really liked Selah, but I didn't say I was ready to marry her. She had yet to even agree to move in. We were still learning each other. Was this what Selah wanted? Were they having conversations about us? I was a big ball of confusion, and clearly, she could sense it.

"I'm not saying marry her today, or at all, silly," she said with the prettiest smile that matched her twin's. Before I did any damn thing, I needed to learn to tell them apart. This shit was spooky. "I know you want her to make the move. This will get it done."

I stared at the ring, but I wasn't feeling it or the pressure she was trying to put on me. Selah definitely had me in my feelings, but I wasn't sure this was the move to make. I still had things I needed to talk to her about. I had a rough past. I didn't even know if she could handle it.

"Let me think about it," I said to her as I prepared to leave the store.

"You think long, you think wrong."

I didn't reply. I just rolled out and made my way back to my car. Sajdah had me feeling some type of way, and now I felt a little pressured. I needed to talk to Selah, but how did I go about it? I couldn't just bust out and say some shit to her. When I got back to my car, I took a second to gather my thoughts. So many memories from my past flooded my mind, and I just had to let them flow out so that I could make the right decision. I swear it was like watching a movie of my own life.

"Put the bodies in the back room and move quick. It's about to get real hot in here."

As I doused the downstairs with gasoline, I had no remorse about what was going to happen next. Don't mess with the church's money— ever——unless you want your entire family to die. I really didn't give a fuck that I had to do this. He already knew the game going in. Come for me, and I come for everybody you know. Real. Damn. Simple. I would take out your wife, kids, the goldfish, and the cat, an entire sweep with no remorse. Believe me when I tell you I had zero fucks for anything.

At this point, I was early twenties, rising up the ranks in the game. I already knew I wasn't planning on doing this shit for long because I was already three years deep. It was too damn stressful, and I despised being stressed out. It made for hasty moves that were sometimes hard to clean up later. Eventually, I would want to settle down with a family of my own, and I knew whatever I did, I would have to move my shit to fucking Ohio or some damn where so that no one would ever find me. I was the reason behind plenty of slow singing and flower bringing, and fate always swung back around to get your ass. I was prepared to die the worst kind of death, but I would have to be found first. You weren't just going to walk up on my ass and take me out. Fuck that.

Rule #3: Never get caught slipping. That was the motto.

I'm not going to sit here and give you this violin-filled tale on how I grew up barely making it with no food and a crackhead mom. I'm not from the projects. My parents weren't on welfare. My dad didn't beat on my mom or vice versa. No one was a drug addict. I wasn't in foster care or molested by my uncle. We were never homeless. I wasn't bullied in school. No alcoholism in our house. I was a spoiled rich kid from Syosset, New York. My dad was chief of surgery at Syosset Hospital, and my mom was head of oncology in the same health system. My brother and I went to the best schools, wore the best clothes, had the best life, and I ended up a drug dealer. It was nothing they did wrong parenting me. They still didn't know how heavy I was in the streets. They just knew that I chose another path that they didn't expect. Yes, they were disappointed, but they loved me unconditionally. I leaned on that love for survival. They didn't need to know what was really going on.

I took full advantage of my opportunity to go to college, obtaining my bachelor's degree in human resources. I used that skill to manage people to keep my team in check. I ran my empire like a corporation minus the medical benefits and ETO. We had money to make, and anyone could be replaced at the drop of a dime. I treated my men well, so either they wanted to feast with us, or they were against us, and being against us wasn't a good thing. I would make it hard for you to survive without me. That was a guarantee.

Don't get me wrong. I wasn't out there just offing motherfuckers because I felt like it. I actually gave folks plenty of rope to hang themselves before I kicked that chair out and left them dangling and gasping for air. I gave progress reports, letting them know if they were on point or messing up. There was no mystery with me. You knew exactly where you stood at all times, and that's why they respected me. They even knew if death was coming. Of course, at that point, they tried to hide, but the goons I rode with would always find you. Always. Where people messed up was they thought they needed to be feared. Fear made people do sneaky shit. Respect made people value you, and more often than not, they were straightforward with you. Lack of respect was what got you killed.

Ten times out of ten, they fucked it all up for themselves. They were either skimming money off the top, getting high on the supply, or flat out lying about why they were coming up short. Not reporting for duty could potentially get you let go, and sometimes they just started to feel themselves a little too much for my liking. I always told them, "Do right by me, and I'll do right by you." My soldiers made more than a hundred grand last year, tax-free. The shorty that kept my books made sure I knew everything that was coming and going, and when shit started to look suspect, she reported it immediately.

Everyone was replaceable. There was always someone ready and willing to take anyone's place or move up in the organization. The best thing you could do was play your part the way you were supposed to. It made life better for all involved. The worst thing you could do was get caught doing some bullshit. Why end your life over a few dollars? You'd be surprised at the amount of people that do.

It started out as a family business. My brother was my right-hand man, and I had his girl keeping the books. My brother was smart as a whip, too, and was afforded the same lifestyle as I had. His mom was from a previous marriage and had died from cervical cancer that had doubled back and metastasized, killing her the second time around. When our dad met my mom, that was how I got here, and she took care of my brother like he was her child from the womb. He was two years old when our parents met, so he took to our mom immediately. By the time I came along, he was five. I didn't know he wasn't my biological brother until we got older, but it never mattered. I just figured he looked like our dad, and I looked like our mom. The love we had for each other cast out all the other shit. We were blood.

When I first got into the game in my freshman year of college, my brother was just finishing up his prerequisites for his biology major. His book-smart game was wicked, but his street smarts were off the meter. He put me on once I realized how the kids at my school would pay top dollar to turn all the way up at a party. They didn't just want weed. They wanted to smoke loud, pop pills, and sip on dirty Sprites all at the same damn time. It was easy money. I just so happened to be having a conversation with my brother about it, and that's when he revealed what he had been up to.

I knew our parents were well off, and I knew he was making okay money at his job, but he was too icy for someone that was barely living above the poverty line. Our parents kept our credit card loaded bi-weekly, so we didn't want for anything. Where was he getting this extra money from? They laced us, but not that much.

"Yo, bro, did you see them in that party last night? They were going crazy." I shot the shit with my big brother, reminiscing about the previous night's adventure. "Whatever they were on had them going crazy. I got my dick sucked by like three broads at the party."

"I hope you used a condom?" he questioned as he flipped through his textbook. He was always very focused on his studies, more than I ever would be.

"Of course," I lied as I half skimmed through my book as well. I never even thought about a damn condom. I was busting off all in them bitches' faces like it was nothing.

"So, I need to make some moves," I began hesitantly. Our parents definitely hooked us up monetarily, but who couldn't use a little more? The way he was flossy made me want to be like him.

"What kind of moves?" he asked, never looking up.

"The same kind you making. I want to walk around dripping just like you. How can I be down?"

He kept flipping through the pages and writing notes like he didn't hear me. I knew that meant he was pondering his thoughts. Hopefully, he would tell me something I wanted to hear. I knew enough to stay quiet and not badger him.

"So, what makes you think you can handle that kind of work? You wouldn't want to disappoint Mom and Dad by getting caught up in some crazy shit, right?" he responded with a smirk on his face. He knew I was a momma's boy and never really got in trouble. My mom was my world. I would never want to disappoint her.

"I guess you wouldn't either, right?"

"Touché."

He kept flipping and writing, and I was really trying to stay patient. I knew this was a test to see how I would respond under pressure. You had to have patience with fiends. They remained loyal to you. A lot of people think because someone is a drug addict that you don't have to value them, but it's the total opposite. How you treat people matters, and that's how I eventually ended up running my business. Don't take any shorts, but don't humiliate them. Drug addicts remember how they are treated, and if you treat them good, they will always come back to you. Hell, even Nino Brown gave out turkeys on Christmas. He was the king of New York, and everyone respected him. I planned to run my shit the same way.

"Okay, let me make some calls. I'll start you out with something small for the upcoming weekend. Once we see how that goes for a while, then we'll make other moves."

I thanked him for his time and continued my studies. I knew how to move discreetly, so I wasn't worried about that, and I also knew that I couldn't let my grades or anything slip, or he would pull everything up from under me. I had to prove to him that I could maintain properly and never lose focus.

Just like he promised, that Friday after classes were done, he met me in my dorm room with the work I needed to get the weekend going. He showed me how to weigh it out and bag it up. Dealing drugs wasn't just about distribution. A successful dealer needed to know how to work the entire operation. You couldn't leave it up to any one individual to get the job done. You had to know all the components of how the system worked.

"So, when you first get to the party, you will hand out a few of the extras to get the buzz going. After that, you let them come to you. Stay patient. They will come to you. You have to trust me on this. Don't fuck this up."

I got to the party off campus around ten. The guard at the door worked for my brother, so he knew not to pat me down as I walked inside. It was lit up in there. Girls half-dressed, dancing on each other, and the guys just taking it all in. I made my way inside and found a spot right by the bar. I was informed that one of the waitresses, who was also on my brother's team, would help me distribute the free samples so that folks knew to come to me. The waitress knew better who the clientele was, as they worked in there and basically knew everybody. My brother made this really easy for me for my first time out, and I wanted him to be proud of me.

As the night went on, the waitress kept coming back to cop more drugs from me, always with the correct money. I was almost out of product, which I was sure was a great thing. This was a nice easy setup, but I needed to come up with a way to remove the waitress out of the equation. I needed direct sales straight to the customer, so that they could buy whenever they wanted and not just party nights on the weekends. In the back of my head, I could hear my brother telling me to move slow and let the grind settle in, but I wasn't sure how much longer his voice would matter to me. I just needed to get put on. I didn't need someone to run shit for me.

I didn't know at the time, but this was the beginning of our separation. I definitely wasn't prepared for it, but I knew whatever came of it, I had to make it out on top.

Sajdah

Desperate Calls

Chase was in no way ready for marriage. Hell, neither was Selah. But if things were going to go the way I planned, I had to make a desperate move. What girl didn't want a pretty ring? As different as we were, Selah and I were the same person inside and out. I knew exactly what to do to get my sister in line because it was all the things I would have wanted for myself. I knew what made her tick. It wasn't like I hadn't met men that could do it. I just didn't want to be tied down in a relationship right now. At this point in my career, it would definitely be forced, and I didn't have enough energy to keep up a façade. All of this shit had me jealous as fuck low key, but I'd rather it be her than some other random-ass bitch.

Truth be told, I hated my sister. Had for a long time. Since we were kids. I loved her just as much, though, so it was a constant battle between the two emotions. You ever want to kill someone, but want them to live? I felt like that every day for the past fifteen years.

She was so much better than me at everything. Well, everything except for schoolwork. I had that in the bag. She just wasn't really interested in applying herself. Making friends, personality, sports . . . all I had on her was that I was damn near a genius. It was so hard for me to make friends back then, and still kind of now. Once my mom started allowing us to not do the twin thing 24/7, I was lost in the sauce. Her fashion sense was impeccable, even as a child. I hated that people were just naturally attracted to her. She got along with everyone so easily, and I was always "the other twin." It was so annoying.

I would never forget when she met Skye and Vice. We were put in separate classes in the second grade so that we could learn to be independent. They tried to separate us well before that, but my mom was against it. It took for my dad to finally put his foot down for my mom to agree. I was just as nervous as she was about the separation, but my dad said we needed to find ourselves.

"They can see each other once the day is over," he told her over breakfast one morning as we got ready to head out.

We knew we were going to be separated. We stayed up half the night talking about it. Selah was so excited about meeting new people and making new friends. She tried to get me on board, but I wasn't feeling it. It was always just us.

"And it will always be us, Sissy. You'll be right next door," she assured me, hugging me extra tight and telling me we should get some rest. I wanted to believe her, I really did, but I knew better. Nothing good was going to come from this.

I had so much anxiety when we woke up that morning. I couldn't even eat breakfast without feeling like it was going to come back up. Our parents fed us good, but out of all the food we had to pick from, all I could manage was a piece of toast and half a glass of orange juice. Selah ate it all—the sausage, waffles, fruit, and cheese eggs with two slices of toast and a big cup of juice to wash it down. Clearly, she was unbothered. I was quiet the entire ride over, while Selah talked enough for everyone in the car.

The drive to the school that morning felt quicker than normal, not really giving me enough time to prepare mentally or physically. We got to Selah's classroom first. She let my mom's hand go and ran inside with no problem. We stood in the doorway as she found the seat with her name on it and immediately started making friends with the people on either side of her.

My mom had to basically drag me to my classroom. I stood frozen in front of the class as the teacher introduced me, begging my mom with my eyes to not leave me there with those people as she stood at the door. She left, and I instantly felt betrayed. How could they do this to me?

I put on my big girl panties and held my guard up for the rest of the day, often wondering how Selah's day was going. I was not about to let those strangers see me cry, although I was on the brink of busting out in uncontrollable frustration at any given time.

By the time we got to recess, Selah was just out there living her best life with her new friends. I was devastated. I just knew she was missing me and having separation anxiety. Clearly, she was having a ball without me, and I was hurt. I knew in my heart that was when the hate began. She didn't even make eye contact with me while we were out there. It was like she already forgot about me. That for sure ruined the rest of my day, and I spent the rest of it just wishing it were over.

When we got home on the first day, she was so excited to share with our parents everything that happened and the new friends that she made. She just went on and on about how cool her teacher and classroom was, and how nice everyone was to her. She wanted to plan a play date and everything. Meanwhile, the little girls in my class were calling me a monster because I had freckles and light eyes, and the boys kept calling me Same Face because I had an identical twin. What did she have that I didn't? We were twins. We were supposed to be the same.

Why did they do this to us? That was the beginning of our separation, and it only got harder from there.

We shared a room for a long time. Our parents tried for a third child for years. They wanted a boy, but unfortunately, it never happened. Before it became my bedroom, it used to be a nursery painted a soft blue, with all boy paraphernalia. I faintly remember my mom's belly getting big, but after a weekend at my grandparents', we came back home and her stomach was flat again. A week after that, all the stuff was stripped from the room, the walls were repainted a soft lilac, and I suddenly had a new space. I was terrified! I had been sharing a room with my sister since birth.

First separate classes, now separate sleeping spaces. This was getting to be too much for my little mind to handle. Plenty of nights, I would get scared and sneak into my sister's room during the wee hours of the morning. She would always scoot over and let me in with no problem. She would tell me everything was fine, and she would hold me until I fell back to sleep. She loved me unconditionally, but my hate grew more as the days went by. I was such a horrible person. The fucked-up part was I didn't care. I had stopped caring a long time ago.

Pretty soon after that, no matter how scared I was, I would force myself to stay in my room by myself, fighting whatever demons my little mind conjured up. Every time I went to visit Selah, she would talk me to death about her day and all the new people that I didn't give a fuck about. She took a particular liking to Skye and Vicerean, and she wanted me to meet them so that we could all be friends. Who were these people that were taking my sister away from me? At first, I declined the offer, but then I got smart about it. I needed to see who the competition was. I needed them to know that I was a permanent fixture, no matter how close they got.

"Make sure you find me at recess, Sissy. I can't wait to introduce you to them." She completely missed the look on my face as she ran to catch up with her new friends after giving my dad a hug goodbye. She embraced them once she got close, and they immediately started incessant chatter about God knows what.

I was already over it. I studied the girls from a distance, already passing judgment on them both. One had light skin like us, the other had a pretty caramel complexion, both with thick long ponytails that matched ours. They seemed pretty nice, I guess. They were definitely getting along with my sister with no problem. I decided I would at least give them a chance and see what would come of it.

Recess couldn't come fast enough. I watched the clock all morning, barely hearing anything the teacher said. I couldn't even understand why I was so nervous. These girls had to be nice people. My sister wouldn't introduce me to anyone that wouldn't like me. She had to be confident enough in their friendship to bring them into ours. Just when I thought I couldn't take another second, the school bell rang, indicating it was time for lunch. I could hardly eat anything, but I managed to choke down half my sandwich and my drink, silently rushing my classmates to finish eating so that we could get outside.

For some reason, the sun was extra bright that day when we got out there, but I was able to zone in on my sister with ease. I half skipped, half trotted my way over to her, ready to meet these new girls that I would be calling friends as well.

You ever meet someone for the very first time and instantly hate them? Something goes through your body, and the hairs on the back of your neck stand up, warning you that something just ain't right about them. You just can't put your finger on it, but you feel it all the way down in your soul. That person ain't to be trusted in the least little bit. You hate them, but you don't know why just yet. I felt just like that when I met Vicerean. It was like I came face to face with the devil, and I knew she and I would never click in this life or the next. I wanted her ass gone, but I immediately put a fake-ass smile on my face for my sister's sake.

"Hi, I'm Sajdah. Nice to meet you."

"I know who you are, Same Face. We put two and two together when you showed up looking like her."

They all busted into laughter, even my sister, and I was shocked. She didn't see anything wrong with what she said? Why didn't she protect me? I wanted to snap her head off at the neck.

"And we are the cutest twins in the city," my sister said, giving me a huge hug, sensing my uneasiness. "Come on. Let's play hopscotch before Tamara's fat ass comes over."

They all laughed again, but I felt uneasy. I was convinced she had my sister brainwashed or something. Every time we made eye contact, she would make a face at me or stick her tongue out. Nobody else saw this bitch but me, and just as I thought I wouldn't be able to contain myself any longer, the bell rang again, indicating that it was time to go back inside. My sister gave me a hug, afterward being grabbed by Vicerean to follow her to get in line. She held on to my sister's arm possessively as an evil smirk came across her face. The three of them chatted nonstop all the way in the building, Vice turning one last time to give me a dirty look before they got all the way inside. I couldn't wait for school to be over to let my sister know what had happened.

When we got into our mom's car after school, Selah just went on and on about her friends and how happy she was that we got along. I was looking at her like, *bitch, please*. I fucking hated them. Skye never even attempted to connect with me, and Vice clearly had some type of girl crush on her. I didn't want neither one of them around her, but she wouldn't let me get a word in edgewise. I decided it would be easier for me to just watch out for them until I could get a solid read on them. If for nothing else, I knew for sure we weren't going to be cool with each other at all. Vicerean and I made sure of it.

Chase

The Rise to the Top

It took about a year, but finally I had a team. My brother was starting to trust me with more work, and I was moving it nicely around campus. At one point, it was starting to be too much, and I ended up recruiting my dormmate to help me make moves. He was just as hungry as I was, if not hungrier. Unlike my brother and I, he actually came from poverty, having arrived on a full ride with the help of a basketball scholarship and unlimited prayers from his grandmother's church family, who stilled prayed for him on a daily basis even though he was away.

He was a very humble person that walked a straight path, even though his was full of ridiculous obstacles along the way. He carried around perseverance like a bible and knew whatever he did affected everyone that meant anything to him. It was a hard choice to make, but I knew he would never cross me. He had way more riding on it than I did. All I had to do was graduate, and my career was practically lined up for me. He carried the entire hood on his shoulders, an honor he didn't take lightly. Not one time did I hear him complain about it.

He was every stereotype I was not. Product of a crack mom and partially raised by an alcoholic father. He grew up in the projects and survived off government food boxes and what food stamps his dad didn't sell to get liquor. This was back when people received paper stamp booklets and not a SNAP card. He was the oldest of three, having two younger sisters to look out for. College was his way out, and even though he knew how to dribble a ball, he was smart as shit, too. We clicked immediately when we met.

He didn't have the same benefits I had of growing up almost rich, so when my parents loaded my card for the month, I always made sure we had the best shit to eat, and a few times I even copped him a pair of sneakers because his were run down and he didn't have anyone back home that he could call to support him. We wore the same size clothes, so whatever I had was his too, and we just rocked out like that. He was down for whatever and even helped me on a few projects for a class that I was having trouble with.

Once I realized that I needed help if I was going to elevate to the next level, there was no doubt in my mind that he would be the one. I was surprised he wasn't already on some shit considering his background, but I wasn't judging him. He made it out, and as far as I was concerned, we would both make it through college. I had my big brother to look up to, who was about to graduate, so my bread couldn't stop once he was gone. I had to secure the bag so that I could still eat once his time was done here.

"How do you feel about going into the distribution business?" I asked him one night while we were playing Call of Duty on my PS3. I knew he was nervous about messing up his opportunity, and I wouldn't want him to jeopardize his future fucking around with me. He had more to lose than I did.

"I'm down for whatever," he responded without hesitation.

I knew for sure at that moment that I would take him with me all the way to the top. He knew exactly what I was talking about, no explanation required. He was loyal, and I'd never heard any shade from him or about him. He was always grateful for my help, and now was my opportunity to set him up so that he didn't have to depend on anyone either. We wouldn't be in college forever, and he would still need to keep getting paid whether I was there or not.

I never regretted that decision. We continued to have the conversation in code as we played the game to make certain no one walking by could eavesdrop and possibly report us to the school. We were about to blow up, but who knew all the bullshit that would come with it.

My brother was not happy that I was starting to recruit a team. My shit with him was, how did he expect me to grow if I didn't make moves? There was no way possible I was going to be able to keep up the type of volume I had by myself. Unless he didn't want me to grow . . . but I didn't even want to think that about him. He wasn't the hating type as far as I knew. People always had a way of showing you something unexpected, though. That was a guarantee.

I knew that college was important, so I made sure to stay up on all my classes, and I made the best grades I could. I'd been on the dean's list since I dropped in on the scene, so nothing I was doing would bring shame to my family by getting kicked out of school as far as my education was concerned. This drug shit was another beast that I kept well hidden. I was so far under the radar I was undetectable. My team was very loyal, or so I thought. At that moment in time, it was like smooth sailing.

My college studies taught me how to manage a team effectively, so it was obvious that was the way to run our team, and my dormmate agreed. My brother's girlfriend was in school for accounting, so it was only fitting to

hire her to keep our books. She loved the idea because it
gave her hands-on practice for when she opened up her
own firm after graduation, and she set up the records
like a fictional company as if it were a part of her cur-
riculum. My brother was pissed, but we didn't care. We
needed an accurate record of what was coming and going so that we knew how to move. I was surprised that
he wasn't already utilizing her services. I dig drug dealers don't do taxes, but you still had to track the com-
ings and goings. How else would you know if shit wasn't
adding up? Maybe I was just underestimating him, but
I had to do what I had to do for me at the end of the day.
This was how I wanted to run my business. The end.
Period.

"Why would you involve Chantel in this shit?" he asked
as he tested our newest product they called Sunday
Morning. I was a little taken aback to see that he was
disobeying the number one commandment: never get
high on your own supply. That's why we had testers.
What good would he be if he was skimming off the top of
his own shit? That would quickly get you dismissed. He
knew this shit, but he was our leader for now, so I found
it best to keep my opinion to myself no matter how taken
aback and disgusted I was with him. He knew better, and
his actions were quickly changing my opinions about him
as a role model.

"She's not involved in anything," I explained to him as
I watched him nod and drool a little. I was repulsed and
couldn't wait to get back to the dorm to run this past my
dormmate. It might be time for us to step up sooner than
later if we were going to keep this thing going without
him.

I was hoping the takeover would be civil, but I was sure
my brother was not going to take this sitting down. We
would have to cleverly phase him out of the operation
altogether eventually. That was a chance I was willing to

take, and I just hoped I wouldn't have to body his ass in the process.

"I'm almost out of here, little brother," he managed to say as he tried to get himself together. "Graduation is only a few months off. I have to get you prepared," was his response, completely moving past the Chantel issue.

I really didn't feel like getting into this shit with him about it. I looked at him like he was crazy. He was graduating to become a dope fiend? Our parents were going to be so hurt when they found out, but I damn sure wasn't going to be the one to tell them. He'd have to figure that shit out on his own.

As he leaned up to take in more of the product, I quickly packed what I needed, taking another brick for myself to flip, and I recorded all but the extra brick in my phone to tell Chantel later. I was so disappointed, but this wasn't a fair game. Sometimes the kingdom had to be overthrown. Sometimes it was by whoever was next in line. Let the chips fall where they may.

When I got back to the dorm, my dormmate was bagging up the last of what we had left and recording transactions for Chantel. We kept thorough books, and I loved that we were on the same page. I never had to double back behind him, and vice versa. We had an open and honest friendship, and we were both in this to gain. He was loyal, and I appreciated him for that.

"It may be time to rise up, Goon," I informed him as I unloaded the product. "Big brother is in a bad place, and if he isn't careful, he might mess it up for all of us."

As I played back to him what I had witnessed, I couldn't help but become sad. I was shocked by it, and I wasn't ready for the reality of what was about to happen. Goon understood all too well what I was feeling. He grew up in that environment, so it wasn't new to him.

We had started calling him Goon because of the way he played on the court. When he had the ball, he was out of control, dunking on people like crazy. His footwork was ridiculous, and the speed on him was supernatural. He was virtually untouchable and had scouts vying for him like crazy. There was no doubt he would be drafted in the NBA.

He wouldn't be able to move dope in the NBA, though, so I was preparing myself for him to go. I cherished what I had found in our friendship, and I wanted to get the team as strong as I could before his time was up. Loyalty like his was scarce, and he would truly be missed.

As I recalled what happened at my brother's spot, he was in disbelief. How could this happen? He was the one that taught us the game, and then he turned around and got caught up in it. We saw firsthand the drop-out and drop-dead rate of students that got hooked on the shit we pushed. We'd only been doing it for a little over a year at this point, and already some of our classmates were missing for one reason or another or didn't make it back from spring break. I witnessed a few pass out at poolside when we were in Miami, so I knew the shit we had was serious. Which was why we *never* sampled it ourselves. There was no way I was about to be doped out and drugged up. We stuck with only smoking weed-packed blunts that we rolled ourselves. We were too cautious to trust anyone else with our shit. We knew we wouldn't fuck each other over, so that's how we moved. Kept that shit amongst us. My brother put us in a weird space that we didn't like being in. The only thing we could do was eliminate the problem.

"Let's just sleep on it tonight before we make a sound decision. This is family we're dealing with, not just some Joe Blow from off the street. It needs to be handled differently than we would with someone we didn't care about," he expressed as he checked the weight of the bricks I just brought in. "Also, you need to speak with Chantel about OG. She said his books ain't adding up and haven't been for a few weeks now. We also have an extra brick. What's this for?"

I explained to him that my brother was so high he didn't even know I had it. He was concerned that it might mess up his count, but the way it looked, his shit was already messed up, and we would have to prepare to straighten his shit out so that we could remain on point. I took the information he had for me regarding his count and then went to hit Chantel for the update.

OG wasn't ready for this type of game. I knew that as soon as we put him on, but he was a friend of Goon's, so we gave him a shot. Goon agreed that he didn't have an issue with letting him go if need be, so we would just handle him accordingly. Hopefully, it was just a misunderstanding, but we would definitely see.

It felt like a lot of shit was dumped on me all at once, but I was a problem solver. Once I had all the information I needed, I would know exactly what to do.

Vice

Because I'm A Good Friend

So, I know how this shit must look to you, but on the realest shit ever, I don't give a fuck. When I became friends with Selah and Skye, I vowed to take every bitch to their grave that crossed them in the slightest way, be it friend or foe. I was dead serious. Sajdah had always been a damn hater, but Chase had to be handled delicately. I had nothing but time on my hands, and I was determined to see what the deal was with him and Sajdah. As far as I was concerned, those two had nothing to discuss at all. He was my best friend's man, and she was the only twin that he should be concerned with.

I must say, God always put me in the right place at the right time. I just so happened to be in Center City and see these two nut jobs down there. They weren't walking together hand in hand and shit. Sajdah was a little smarter than to not be so obvious in broad daylight. To the clueless, it would just look like they were two people downtown at the same time on a weekday afternoon. It didn't even look like they knew each other. I knew better than that.

Just so happened, I was enjoying a little lunch right across the street from the jewelry store I watched her go into, then shortly after, he went in. They spent some time in there and then left the same way—her first, and then him. I couldn't grab a pic of them together, but I made sure I got pics of them at the same location, time stamped just minutes apart. Oh, I was definitely building a nice portfolio for these fuckers because I wanted them all the way caught with no way to squirm out of it. Pictures and video have never told a lie.

I packed my lunch away quickly and trailed behind him a little as he made his way back down the street, no bag in hand to indicate he made a purchase. As luck would have it, we were parked in the same lot, so I hopped in my car and waited for him to bust a move. When he pulled out, I pulled out. When he switched lanes, I switched lanes, being sure to stay a car or so back so that it wasn't obvious that I was following him. He took me all the way out of the city, and that's when I found out where he lived. I made sure to store the number of his house and a picture of it on my phone for later use. Stalking came naturally to me, and if I had to camp outside this bitch every day for the next year, I would. He was not about to play my homegirl and get away with that shit.

It could be that it was nothing at all and I was reading too much into it, but I saw the way he hugged up on Sajdah that night. You don't touch people that you're just friends with like that. Try that lie with someone who doesn't know the whole truth.

I parked my car down the street to see who would show up after me. Chase saw me around, I'm sure, but he didn't really know who I was for real. I was the one to watch out for out of the entire crew. I saw everything at all times. I waited for about a half hour, then I crept down to the condo I saw him pull into. First glance didn't produce any cameras on the property, but that didn't mean that the neighbors didn't have any. I still kept it very cautious as I got close enough to zoom in on the license plate and the keypad that was attached to his door. I wasn't exactly sure how I was going to use these flicks, but I had them in the tuck just in case it was necessary for me to pull them out. Satisfied that I hadn't seen anything suspicious, I tipped back to my car and made my way back down to familiar territory.

Shit was just too squeaky clean with him for me. I needed to know about his past so that I could handle him properly. I knew a few dudes off his team, but them soldiers were tight-lipped when it came to him. That was a good thing, and I wasn't completely mad about it. Loyalty is hard to find nowadays, especially when the person in charge could take out your entire family with a text message. They were right to fear for their life if they valued what was dear to their hearts. There was a weak link in every chain, though. Someone was bound to feel like they were being treated unfairly and had nothing to lose. That was the one that I was looking for. The one who thought he was Superman. The one that would let me know the real tea. I was willing to give up the pussy to get it. That's the kind of friend I am. A quick fuck for quick information has more power than you think.

I had my eye on this one dude they called Sniper for a minute now. I dug in his pockets a few times last summer, but I never gave up the box. Let's just say he taste-tested the menu but never got to the full course. He let me do that shit to him five times, so he was just an easy target that I got a nut and a buck from when I was bored out of my mind. I never really had any other use for him before now. He had a baby mom that I didn't feel like dealing with, and he tested his product here and there, so I wasn't dealing with that shit either. He would probably get suspicious if I showed interest now, so I would have to let him think he came to me. It was a control thing with men that had no clue, but I was ready to play the game.

As luck would have it, when I made a right on Woodland Avenue, I saw his raggedy ass standing outside of Sammiches, this sandwich shop that sold the best stuffed turkey burgers in South West. He was looking more raggedy than usual as I peeped the scene before spinning the block again because there was never any parking right there. Maybe he was doing more than testing the product nowadays. Either way, I needed to see what I could get out of him while I could.

By the time I got past the medical center and around the block, I didn't see him anymore, but knowing him, he was headed out the Ville to move product. That's where most of the drug dealers and drug users hung at. That bitch Shanna that I didn't like lived out there too, so I had to move with caution. I fucking hated that she was even cool with Selah, but I might have been able to use her to my advantage.

As I made my way over to the projects, my mind was really on what was best for my friend. Did she even deserve a dude like Chase when she had so many other options? He was a fucking scumbag as far as I was concerned, and I really felt like, if given the chance, he would fuck the entire crew behind her back and not say a damn word if we didn't.

That's when that shit clicked. I was going about this entirely the wrong way. If I was going to really put my pussy on the line for this bitch, it had to be done right. I was taking the scenic route when the expressway was right in my face.

Busting a left at the gas station on 54th and Elmwood, I headed back to where I followed Chase to begin with and hopped on I-76 at the University City entrance. He didn't know how close Selah and I were in real life. I wasn't even sure how much she told him about us, but I was good at everything I did. I promise I can sell fire to the devil, so this was going to be easy at best. I had to catch the big fish but keep myself in the clear in the process.

Rush hour traffic was a whole mess, but I sat patiently and drove like I had some sense until I got back to his door again. I was happy to see that his car was still there because I would have been salty as shit had he left before I got there. I didn't even know what I was going to say to him. I had to let him believe that he and I were on the same page if he was going to trust me enough to tell me what I needed to know.

I pulled up in an empty space a little farther down from his door but on the same lot, just in case some shit popped off. For some reason, I was feeling brave and unbothered. I could see who was coming and going from my vantage point, and I was able to see some random woman leaving from his door that wasn't Selah or Sajdah. This dude had more shit going on than I thought, which would make this entire sting that much easier. I snapped a few pics of her to add to the collection but allowed her time to get in her vehicle and leave before I went up to his door. I didn't need any witnesses to see me coming and going.

I stood outside his door to listen for more voices, but it was quiet on the inside. I did notice that he had a doorbell camera, only because my mom had the same one on her door, which meant there were other outdoor cameras that I couldn't see at the moment. I wasn't too worried about that. Chase struck me as the type that had a lot of traffic in and out, and he probably wouldn't want Selah to know I was there anywhere.

I tossed it back and forth in my mind about what I was really doing there. I could easily just mind my damn business, but I knew for a fact that if it were the opposite situation, Selah would go all the way out for me.

I rang the bell before I changed my mind. I could hear him shuffling around a little on the other side before he got to the door. The hesitation before opening the door took forever, because either he knew who I was, or he didn't and was wondering why I was there. I pushed him back and stepped inside, closing the door behind me. The look on his face was both amusing and worrisome at the same time.

"So, you think you're just going to play in my friend's face, huh?" I asked, leaning back against the door and crossing my arms under my breasts, waiting for the lie.

From what I could see, the place was very nicely decorated. He definitely wasn't like your typical hood boy. He had a little class with his shit. Clearly, he was the one running the business.

"Who are you again?" he asked, a slight smile tugging at his full lips.

I had never realized how handsome Chase was. I never really saw him close up like this. I had to tell my body to simmer down before I was wrapped around him. I could definitely see what had Selah all head over heels with him. He was gorgeous.

"Vice," I offered as I stepped around him and made my way farther into the house. I didn't see any obvious signs of a girl being there, aside from actually seeing one leave the premises. He was good at this shit.

He stayed in his spot, watching me walk around some. No person is just going to let a total stranger come into their house and roam freely, so he had to know me to some extent.

"So, to what do I owe the pleasure of this visit?" he asked, leaning against the door himself now, with a calm expression on his face.

I turned to look at him, and I wondered how much he really loved my friend. He was already fucking her sister and apparently a few other randoms. Where did his loyalty lie?

"I'm watching you. I see how you're moving. Selah really isn't to be played with," I warned him as I walked back over to him and stood breasts to chest.

The smirk never left his face. I promise the heat that radiated between us had me breaking out in a sweat. I had to stay focused, but my inner thot was starting to seep out. I needed to leave.

"You're watching me, you say," he responded, licking his lips.

I couldn't stop myself from imagining his tongue in other places.

"What you watching me for?" he asked, reaching out and running the back of his fingers across my erect nipples. The sensation sent a shock right down to my clit. This guy was dangerous. "Seems like you're the one that needs to be looked after. I didn't invite you here."

For the first time ever, I was speechless. I knew what my mission was, but he was throwing me off guard. Selah was my girl! There was no way I could do her the way Sajdah was, but he was so damn tempting. The way she talked about the dick-down, it definitely made you want to test it out. I was stuck between making a clean break and testing the damn goods. What kind of friend was I? Low key, I was no better than her messy-ass sister.

"If you not letting me in, love, you might as well leave," he said in a tone low enough for just me to hear, as if someone else were home.

My body felt like it was on fire, but my damn legs wouldn't move.

"I won't say a word to Selah. Scout's honor," he said with a devilish smile on his face that made him even harder to resist.

I swear I got the slimeball of the decade award for this shit here. I was wrong on so many levels. Letting my eyes take in his entire body, I was impressed with the muscle definition I could see pressed against his T-shirt. He had a nice, meaty package that poked out in his sweatpants, just begging for me to grab it. Even his manicured toes in his Adidas flip flops looked suckable. He had my weak ass, and he knew it. I don't even remember putting up a real fight.

Before I knew what was happening, I was upstairs, asshole naked in his shower, getting beat down from the back. He had a strong grip on my hair right at the scalp, just the way I liked it, and had my back arched so deep I thought my spine would snap in the middle. He completely filled me up, and my greedy ass was taking it like a champ. He was talking all kinds of ignorant, dirty shit to me that took my orgasm to the next level as he lightly choked my neck from the back and grinded deep into me, feeling like he was in the pit of my stomach. He made me promise to keep our secret as I exploded over and over again. I couldn't even look at him when we were done, the same sly smirk still on his handsome face.

As I drove all the way back to the hood, I sat in silence, not believing what I had done. That shit just changed the game, and I had to definitely make sure moving forward that Sajdah's dumb ass got caught up. Selah could not know that I got to experience that yummy dick she was always bragging about. Just thinking about what happened still had me pulsating and on fire, and I wanted more.

As I pulled up to the block, I saw the little honey dip that I broke off sometimes outside. I motioned for him to come to my house as I went inside. I couldn't get Chase again for round two, so he would have to do for now. I was such a horrible friend, and it was heartbreaking. I just wasn't about to get caught out there, though.

As I thought about Chase and gave my honey dip my best work ever, I slowly started to formulate a plan that would clear me of everything. For the first time that night, I had a smile on my face.

Chase

The Informer

There's nothing worse than a lying-ass snitch. People like that just do something to my spirit. When a man goes out of his way to make sure you eat, never ever bite his hand. Unless, of course, you want to get slapped upside the head with it. I really liked to run a tight operation, but folks always needed to be made examples of, even though I tried to keep shit peaceful at all costs.

Once Goon brought the issue with OG to my attention, I set my radar on him to see what he was really up to. I had questions, but I didn't necessarily want to speak to him about it. I needed to see things with my own eyes. Give them enough rope . . . then come back and kick the chair. One thing was for certain: people would always tell you exactly what you wanted to hear, but would also show you exactly what you needed to see. Don't take anyone's words for law; always watch their actions. Actions haven't told a lie yet.

He was an acquaintance of Goon's, so when he asked to get put on, I gave him the opportunity. He lived in a neighborhood near the college where we sometimes played ball, so I figured he could get those off-campus sales, and the glow up would be real. Because we were men, I didn't micro-manage any of them. I was expecting them to live up to the goals we set on our initial meeting. I don't just scoop any old body off the street and give them drugs to sell. It was a process. It was not like they were getting hazed or anything, but we just needed to know that you were trustworthy and wanted to work your way up. No one sold drugs forever; you had to have a way out. This was supposed to be a temporary thing, and that was a part of the conversation when they were first bought on board.

There was a stigma to being a drug dealer, one that I was not just going to lay down in and get comfortable. Silly me, but I truly believed that there was a way out of the game, and my team was not going to be the average Joe Blow drug boys. This was supposed to be temporary, I mean, to make ends meet until we moved on to bigger and better. Unfortunately, it didn't always work out that way, and that's when that example came rolling in. Someone always tried to fuck up the church's money. It's like we could never just have good days without someone throwing salt in the damn pot. It was very annoying and disheartening.

Why are you here? They always looked astonished when I asked them that. Dig, we all had hard times. Okay, maybe not *all* of us, but if you were turning to illegal distribution of a narcotic or something similar, there was something going on. No one dealt because they ain't got shit else to do. There were way too many options to choose from. Dealing drugs was at the very bottom of the totem pole. Nobody wanted that Walmart and McDonald's money, even though it was the most legit way to go. How could you say you didn't want to make $11 an hour when at your current state, you were bringing in zero? That logic had always been lost on me, but instead of getting that little bit of money, they'd rather put everything at risk. At least at an establishment you have set hours. The drug game was 24/7/365. We didn't get no days off. This was a nonstop grind where you were expected to report every day, weekends and holidays.

"I need to feed my family."

That's the answer 99% of them gave. They either had a kid or ten, one on the way, mom sick, behind on bills, no education, so they can't find a job that pays enough, too proud to work at McDonald's or Walmart . . . the list goes on forever. However, none of that meant a damn thing to me. What was the plan to get back on your feet so that you didn't have to do illegal shit to survive? Silence . . . and a confused-ass look because they never had a plan.

At this point, the test began. I calmly explained expectations. We got rich so that we could move on. Build your team so that you were out of the line of fire. Stay honest because that was the only way I wouldn't kill you. Some of them got it; some of them we put in the dirt. That was the nature of the business, unfortunately.

OG seemed different. He was a little dusty, but I could see that he could be polished up and groomed if he were willing to put in the work. He worked at FedEx overnight and had a second kid on the way by his girl since middle school. He did graduate from high school but wasn't beat for that college shit. (His words, not mine.) His goal was to stack enough bread to buy a FedEx truck. From the way he explained it, a lot of the guys that drove for UPS/FedEx owned the truck and got paid for the route. That was where the real money was, not sorting packages for four to six hours a night.

I was glad to see he had an agenda, but with drug money, if played right, it would look way more appealing than what he could make at FedEx. The idea was to keep them focused. He also had an advantage with the truck because he could easily move weight across the borders while delivering packages. Some drivers were local; others drove as far as DC and Virginia. If he were smart, he would get some shit started out of town away from home base that no one could tamper with.

I had to always remember everyone didn't have my business sense, and trying to teach these dudes the hustle was tiring. I led them right to the water, put they damn lips up to the shit, and these dumb asses still wouldn't drink.

So, my operation was a family business, and these men were my brothers. What happened to one of us affected all of us. I drilled that in their heads constantly. What you did on your own reflected us as a whole. If you found shame in any act, do not, under any circumstances, bring shame to the family. Most times, if a person just asked for help, we could come up with a plan that was best for everyone involved. It was when these fools tried to take matters into their own hands that shit got messed up. It happened every single time.

OG was pretty cool at first. He stayed focused, even opened an official bank account to stash his money in. He flossed a little, but that was to be expected. Once those bills get caught up, breathing became a little easier. Life hit different when you were back on top. His girl even found a job to help out, and they were on easy street. They even copped a whip to get around in, and I was just happy that he was sticking to the course. It seemed that he was on track to building a team, too, and this meant that eventually I could branch him off and let him do his thing. He'd have his own truck for FedEx, still getting drug money, kingpin status, and life would be easy. Everything was going in the direction it was supposed to.

What I didn't know, and found out later, was that OG was a drug addict himself—a functioning addict, but an addict nonetheless. Goon was just as surprised as I was. I thought maybe he was just smoking weed. Damn near the entire team did that. We had the best loud selection in the hood. I just wasn't interested, and Goon had to stay clean to get into the NBA. It wasn't until OG's account started coming up short that it became a concern.

When I sat and looked at Chantel's books, I could see over the course of a few months that his count was getting lower and lower. He went from turning in his cash on time to turning it in late. That later turned into it being late and short, or sometimes not at all. When Goon approached him about it, he got all defensive, claiming Goon was calling him a thief. What I appreciated about Goon was he didn't fly off the handle right away. What we did affected *all* of us. Goon got that, and since OG was on his team, that made them as a team look crazy. None of them appreciated it, so he had to be dealt with accordingly.

"His eyes were bloodshot like shit, and he could barely stand up straight," Goon reported as we conversed about him one night. "Weed ain't never had me like that. Not even the loudest of loud. Clyde told me OG was using the product, and I didn't want to believe it, but when I saw him like that, I felt like it was true. When I saw the video, I knew for definite."

He pulled out his phone and pulled up a video in this Facebook group called Spice Gang. Lo and behold, there was OG at a party, sniffing lines like a pro. That definitely wasn't his first time at the rodeo, but I wasn't angry. I was more so disappointed. I told Goon I would handle it, and we moved forward with no questions asked. The trust level Goon and I shared was undeniable. We didn't have to hash out everything. He knew I was good for my word, and when I called to make the move, he just showed up. Everything I did was for the team. There was no doubt in anyone's mind about it as far as I knew.

When I showed up at OG's house, his kid's mom answered the door, looking miserable as hell. Her belly looked like it was going to pop any day, and she looked like she had been crying nonstop. I had never seen her before that day, and I almost felt bad about what was going to happen to her if her dude didn't come correct. I didn't feel too bad about it, though. He dug this grave for himself. He knew he had a family at stake. In this business, none of that mattered. She was about to find that out whether she was ready or not.

"Hey, love, I'm looking for OG," I explained to her once she answered the bell. I had a smile on my face, but I was really not in a happy mood. I knew enough to know that it wasn't wise to alarm folks that had nothing to do with the matter at hand. She didn't need to know there was a problem brewing.

"Me too," she responded with an attitude.

I didn't want to jump to conclusions. After all, she was pregnant and emotional. He could have been gone for a few days or a few hours. I wasn't going to jump to conclusions just yet. I needed to see how much information I could get from her first. From the looks of her, she was already stressed to the max, so there was no need for me to add anything extra.

"Word? I thought he said he would be here. When was the last time you saw him?" I asked as I made myself comfortable against the door jamb. Staring at her, I could see that she used to be a dime. Now she was more like a six, but that could be for any number of reasons. A baby would do some strange shit to your body. Everyone didn't get that happy pregnant glow that I've heard about. Coupled with her now drug-addicted baby father, she was going through it.

In the midst of our conversation, another kid walked up and grabbed her leg. He looked just like OG. I quickly prayed that we could rectify this situation without bringing harm to everyone.

"It's been a few days. Ever since he got on this shit, he been missing in damn action. He supposed to be selling drugs, not using them. This baby due any day now, and my son—"

At that point, I tuned her out. She pretty much confirmed what I needed to know. He was getting high, more than likely on our product, and that was simply against the rules. I didn't care how much weed they smoked as long as it didn't affect their work flow. Our product definitely would. Now it was time to put the hit out on this fool. I didn't have time to be dealing with a coke addiction. I didn't hold addict meetings and shit for folks. Either you could handle your shit, or step off until you could. Don't put me in a compromising position to have to lay hands on you. Goon would be very sad to hear this info, but we knew going in what the deal was. We handled everyone accordingly, all feelings aside.

"Thanks for your time, love. I'll send him your way if I see him," I assured her, cutting her rambling off mid-sentence. She was saying some more shit, but I was already down the steps and in my car, putting the word out that I needed him found as soon as possible. With drug addicts, you gotta move in silence, but quickly. We didn't want him trying to jet out on us before we got what we needed from him.

As I was making my way back to campus, I kept getting calls and texts from Chantel. I figured it might be something up with the books, but right now, I had bigger fish to fry. I was irked that I even had to take him out like that, but I had to set the example. If I let him get away with it, they would all think it was free reign. My phone buzzed again, and I decided to answer this time. Whatever it was apparently couldn't wait.

"Hey, Chantel, tell me something good." I spoke into the phone, preparing to hear that OG was found.

"It's your brother. It's not looking good. You need to get here now."

My stomach instantly tied up in knots, and I felt like I would vomit. What happened? I turned my car in the direction of his off-campus apartment and gunned the gas. I couldn't do this without him, and I hoped I wouldn't have to go on a rampage for someone causing harm to him. All kinds of crazy thoughts ran through my head, and I could only hope I was overreacting.

Chase

The End of The Road

By the time I got to his apartment, I barely made it
through the door. My brother was lying on the floor,
foaming at the mouth, and I already knew he had over-
dosed. I had the foresight to call Goon on the way to meet
me at the spot just in case it was more than I could handle.
He had already started packing the crib up before I even
arrived, and that's why he was my number one man. He
knew what to do in any situation that I wasn't around for.
There was no way we could invite the cops in with the
amount of drugs we had on the premises. This shit would
have the entire book thrown at us a hundred times, and
we'd all be under the jail. Chantel was freaking out, but I
told her it looked like he was already gone well before we
pulled up. As they were taking the last of the product out,
I called the cops to let them know we found my brother
on the floor.

"You don't know shit," I instructed Chantel as she cried
with his head in her lap. The sound that came out of her
would not be easily forgotten. She cried from the pit of
her stomach, and I knew everyone in the building could
hear her. I didn't bother to stop her. She cried for both
of us and just didn't know it. The pain she was feeling, I
felt a million times over, unwilling to believe what I was
seeing in front of me. I sat down on the floor next to
her for appearance's sake and to give her support. I was

ready to run screaming through the campus, but I had to keep things together. If I was going to be running shit, I could not show weakness. Not even in death.

I already knew this day would come, so I was kind of prepared for it. That is taking into consideration that you can actually prepare for this kind of thing. I had been getting word about my brother being high when the squad came to cop up with him half the time passed out on the couch. Thank God for loyalty. They could have easily just dipped out with some extra shit, and he wouldn't have been the wiser. He didn't keep the best books, so he would have been trying to recoup either way. He was starting to look like a fiend the last time I saw him, so I had mentally begun to prepare myself for this day. It actually took longer than expected. At the rate he was going, he should have dropped a long time ago.

We even conversed about it, and I asked him why he was doing this to himself. He had a lot to live for. He was graduating at the top of his class, and our dad had already secured a spot for him in the biomed program at Temple. His future was set up lovely, and the rest of his life was going to be just as breezy as the first half was. We came from privilege and didn't have to work hard to obtain anything. We were kids of the wealthy. We didn't struggle. That's why I couldn't understand what was really going on with him. We were living the best life possible, yet he was unhappy.

"I'm really not beat for that kind of life, bro," he revealed to me one night while he distributed packages to the team. He was including me more on the running of the operation so that I could eventually step in when he was ready to step out. I was grooming one of my men the same way. We would still report to him, but he would be untouchable under the radar. That's the way you run an empire. I learned best from his example. "I'd rather just let this money work for me until I'm gone. I haven't spoken to Dad about it, but I will. I just wanted to let you know that it's almost time for you to step up. I'd rather plane hop to exotic islands than be sitting on someone's office. I'm not that dude."

That was three weeks ago to date. Did he do this shit on purpose? I thought I had more time, and this OG mess had me occupied, so I wasn't able to put much thought into what he was saying. I felt so guilty. There had to be more to it than what he was saying, but from what I could see, my brother was truly living the life. What secret was he holding on to? What happened that made him not want to be here anymore? I had tons of questions, but they wouldn't be answered.

By the time the ambulance got there, he was pronounced dead. I was so angry with him. He was supposed to be calling me from some pink sand beach, telling me about all the hoes he bedded since he was overseas. He was supposed to invite me out to enjoy the fruits of our labor, and I was supposed to decline because it was business as usual. We were going to be large in this game, but he copped out on me. That shit had me pissed.

I felt horrible for Chantel. Yeah, the EMT workers probably could have saved him if we had called sooner, but my brother would have wanted us to protect the operation. People overdose daily, so they knew how to bring them back, but letting them in was too risky. She didn't get that part. We still needed to eat even after he was gone. I tried to comfort her, but she wasn't checking for me at all. She blamed me, and I wasn't sure why. I knew my brother pep-talked her about the business as well. Maybe she didn't believe him. She called me every name she could think of, a few times charging into me and swinging wildly, trying to cause bodily harm, just to turn and collapse in my arms, her cry echoing off the walls. She loved my brother. We all did. It was just that sometimes, things happened out of our control. This was one of those things.

When I called my parents to tell them of his passing, they were devastated. My mom's cry sounded just like Chantel's but worse. They didn't know the life we were leading on campus, and I damn sure wasn't about to tell them. I pretended that I had no idea of his drug use and was just as shocked as they were when the doctor told us there was cocaine found in his system. Of course, our dad was in denial and demanded a full toxicology report. My mom fainted at the news and ended up in urgent care to get herself together. Come to find out, she hadn't eaten or drunk anything since she got the news and had become dehydrated.

My mom seemed to shrink before my eyes, the tears escaping her eyes in buckets. My dad just had a look of disbelief on his face, and he seemed smaller in stature as well. He had to be wondering where he went wrong with us. They gave us the best of everything. How could his son, out of all the people's sons in the world, die of a drug overdose? It was a huge pill to swallow for him. He didn't want to accept it, and I understood. I saw it happening and couldn't accept it either. All of this was some bull-shit, and the guilt just ate at me. I was so busy trying to get mine that I left him to his own devices. I should have been more attentive.

They set it up so that we would never have a worry in our lives. We absolutely wanted for nothing ever. Even my shit was set up properly to run one of my dad's doctor's offices once I graduated. They didn't ask much of us, just to maintain our grades and graduate. The rest would be handed to us on a golden platter. I felt horrible having to keep all of what I knew inside. Knowing the truth would be more painful than not, but they wouldn't be able to handle any of it. They didn't grow up in the hood, so they didn't understand hood struggle. They were an elite bunch. This shit we were into was not a damn tea party.

By the time we left the hospital and I got my parents tucked away in the hotel for the night, I was ready to just fall back. I had a lot to process and a lot to take on. I dozed off for what felt like the first time in days, and the insistent buzzing of my cell phone finally woke me up. Further inspection showed that I missed over twenty calls and even more texts from Goon.

OG tried to rob the warehouse.

I jumped up from my bed and ran down to the car, calling Goon back as I moved. I saw I was going to have to make an example out of this dude when I really didn't want to. Why was everyone being difficult at one of the most difficult times in my life? I needed to be mourning my brother, comforting my parents, and making sure Chantel was okay. All of this shit was happening at the wrong time. I promise you when it rains, it storms harder than a motherfucker.

Meet me at his house. They already tied up.

I backtracked to the same place I spoke with OG's baby mom the day before. When I walked in, I saw OG strapped to a chair with blood everywhere. His left eye was swollen and damn near closed. Goon looked heated, an emotion he barely showed. I figured it was because he personally bought OG to me and he was feeling betrayed. Of the two of us, he was definitely the more levelheaded one. I would comfort him later, but now it was time to handle business. We had a situation on our hands.

Furniture was flipped around like shit got real before I got there. There was also a body with a huge amount of blood around the head lying in the dining area. I could smell blood in the air, and it made me uncomfortable.

I could never get to be okay with killing people. It just wasn't in my makeup. My parents didn't raise me like that.

"OG, tell me what's going on?" I asked as I texted another member of the squad to get the container and bring some gasoline over. I wasn't even about to get into a long, drawn-out discussion on the why's and why-nots. It didn't matter. When you went against the grain, you died. No exceptions. I hated that this was the person I had become. I was allowing people to bring out the worst in me.

"I needed more. I wasn't making enough," he said as his head hung low. He was embarrassed.

I liked OG, and this shit made it harder than it needed to be. He tried to rob the warehouse. What the fuck was I supposed to do with that? We could work out him being short and even losing clientele, but trying to rob me changed the game. There was no way I could let him walk after this. It would change the dynamic of the team, and I couldn't afford it.

"Did you make enough to buy your truck?" I asked as I began to walk through the house. I saw that Goon had already bagged up what little bit of product OG had in the crib. Wasn't any use in losing it all in the fire.

At this point, it was like 3 a.m. My parents were in town, my brother was dead, and I wasn't really in the mood for anything else at the moment. In hindsight, I probably was thinking irrationally, but what was done was done.

"Yes, but—"

"Was trying to rob me worth it?" I continued to quiz him as I began to pour the gasoline on the kitchen floor. "Put the bodies in the back room and move quick. It's about to get real hot in here," I instructed Goon as I totally ignored OG's pleading. The pregnant baby mom, the son, and him would all be unrecognizable by morning. I knew at that moment I was truly a monster.

As I circled him with flammable fluid, I made sure not to actually get any on him. I wanted him to feel the heat before it hit him. I wanted him, even in death, to never forget this moment. More importantly, the people that were there to witness this wouldn't forget it either.

"Can we spare her and the kids? It's not her fault," Goon pleaded when I first got there.

This shit was tugging at my heart strings, but I had to set the example. Everybody got it—cat, dog, mom, and goldfish. No one was off limits. I knew this made me seem heartless, and at the moment, I probably was. I had other shit going on. He definitely caught me at the wrong damn time.

Once Goon secured the bodies, I set the blaze in the kitchen, then tossed a match at his feet before exiting. I could hear his screams from blocks away as we hastily made an escape like OJ Simpson in a white Bronco. Even if they got the other body, the goal was to make sure he didn't make it out alive.

Goon and I went our separate ways, planning to meet up the next day. He stayed in his girl's dorm, and I stayed in ours.

When I woke up the next day, I saw it on the news that there was a bad house fire overnight. The bodies found inside were completely charred and unrecognizable, and they would have to use dental records to identify the victims. When I looked at my phone, Goon had sent me a black heart in a text, indicating that all would be good. Tears filled my eyes for the first time since my brother passed, and I could barely breathe. I felt like I was losing it completely. I lay back in the bed, trying to decide how to move forward when my phone began to ring.

"Hello," I answered, pretending like I was still asleep.

"Chase, I'm pregnant," Chantel revealed, busting out in tears.

Did my brother know? I offered to meet her at her house, where we could sit face to face. All of this was just too much, and I just wasn't ready for it.

Selah

Fast Forward Eye Opener

This man was a real live killer. Like, what the fuck?

The bath water had gotten cold as we sat there and I listened to him pour his heart out. For the first time in our relationship, I was scared of him. If he could kill a pregnant woman and her child, who in the hell was I to think I was any different? Shit, I still had questions. How did he end up in Philly? What happened to his friend Goon? Was he one of the guys I saw him with sometimes, or did he make it to the NBA? This man of mine that I loved with everything in me was a fucking murderer . . . just like me. I was scared for my life, but I didn't want to leave him.

"I've made a lot of mistakes, babe," he said as he let the water from the tub and stood so that we could get clean. Tears ran from his eyes, probably for the first time ever. He probably didn't have time to grieve his brother or process having to kill other people after. He scared me, but I loved him. I had to be there for him. He probably never spoke all of this shit out loud before, so it had to be a shock to his senses as well. Imagine holding in years of hurt that haunted you at night, and you finally got to release it. It would feel amazing and petrifying at the same time. I was glad he trusted me at this level.

Taking the loofah from his hands, I soaped it up and began to scrub him clean. It was almost ceremonial, as if

I were washing away all the stains from his past. I did the best I could as tears began to run from my eyes too. We both had shit we weren't proud of. I was not there to pass judgment, and I was glad that he had even shared what he did with me. That had to be tough.

I needed to share some demons with him as well. I wasn't the goodie-two-shoes he thought I was. I took lives as well. Maybe not to the same extent, but people were not here anymore because of me. We were the same person.

As the water ran down off of him, rinsing the soap away, I took him into my mouth until he began to stretch and harden. Now probably wasn't the time to give him head, but I wanted him to know that he had me regardless. I loved this man and would do what I could to take away his pain. He leaned against the shower wall to keep himself steady. I could feel the stress slowly lifting off of him as his grip on my hair loosened some. I took him in once more, moving my kisses up his body until we were standing face to face.

He picked me up and pinned me against the wall, pushing deep into me in one swift swoop. I gasped, not ready to take all of him in like that.

He looked me in my eyes, and I could still see sadness. He wasn't a monster at all. He was a man that had to make tough decisions sometimes—the type of man that I knew would protect me if I needed protecting. I could give my heart to him and know he would keep it safe. He needed someone to forgive him for some of the shit he did because he probably felt like God wasn't hearing him anymore. All of this shit was overwhelming, but I would not dip out on him like the women in his past. We were going to get through whatever it was together.

We really made love that night. No fast fucking, pounding me against the headboard, carrying me around the house type of shit. I'm talking real, live soul-connecting, it's-me-and-you-against-the-world, I'd-kill-someone-for-him type lovemaking. Chase made me believe that being with him was the only place in the world I needed to be. It was time for us to make major moves, and by the morning, I knew that it was time for me to pack my room up and become a full-fledged adult.

I couldn't wait to share the news with my mom and dad. I was hype, but I knew once I spoke with them, their reaction would let me know if I was making the right decision. He deserved all of me. I deserved all of him.

I forgot all about Sajdah and her bullshit. She would have to live in her misery by her damn self. I really tried with her to make things what they used to be, but she was not budging, and I was done begging, especially since I had no damn clue what the real issue was with her. How did she expect me to rectify a situation that I didn't have details about? That shit was so stupid to me, and I didn't have the energy for it. Fuck her. When she decided to get back regular again, maybe I would be in the mood to let her back in. We would just have to see when the time came, but I decided I wasn't going to sweat her for info that should've been readily given. Just because she was ready to talk didn't mean that I would be willing to listen. She should have taken the time when she had it. Now I didn't even care if we ever spoke again at this point. I would miss her, of course, but I'd be fine. I always bounced back, regardless of the situation.

The next day after work, I went to my parents' home to begin the process. I had sent a text to my mom while at work, letting her know I wanted to talk, but we were both tied up in meetings and couldn't get out for lunch. When I got there, she had the kitchen popping with something that smelled amazing. I was hungry, too, so I was happy I showed up when I did.

I kissed her on the cheek and greeted my dad in the living room as he worked on his laptop until dinner was done. I would miss him the most. I was truly a daddy's girl, so not seeing him on a daily basis would be weird for me at first.

I was glad they were understanding and support-ive of what I was trying to accomplish. Not that they would mind, but I didn't want to stay at home forever. Eventually, as adults, we would move on and obtain our own house and family. Sajdah just didn't see it that way. She was acting like we were supposed to shrivel up and die in this damn house.

Once I got to my room, I sat on my bed and looked around. I made the decision that I wouldn't take every-thing right away, just in case I needed to double back. I wasn't about to get a U-Haul or no shit like that. I would just take some clothes, shoes, and makeup to hold me over. I'd come get more things as needed. I basically packed as much as I could in a duffle bag and the few pairs of shoes that would fit in a bin. I grabbed most of my makeup for sure, and a few perfumes off the vanity. This would be a ninety-day trial period. If shit didn't go the way I needed it to, my ass would be jumping ship like I never got on.

After I packed, I went to speak with my mom in the kitchen before everyone gathered around. I was hoping Sajdah was working late again. I really didn't feel like her shit that night. It was better not to deal with her at this point. I wasn't going to be made to feel uncomfortable in my own damn house. She could very well keep her negative ass right where she was.

"Hey, Ma." I spoke to her as I started setting the table for myself and my parents, purposely leaving Sajdah's place setting out. My mom gave me a quick glance to say that she noticed, but she refrained from saying anything about it.

"Hey, ladybug. Sorry I couldn't meet up with you at work. We are wrapping up our fiscal year, and they got us working like slaves," she said with a slight chuckle, wrist twisting like stir-fry as she maneuvered multiple pots and pans.

"Us too! I can't wait until this month is over," I replied. Fiscal time was a mess. We always kept books in order, but it was so much work wrapping up year-end paper-work that we had to do mandatory overtime. I could totally understand her exhaustion.

"What did you want to discuss?" she asked as she walked to grab another ingredient from the fridge.

Just as I began to tell her, my dad walked in the room and took a seat at the table.

"It was nothing important. I plan to start spending a little more time with Chase at his house. I didn't want to just bust out and move in with him not knowing how it would really be."

"That's not a problem. You never really know someone until you are constantly in their space," my dad chimed in as he filled our cups with homemade lemonade. I was nervous that he would be upset, but he seemed pretty chill with the idea.

"Your room will always be available as long as we have a house. No worries, dear. I'm excited for you," my mom jumped in, given me a quick hug in the process.

The amount of relief I felt completely calmed me down and gave me that extra reassurance.

"Now, I won't get into my views on premarital sex," my dad began with a solemn look on his face. "Especially since I tapped your mom well before marriage."

The look on my mom's face was priceless. We both busted out laughing as she pretended to beat him over the head with a spoon. My parents definitely came from the old school, but they were very modern in their views

on how the world worked in 2019. They definitely weren't
stuck back in 1970. Thank God. The way Chase had been
chasing this cat and catching it, they would be astonished
to know the real deal.

"Chase seems like a nice guy. How do you feel about
him? Aside from anything sexual, what are your true
feelings about him? Will he be a good provider?" my dad
quizzed as we settled in to enjoy this good meal my mom
whipped up.

Sigh. I knew that question was going to come up. Let's
be clear, our parents raised us to be independent women;
however, we were also made very aware that was not a
sign of weakness to allow the man of the house to be the
man of the house. The woman's job was to be the woman
of the house and be strong in the areas that he was not.
Like, if he had trouble paying bills on time, he allotted
the finances to his wife, and she took care of it. This was
not about to be some unwed, barefoot-and-pregnant,
waiting-for-him-to-make-a-move type situation. This
was an equal effort. I wasn't sure how Chase wanted me
to contribute since my parents refused to take our money,
and aside from personal expenses and us sticking cash in
our mother's pocketbook, we basically banked our checks
and kept our credit in pristine order. I had never paid a
utility or mortgage in my life, so I would have to figure
out how Chase wanted to handle things. Apparently, he
had been doing these things himself prior to me moving
in, so I made a mental note to converse with him about
it later.

"Well, that's kind of why I'm not rushing to move all
the way in. So far, he has been wonderful at providing for
me. He hasn't given me any reason to suspect he can't.
His home is gorgeous, located right off of the Main Line."

I didn't want to get into the fact that he was a trap king.
My dad would flip if he knew that much. He saw that

Chase drove a very fancy car, so he knew he had money. I opted instead to tell them what little I knew regarding his background. His parents were physicians, so even if he were merely living the life of a spoiled rich kid, he appeared to have some stability.

"It sounds like you did your research," my dad responded, sounding satisfied with my answer.

At that moment, my mom set his plate in front of him, so I knew it was time for us to indulge. Saved by the food indeed!

"Just know you never have to hesitate to come back here. Ever."

"Yes, Daddy," I replied, getting up to hug them both. Now that I had their blessing, I felt a little better about the move I was about to make.

I enjoyed great conversation with my parents about everything under the son, my mom and dad just as flirtatious as they always had been. After dinner was done, I double-checked to make sure I had everything I wanted to take with me packed, and after chatting with Chase about a few things, I let him know that I would come the next day after work. He was hype as shit on the phone, and that set my soul at ease even more. I felt like this was going to be a good thing. I couldn't wait to begin my new life with my love. He wanted me there; I wasn't forcing my way in.

They always say that everything that glitters ain't gold. What they didn't tell you is diamonds sparkle as well . . . but so does aluminum. This step was the beginning of how Chase and I would co-exist. Let's just say I wasn't ready for the journey, but we'll get into that at a later date. For now, just ride this thing out with me because it's about to get real.

Sajdah

Your Man Is My Man Too

"Chase, slow down," I moaned into his ear as he went deep. I had been getting the dick long before him and Selah became an item. Yeah, that's shady as fuck of me, but oh well. I wasn't ready for a commitment. I was truly focused on concentrating on my career. Chase understood that. He also understood that there was no way in the world Selah would agree to us sharing him, so I helped him out with an alternative. He could smash whenever I wanted him to, no strings attached. He was never to call me, though. That was the rule. I'd be the one doing the calling.

Chase liked to be controlled. I found that out early on. Selah would never know that because she was easily controlled. That's what made this entire thing so sweet. My terms, my rules. It didn't look like it at the moment, but I actually looked out for her best interests. She would be waiting forever on Chase to make a move in her direction if it weren't for me. As far as I was concerned, I should be getting the sister of the year award.

Most nights, when I got in late, it was because I was riding his dick all crazy. I didn't even get upset when he called me my sister's name by accident. Hell, we looked just alike. It was easy to mix us up. He really couldn't tell us apart, so whenever I showed up, I would greet him a certain way so that he knew it was me. The crazy thing was, he really did truly love my sister. He *loved* that girl, so much so that he even tried on a few occasions to break it off with me. As you can see, it was unsuccessful. The moment Selah became unavailable, he let me right back in. That shit was too easy.

Why was I really getting in the way of whatever it was they were trying to build? I would never admit to being a hater, but that's exactly how it looked from the outside. For the moment, I was willing to take that hit. It was about me for the first time ever, and no one else was stepping in on that.

I wasn't completely telling lies to my parents, just in case you were wondering. I did just score my second Comcast account. It definitely had me at the office late most nights. It was a very demanding job. However, every so often, I had an itch that I couldn't scratch myself, and that's where Chase came in. Toys could only take you so far. Eventually, you needed the real thing, something with a pulse. They hadn't invented a toy that pulled your hair and spanked you from the back just yet, and a sistah had needs.

Of course, he was nervous at first, but once I assured him that I would keep his secret, he was all in. Men rarely turned down pussy. Trust me on this. Chase was no exception to the rule.

I was the reason why he knew so much about Selah. I made sure that her coffee and cinnamon bun were ordered every morning. I set up his condo for her engagement surprise and hired the chef to cook the meal. I picked out that gorgeous-ass ring that she was currently wearing, and I had access to his checking account (that I helped him set up) to make sure his bills were paid on time, and to buy whatever my heart desired as long as I cleared it with him first. Her gullible ass thought he was on top of his shit when, in reality, it was all me. He provided the money, don't get me wrong, but I was the brain behind the romance. I set her up to live a lovely life, and she didn't even realize it.

Oh, do know that if she ever knew any of this, she would definitely kill his ass. I may be spared because we shared a bond, but that was a strong maybe that lately, I wasn't really sure I could bank on. It was definitely due to my attitude, though. I was so busy setting up shit for her that I never even considered my own happiness. What would I do once they got married? Would I continue to fuck her husband when she wasn't around? At what point was enough just that? What happened when she got pregnant? Where did Sajdah fit in the picture? I didn't, and the reality of it all was starting to piss me off. Most importantly, why didn't he just choose me? I was already playing the part. What was I lacking? Oh, wait. He did choose me, but I pushed him off. The shit bugged me to no end, but I knew what I signed up for, so I had to roll with it.

Funny thing was, I had the opportunity to let her know I was crushing on him. She did ask, and I blew her off. I knew if I told her the truth, she would have never pursued him. This mess-up was my fault. It wasn't like I didn't have dudes checking for me. They were definitely feeling the kid, but I wasn't interested in a work relationship or some stuck-up corporate man. I liked them thugged out, just like Selah did, but they were intimidated by the book smarts. It was hard being beauty and brains, and I was still trying to master it. I definitely wasn't about to dumb down for anyone. Fuck that. This shit was frustrating, and I had clearly started taking it out on my dear sister.

"Lay down. Let me ride," I demanded as he pushed my legs back until my knees touched my ears. I had to definitely stay up on my birth control with this dude because even from the beginning, we never used protection. He was cool with getting tested for HIV, and once the results came back non-reactive, I busted that shit right open for him—after being certain that he was only fucking my sister and me. I didn't have time to be worrying about some random bitch, too. Between the two of us, he got more than enough pussy for any man. We made sure of it, unbeknownst to Selah, of course.

I had a scare about a year ago that changed the dynamics of our relationship. I had been fucking up on my birth control, not really taking it the way I was supposed to, partly because Chase and I weren't hooking up a lot. Around that time, Selah was going hard with finishing classes so that she could graduate early, so she wasn't checking for him at all, and I had landed my first Comcast account, so I was focused. They were spending some time, but not like he wanted. That let me in to cum all over his dick as often as I wanted to. Chase was not about to pull out and waste his nut. He told me that from the rip.

"So, make sure you got that birth control thing figured out. I'm not ready to be a dad."

He made that shit very clear, and I agreed. Well, all that boot-knocking got my ass knocked right the fuck up. I thought I had the damn flu. I felt like my life was ending. One day while at work, I just couldn't take it anymore and finally dragged my ass to urgent care, who ended up sending me right to my doctor's office. The dizzy spells were overwhelming, and I could barely concentrate. I didn't think much of the doctor asking for urine. Even when you weren't having sex, they asked you to piss in a cup to check for sexually transmitted diseases. I first thought this nigga gave me some shit, and I was prepared to go clean the fuck off on him. When the doctor said they had to do an ultrasound, I thought maybe I had developed some shit I couldn't get rid of.

"Looks like you're going to be a mommy," my doctor said with a smile on her face.

I promise if I wasn't already lying down, I would have passed out. Pregnant? What the fuck! I didn't even bother telling Chase. I immediately contacted Planned Parenthood, and by the end of the week, that shit was a wrap. Wasn't any use in complicating shit. This was sex. Anything that happened after that was on me.

I lay in bed the few nights leading up to the abortion, trying to figure out if I was really going to do it. What choice did I really have? It wasn't like Chase wanted in on it, and I'd be damned if I was going to be somebody's single baby momma. Even if I wanted it, how would I explain that shit? And just my fucked-up luck, the child would come out the spitting image of Chase's dog ass. It was just too much risk involved, so when Friday rolled around, I got my ass up like I was going to work and made my way to Planned Parenthood by myself. They wanted me to have someone with me, but I didn't have anyone, and that shit really opened my ass to where my life was at the time. I couldn't tell my family, and I didn't have any friends to lean on. The one person I did have I couldn't say shit to because it was her man's baby. As depressing as it was, I took that shit like a champ and handled my business. This was no one else's problem but mine. My parents would definitely try to talk me into keeping it, and I didn't need that kind of negativity in my life right now.

I didn't call him for about a month. Complete disappearing act. He sent flowers to the job, amongst other things, because I practically fell off the face of the earth. He thought he had done something, but the last box I got from him surprised me. At that point, I was getting tired of him sending me stuff and had mentally made plans to call him that afternoon. When I got back from lunch that day, I had yet another bouquet of roses, this time with a note attached to it. Upon opening, a piece of paper from Planned Parenthood that listed my pregnancy termination fell out. Chase's note read that basically, if I didn't come to him, he would come to me.

Shocked wasn't even a strong enough word to describe what was going on in my head. Which one of his hoes got this info for him? How would he even know to dig up this kind of shit on me? I never mentioned even being with child to him. The more I thought about it, the madder I got. Who in the hell did he think he was? I did what I wanted, and I thought I had made that clear. I was definitely going to see his ass. That, he didn't have to worry about. This type of shit was unacceptable.

Chase really didn't know who he was fucking with. Him popping up at my house or some shit in Selah's presence would not only blow up both of our spots, but it would definitely get a bullet put in his ass. At first I was pissed and started to let him find out the hard way, but I didn't want to have to go into why I had overstepped boundaries with him to Selah, so I sent him a text, letting him know I got his message and I would stop by to see him after work. He didn't reply. That shit made me nervous. What if he killed me or some shit when I got there? I had been keeping him a secret from everyone, so they wouldn't even know to look for me there. This was all just too much, and I wasn't ready to deal with it then, but I knew the best thing for me to do was just go and get it over with. I was sure this wasn't something a good dick suck could fix; he was just in his bag right now. I felt more confident as the day went on because I knew who I was dealing with. Little did I know, Chase wasn't to be fucked with either.

"So, you killed my baby."

It was more of a statement than a question. I was standing at the door of his condo, only able to make it to just past the entrance. He was steaming mad, but his exterior was cool as a cucumber. You weren't allowed to show emotion in the game he was in, so he clearly learned to have that kind of control from that environment. His face was a dead giveaway for me. His jaw was clenched so tight I was surprised his teeth hadn't broken, and his eyes were bloodshot.

I played myself this time, and there wasn't much I could do to make it up. I tried to flip that shit back on him, but he wasn't having it.

"Chase, I did what was best for us. How would we have explained it to Selah? You made it very clear that you were not ready to be a father."

"You tell me that you're pregnant, and you give me that choice. You don't just take shit upon yourself and dip off like what I have to say doesn't count."

Mute. He was right, and I had no argument for him. I could have at least sent him a text. It wasn't like he was going to convince me to keep it. I took the money out of his account to pay for it because I was still under my parents' insurance, and I didn't want it to pop up on their statement. I was just walking around lying to every damn body.

I tried to reason with him. As sweet as she was, low key my fucking sister was a damn lunatic. It was no way she could go through this shit again. Kev did this exact same thing to her with another girl she used to run with in her little clique. *Devastated* isn't even a strong enough word to describe how her world crumbled. It took her months to bounce back from that. There was no way I would be responsible for causing her that kind of pain for the second time in her life. Not for anyone in this lifetime or the next.

"We could have figured it out, Sajdah. You didn't even tell me. I had to find out from some broad in the street that clearly had my best interests at heart. Hell, I would've given you the money and held your hand through the process. You didn't even give me a choice. You know how the hood talks. I'm surprised your sister doesn't already know."

Pause. Who the hell did he have keeping tabs on me? Maybe I underestimated Mr. Warren. I had no idea that he had connections all over. Apparently, he didn't trust me as much as I thought he did. Hell, he probably didn't trust anyone fully, but still, I was offended.

"You're right. I should have said something to you," I agreed in an effort to soften the blow and get him back in line. "It's just that—"

"No excuses. That's some snake-ass shit you did," he spat out, barely able to control the anger bubbling up inside of him. "I don't trust snakes. You can let yourself out."

"But, Chase . . . I can explain!"

"Sajdah, if I were you, I would leave. It's beneficial for both of us that you do. Right now, I'm just trying to make sure your sister doesn't find out."

He turned his back to me and walked away. I started to take a running start and drop-kick his ass, but I honestly didn't know what Chase was capable of. No one knew I was there, so if he killed and buried my ass, I'd just be another hashtag on the missing person's report. My feelings were hurt, surprisingly. I thought for sure I had secured the bag with him, but my grip wasn't as tight as I thought.

I figured I'd just give him some time to cool off, so I left. When I got home, I decided to send him a text. Honestly, I really didn't think he would be this upset about it. I saved his life! There was no way we were going to be able to sneak a baby past my family, and they would definitely grill me for the facts. He didn't see it that way, though, and I learned enough in my psych class to know that you had to allow people their time to be in their emotion. Otherwise, they wouldn't be open to hearing you.

I did decide to text him to let him know I was sorry. After shooting the text over, I got a message back stating the number was invalid. I checked his contact info to make sure I hadn't changed anything and tried it again. A second or so later, I got the message again. I called next to see and received a message saying the call could not be contacted. This dude blocked me! Was he serious right now?

I jumped up out the bed and got dressed real quick. On the way down, my mom and dad were cuddled up watching *Jeopardy* on TV. I told them I had to make a run and that I left something at the office. When I got to Chase's condo and tried the code, it said it was invalid. I tried it again and got the same message. I didn't see his car outside, and I knew if I tried it again, it would set the alarm off, and the cops would show up. This man shut me all the way down. I was hurt.

All this time, I thought I might have meant more to him, but I guess not. Turning back to my car, I totally missed him peeking out at me from the living room window. Chase definitely hadn't seen the last of me. He was not just about to shut me out and think everything was cool. I would have to show him better than I'd been telling him. He fucked over the wrong one this time. This revenge was going to be sweet.

Chase

They Always Think It's A Game

I didn't know what kind of karma I was dealing with, but something had to give. Too much shit was coming at me at once that I really didn't want to deal with. I already had the shit with Sajdah and this aborted-ass baby, and now I just added her homegirl Vice to the mix. I wondered if she really knew what kind of snake-ass bitches she had in her camp. I damn sure wouldn't be the one to tell her. There was no way I would even step to anyone on my team's girl. That shit was a big-ass don't-do-it-or-die-if-you-do situation. I was not about to let some pussy get in the way of this bag.

Vice was a different breed than the rest of them. A hood booga at best, but pretty to look at. She came back for repeat dick downs just like Sajdah did, but she wanted me to line her pockets to keep quiet. She kept telling me that she had a plan and that all of this shit would fall on Sajdah's head. I didn't give a fuck who that shit fell on, as long as it wasn't on me and I got to keep my girl. I was not a complete monster, and I didn't want Sajdah to fall out with her people, but at this point, I just wanted to be done with all of their asses. We were all dead-ass wrong, and the only person that had a right to feel any type of way was Selah. She was the clueless one, and that's how that shit always was.

I felt like shit and decided moving forward that it would only be her. Either that or let her go completely and just be rid of everyone. The other two made it difficult to just say no. Sajdah was demanding but could ride better than a cowgirl, and Vice's throat was so deep she could damn near fit my entire dick and my balls in her mouth. Selah was a freak, too, but I had the other two fucking on me like crazy and causing mad competition. Selah had no clue about either of them. Sajdah only knew about Selah, and Vice had the drop on both of them. She was the real MVP. All of this had me exhausted.

I saw that Selah had started to move some of her things in. I was shocked that she hadn't shown up with a damn moving truck because I knew she owned more than that little bit of shit she had stuffed in a tote bag and storage bin, but I decided to let her be great and move at her own pace. She was playing it safe, and I couldn't blame her for that. The way this shit was looking right now, I wouldn't trust my ass either—but I was willing to put in any work that was required to make sure she was straight. Fuck all them other hoes.

The crazy shit was, every time I tried to put some distance between me and them, one of their asses showed up. Maybe once she really got herself settled in, they would just leave us be. It was no way they were that bold to still try and slide through if she was living there. Obviously, me telling them it wasn't working didn't mean a damn thing to anybody. I wasn't exactly ready for marriage, but I borrowed a page from Sajdah's scheming ass and went on ahead and copped that rock from BB&B. I wasn't about to give her some cheap-ass Center City ring. She deserved more than that, even if it was partially a lie.

I was enjoying her being there, I'm not going to lie, but it was a definite adjustment having someone constantly in my space. I made sure I went through the crib to get all the bullshit out that any chick had left there. They were a very crafty bunch, so I made sure to check every obvious and not-so-obvious spot. Chicks would hide a damn hair clip on a lampshade in a dark corner, and that shit would just bust out and appear after ten months. I wasn't in the mood for the bullshit. I even considered changing my number, but it would be too much to make sure everybody got the new one. It was easier to just block they simple asses. That way, just in case I ever needed their services again, I could always unblock and get right back at them. Yeah, they would be mad at first, but they always came back around.

As for the team, I had plans to fly out to L.A. to see my boy Goon. He did the damn thing while in school, and I hated to see him go, but we knew that was the plan going in. He was a beast on the court and was the number three draft pick for the L.A. Lakers. I was happy for him, and I was glad he made it out the hood. We both walked across that stage and grabbed that degree, and even though he tried his hardest to get me to see past the streets, this was what I was doing with my life. My father was not happy about this, to say the least.

I was genuinely happy for my boy. He made it out the hood. He fought against adversity. He built a solid team. He made it to the big leagues. That was the type of shit that made all of this worthwhile. The turn-up for his sendoff was major. I got the baddest bitches on campus, the best food our city had to offer, and we shut the club down, popping bottles all night. I surprised him and flew his grandma and siblings out to see him graduate, and the smile on his face showed me that he was eternally grateful. He taught me a lot during his reign, and I would definitely miss him.

What I loved about Goon was his loyalty. He wasn't even in L.A. a good month before he was calling me down there to see how he was living. I stayed at his condo while I was there, and he made sure I had courtside seats to the games. He introduced me to other players on the team, and I definitely made sure I got an autographed jersey with his number on it. He was the brother I still had after my brother departed.

I couldn't wait to introduce him to Selah. She heard stories about Goon, but I needed her to know he wasn't a monster either. I trusted him with my entire life, and I needed her to have that same trust. Aside from my biological brother, who was already deceased, Goon was all I had.

It was weird for me not to just get up and go. I was used to just packing a bag and jetting, or just grabbing my passport and getting what I needed once I landed. As long as my team was solid, I was good to go. This having to check in shit was taking some adjusting, and quite frankly, I was over it. I hadn't had a curfew since I had a curfew, and I was not about to be put on a schedule. I also didn't feel like arguing with Selah about it, and I thought the best thing to do was invite her along. That way, she could meet my boy and let me have some peace.

That shit did not go as planned, and I ended up regretting even offering the damn trip. I was willing to give her the rest of my life, but not if it had all these stipulations.

"Chase, some of us have a job we go to. I just can't up and call out for two weeks without getting fired. Vacations are planned, not impromptu for a half a month."

The look on her face said the most. She didn't trust me to take care of us, and I completely understood it. We weren't on that type time just yet, and she was the independent type. That was smart of her not to jeopardize her bag, but where did that leave me? I wasn't about to sit around there when I didn't have to.

"Selah, I dig that. I wasn't asking that you sta[y] entire. Just come out, meet my boy, party a little, a[nd] have you on a flight back here Sunday night."

"You'll have me on a flight? So you plan to sta[y] there without me?"

I wanted to scream. What part of a two-week va[cation] did she not get? I wasn't going out there just to b[e with] Goon. I was trying to develop some connects over [there] to get cash flow rolling in on that part of the glo[be.] shit was bigger than just Philly. I wanted global [reach,] and I wanted it for my team, as well. I believed in l[eading] by example, and this was how moves were mad[e, but] she kept hollering about a legit business. I was pl[anning] on surprising her by showing her a few nightclub[s I] wanted to invest in while I was there, but she was [on] up the church's money. What had I gotten myself [into?]

"Selah, let's just have this conversation a litt[le bit] when we are both less tense. My only priority is [to] remain happy. This is such a minute circumstan[ce.] We can get through this. I promise you."

She looked like she didn't want to believe m[e, but at] least I got her to shut up for the moment. I ha[d to find] something to occupy her time so that I could [make my] money with the least amount of stress. She [was my] people; she just had to adjust a little to dealing w[ith one] like me—or I would just have to let her go.

Selah

Life With Chase

This man was so happy to have me there. When I showed up after work the next day with my suitcase and duffle bag, he had already made room for me in the bedroom, and he gave me permission to turn his third bedroom into a walk-in closet. It was initially going to be an office space, but he never got around to it. He gave me his credit card and a $10K limit. I was in love.

I thought it would be weird not being at my parents' house on a regular basis, but after a few weeks of waking up there and returning after work, I was slowly starting to get used to being in his space, or *our* space, as he insisted. He made sure we had plenty of food and things to drink, and I had my room furniture already ordered and ready to go. What I couldn't order, he promised to take me out over the weekend to shop for it. I was impressed.

It was actually fun to cook dinner for him at night. I would pretend I was my mom in the kitchen, whipping up meals like she did for my dad on a daily basis. This was not about to be a takeout-dinner-every-night household. I learned from the best, and I was about to show him. My dad even shared his famous sweet peach tea recipe with me, and when I made it for him the first time, he was hooked. I knew then, I would definitely have to keep a carafe for him in the fridge.

It appeared that life with Chase was going to be good. However, there were some things I just couldn't get used to. I don't know what I was expecting, but him coming in at the wee hours of the morning bothered me more than I thought it would. I thought the purpose of him having a team was so that he could live a normal life. Since he didn't have a typical nine-to-five, I wasn't expecting him to just be sitting home all day, but I was expecting him to do something other than trap all night. He had a bachelor's degree, for God's sake. Utilize that shit and open a clothing store or something—anything to normalize his life and not have him on the run all the time. We were not Beyoncé and Jay Z. I needed a normal life.

What irked me a little was he thought buying me things would shut me up. I could buy my own shit; I wasn't that girl. You couldn't just silence me with diamonds. I knew what I was getting into when I got with him, though, so I was either going to have to shut up and take that shit or deal with it until he put a plan in action. Either way, something was going to have to give sooner than he thought.

Second thing that irked me—him waking me up to fuck when he came in. Every. Damn. Night. Like, okay, dude, you put a ring on it, but you don't own me. I have to get up in the morning to go to work. I didn't have the energy to be riding dick every single night and sometimes again in the morning. We would have to have a talk before we burned each other out before we even got started. Was this man a sex addict, or just happy to see me? I really wanted this thing to last with Chase, and if it were going to last, we needed to set some boundaries ASAP. It could be that he was excited to have me on a regular basis, so I dug it, but we were going to have to space this shit out. Good thing you can't run out of pussy, because the way this man was in me all the time, he would deplete that damn supply in no time.

The old saying goes, "If you look for dirt, you find dirt." The type of shit that happens when you are home by yourself will get you in a world of trouble sometimes. So, I was bored as hell on a Friday, and Chase was out on the block yet again, doing what trap boys do. Of course, I took some time to set some things up in my walk-in closet, but I felt like I needed to familiarize myself with the entire house since I was living there now. Nothing looked out of the ordinary as far as I could see. Chase was very anal about things having a proper place, so there wasn't anything just lying around haphazardly.

I looked in the drawers to see that his clothes, all the way down to his underwear, were folded neatly. Everything was checking out, and I was impressed until I stumbled upon a pair of panties and an earring shaped like an S on the floor in the back of his closet. Now, I didn't immediately go off because, for one, they were in the back of the closet, which meant they could have been there forever and he had no idea, or they could have just gotten there and he still had no idea. Women were so petty and strategic. Chase would have just thrown the shit in the trash had he known it was there. Women hid shit knowing another woman would search for it. Most guys didn't think to look that far into the closet for anything, but the person that put that there knew for sure that women were detectives and would peel the fucking carpet back looking for a stray hair to have evidence before we ended up wrong about some shit.

I was a little upset, not because I thought he was currently cheating, but because obviously, at some point, someone else was there. Again, who knew when? I wasn't about to appear insecure in front of him, though, so I placed both items in a sandwich bag and stuck them in a basket in my room until I had time to further investigate. When I decided the time was right to go to him, I needed stone-cold facts that he wouldn't be able to deny.

As I continued my little search, I didn't come up with anything else that didn't belong, so in my head, it further proved that the panties and earring were planted. The mystery was by whom and how long ago? What did they want me to know about him that I didn't know already? I had to keep my cool with this, though, because if it were some shit, I needed it to be without a doubt. That's how I played myself with Kevin, and he almost got to wiggle out of the bullshit he put me in. I didn't have all the info when I first stepped to him, but it didn't take me long to hunt it down and gather it up. When I was on a mission, I didn't stop until it was complete.

Of course, I shot a text to my girls of the stuff to put them on alert, being sure to get clear pictures so that we knew what we were dealing with. If we were going to have to body this dude, we needed to be on point; but for now, I was just going to enjoy the amenities. There was no use in causing drama in the household that didn't need to be there because when it was time to wreak havoc, there was no room for doubt.

Peeping at the clock, I saw that it was almost seven, which meant if I were going to get in bed at a reasonable time, I needed to get dinner done. I had no idea what time Chase was coming in, so I just made enough for myself. It was almost like he didn't appreciate a home-cooked meal.

I tried blinking back tears as I rinsed pasta off to boil and prepped the chicken. I was so fucking lonely, and I wasn't used to it. I was used to being around family. We had dinner as a family every night, with lively conversation about what happened in our day. The only thing I had to talk to were the damn walls because I was there by myself. I did not want this type of life.

I had no idea this was what I was signing up for. A part of me wanted to go and pack up the little bit of shit I bought there with me and go back home. Then again,

I knew this was how he got his money. How else would we be able to afford all this shit we had if he didn't do what he was doing? I made okay money, but not enough to afford us living there. I was so torn, and my appetite was completely gone. I knew he would bitch, but I just turned the stove off and left everything where it was as I ran into the bedroom and cried on the bed. I did not like this shit, and I didn't think I would ever get used to it. I didn't want to seem ungrateful, but what was I supposed to do? I needed to adjust quickly, but it was too much of a struggle.

I eventually cried myself to sleep, and I was awakened by Chase. By the time my eyes adjusted to the light, I saw a big box siting on the end of the bed. I broke out in tears instantly, and he had the most confused look on his face.

"Babe, what's wrong?" he asked as he tried to wipe my face.

I knew I was looking crazy at the moment, and I didn't care. I wasn't built for this shit. I wanted to go back home. Maybe I made the jump too soon.

"I have to go back home. I can't be here by myself," I cried out as he held me even tighter.

"Babe, I know I have to do better," he began to explain as he tried to comfort me. "I'm setting things up now so that I can spend more time with you. I just need you to be patient, ma."

I cried so hard I could barely catch my breath. Did my mom and dad ever have to go through this? What did she do? I wanted to give us a fighting chance, I really did, but I didn't feel like I had any fight in me at the moment. He could have at least stayed with me the first week to help acclimate me to my new living situation. It was like he just threw me in the middle of the ocean, knowing I couldn't swim and leaving me to figure out how to survive. I was not ready, and I was not happy.

"Babe, look at me," he coaxed as he lifted my chin for me to look him in the eyes.

I tried to fight it, but finally, I gave in and looked up, his face a blur from the tears in my eyes.

"I will never purposely hurt you. I should have probably thought this through a little more before I asked you to uproot your life like this. I should have been more prepared, but I promise you I will not make you regret coming here."

"But, Chase, I'm—"

"Selah, give me a chance. I'm begging you." He pulled me in so close I could feel his heartbeat against my cheek.

I was supposed to be there with him. I just had to chill the fuck out and get with the program. He said things would change soon. I had to at least give him the opportunity to do the right thing. He was not Kevin. I had to keep repeating that to myself. I was not a princess locked away in a castle, waiting for a prince to come save me. I could come and go just like he did. I had to find better ways to occupy my time, maybe take another class, hang out with my girls more, find a hobby, something that wouldn't have me stressing about him.

"Babe, I got something for you," he said, gently placing me back on the bed and getting up to reach for the box. He set it in front of me with the most genuine smile on his face. He set the box down between my legs, and all I could do was smile. He was thinking about me even when I thought he wasn't. I needed to start giving him more credit.

I went to pick the box up to shake it, but it was a little heavy. I had no clue what it was, and my face showed it. First removing the bow, I gently took the lid off, and the cutest little puppy was asleep at the bottom of the box. I busted out in tears again as I reached in to grab it. I'd always wanted a teacup Yorkie. She was so precious. This was just what I needed, for right now at least.

"Chase, are you kidding me?" I asked as I held the dog to my chest. She had the cutest little pink-and-white bow on her head with a diamond-studded collar around her neck. It was love at first sight.

"I know this doesn't take the place of me being here," he explained as he took a seat next to us on the bed. "But I figured you might need some company until I get in."

His smile . . . I promise it got me every time. I pulled him in for a kiss, and I assured him that I would give us a chance.

We all cuddled in the bed together after he reminded me that he was taking me out shopping in the morning. I mentally added stopping at Monster Pets while we were out so that I could get some cute stuff for our new addition.

This man really loved me. He'd been proving it to me since the beginning. I had to learn to be more patient with him. We were going to be great together. We had to be.

Although this was a nice gesture on his part, I didn't forget about the panties and the earring. That shit almost slipped out with my emotional ass, but I pulled it back in. This very well could be nothing at all, but until I found out the truth, I was holding that ace in my back pocket.

Vice

Shade Comes In All Shades

"You have got to be fucking kidding me!"

When I received the picture text from Selah, I almost lost my mind. A pair of panties and an earring shaped like the letter S. Who the fuck else would that shit belong to besides Sajdah? This bitch was really playing on my sister-friend's face, and I was not about to just let this thing slide. It was time to put some shit into action because obviously, Sajdah didn't think she had anything to lose at this point. We could body both they asses in any order Selah saw fit.

I ain't gonna lie to you, though. When the text first came through, a bitch was nervous. I felt like I took all my shit the last time I was there, but you never knew. It only took a strand of eyelash hair to connect the damn dots. Low key, I was falling for Chase, and I felt horrible about it. I knew I couldn't have him, though, so I allowed that fact to keep me in check while I still enjoyed the benefits of a good dick down.

Chase made this shit too easy. He was the easiest target on the damn map, and I was shocked that Selah hadn't clued herself in to that fact before now. She was usually very specific about who she dealt with and always alert. I don't know how in hell we'd been getting away with fucking her man all this time, but I wasn't about to be the bitch to bring it to her attention. I just played my position like the queen that I was and played my part as her friend, like I always did. Never switch it up on a bitch. That was my story, and fuck whoever didn't believe it.

I texted Skye to gauge her reaction, and she was just as pissed as I was. When did Sajdah get so bold? I at least hid my shit well. I crept up on that nigga during the wee hours in the morning while he was out trapping. Once Selah moved in to the house, I made that my absolute last time going there. As far as she knew, I had no clue where that man resided, and I would act just as shocked once she invited us over to see her new digs. You had to wake up extra early in the morning to catch me with the bullshit. Now, before she moved in, I busted plenty of nuts on that same mattress she was sleeping on at night. I had my naked ass on the counter where she ate, and even busted it open in that gorgeous-ass shower they now shared, but I was content in the trap house for an hour or so. I was from the hood, so none of that shit bothered me in the least.

I texted back to ask her where she had found the stuff in the house. She just sent the pics, but no explanation as to the source besides that it was somewhere in the crib. I was fuming mad and ready to go to their mom's house to fuck shit up. Sajdah was about to fuck shit up for everybody. Little did she know, it wasn't just me and her floating through there. Luckily, I had more respect for her parents than that, but I was not above being petty. I had to get something solid, and I didn't have time to wait on Skye to figure shit out.

The next morning, I was up bright and early. I had to sleep on it for a second because that shit right there had to be perfect. I couldn't afford a mess-up because I didn't want to possibly fuck up our friendship over inaccurate accusations. I had to somehow get Selah to see her sister as the culprit. This could not fall on anyone else but her.

Yes, this would fuck her up royally, but better now than after marriage. I dreamt up the perfect plan, and now I was up to put it in action.

I didn't tell Skye because I knew she would try to talk me out of it. I had to take this one for the team, and if I were wrong, then I'd rather not have a bunch of people involved. If for no one else, I just had to be sure my ass didn't get caught in the crossfire.

I got to Selah's parents' house around 10 a.m. I remembered Selah saying that Sajdah was working on the Comcast account again, and from what I remembered the last time, she worked on Saturdays. Hopefully, that was the case, because I would definitely have to go in her room.

When I got to her parents' house, I pulled up behind her dad's car, not seeing Sajdah's anywhere in sight. Hopefully, that meant she was already gone for the day and didn't merely just park it in another location. Taking a deep breath, I hopped out the car before I changed my mind. It was mid-morning, so I knew her parents were up. I ran up to the door and rang the doorbell, hoping they wouldn't think it too crazy of me to just pop up. I really only came by when Selah was there and had no reason to any other time.

"Good morning, Mrs. Tracey." I spoke to Selah's mom as I leaned in to hug her. I loved their mom more than my own, and it killed me that I was at her house to do some shady shit for the sake of my friend. I was sure she would understand if she knew the story. For friendship, sometimes you had to go above and beyond to keep that shit together. I was willing to risk it all. That's what made me a different kind of friend than the rest.

"Vicerean! Hey, love. Long time no see! Come on in. What are you doing in my neck of the woods?"

Gosh, she was sweet as damn peach cobbler. Why couldn't she be a mean bitch? Then I wouldn't even give a damn about busting up in her crib like a damn private eye.

My shady ass maintained eye contact like a real goon because I was not about to pop up there looking all suspicious and shit. I couldn't have her going back and telling Selah she couldn't trust me for any reason.

"I had to pee so bad and couldn't make it home," I lied as I did an over reactive pee-pee dance. "Do you mind if I use your bathroom?"

"Sure! You know where it is," she replied as she turned to go back to the kitchen. "I just finished making brunch for David and I. Are you hungry?"

Lawd, why was this lady doing this to me? There was no way I could turn down brunch! Selah's momma knew how to whip them pots up just right. I had to have it. It would be deemed disrespectful if I didn't take the plate, and I was not about to disrespect my bestie's momma any more than I was about to by snooping around in her damn house.

"I can't stay, but I would definitely like a to-go plate," I responded as I made a dash toward the steps like I really couldn't hold it. "Good morning, Mr. Dave!" I yelled into the living room as I passed by, hoping that he wouldn't catch any guilt on my face. They were such nice people. Selah definitely got her kindness from them.

When I got to the top of the steps, I paused, trying to decide if I should go straight for Sajdah's room or should I just go to the restroom to try to figure it out. Deciding to just go into the restroom, I had to really sit on the toilet to gather my thoughts. I was shaking like a damn crack fiend who stole her man's pack. This shit was not going to end well. I was so nervous my damn bowels were loose, and I felt bad about having to take a shit in her bathroom.

I started to text Skye to tell her what was happening, but I knew that I had to hurry the hell up. Just as I was reaching for the toilet paper, I saw the fucking earring on the floor. It was the same damn earring that Selah sent us in the picture. Jack-motherfucking-pot! Her dumb ass probably thought she lost the fucking earing somewhere else and had no clue it was even at Chase's house. I really wished I knew where the stuff was when she found it so that I could connect the damn dots. If it was out in the open, it was definitely left by mistake. Sajdah wasn't that bold last time I checked. However, if she found that shit in a random closet or stuffed in a damn crack, Chase was trying to hide it from her. Either way, I had they ass, and it was about to go down!

I was screaming on the inside. What do I do? Do I take the earring? Do I leave it there and just take the picture? I was so confused. Why would Sajdah do this to her sister? Why would she put us in a position to have to get her ass?

I decided to do both, just to be on the safe side. I picked the earing up and set it on the sink so that I could get a pic of the entire bathroom sink area as proof that I was there. Selah would want stone-cold facts. I had to make sure I was on point.

After sticking the earing in my jacket pocket, I turned to wash my hands and found piece of evidence number two. The fucking bra that looked like it would match the panties in the picture was lying on top of the dirty clothes hamper in the corner. What kind of luck was I having today? This was too much even for me to handle all at once.

I almost starting shouting like I had the Holy Ghost when I saw this. Now, there was no way to even implicate me in this shit at all. Sajdah had no clue about me, but even if Chase tried to throw me under the bus, she wouldn't want to hear the shit. I was twerking like I was in an Uncle Luke video from the excitement. This was coming together better than expected, and I was suddenly glad I took the chance and went over there.

I snapped a pic of that, too, since taking the bra was out of the question, kind of. There was no way to get it out the house without a big enough bag. I thought to maybe put it on over my bra, but that was just too much work, and I was already taking forever in there. I was basically stealing out of Selah's momma's house, so I needed to keep it basic and easy to hide, opting to just roll with the picture I took.

By the time I got downstairs, Mr. David and Sajdah had joined Mrs. Tracey at the table for brunch. I had to keep myself from choking this bitch out in front of her parents. How dare she do her fucking sister this way, sibling rivalry to the side. How could you be so fucking vicious toward your own blood? I swear, family ain't shit, and Sajdah just made me even happier to not have real-life sisters. If family would do you like this, strangers most definitely could not be trusted as far as you could throw their ass. Oooooohhhh, I couldn't wait to get her! She was so fucking conniving, and I couldn't stand it. I briefly wondered if her mom would be mad if I banged her fucking head against the table just once, but I wasn't here for any drama. She had hers coming sooner than she thought.

She looked like she almost lost her lunch when she saw my face pop up in that doorway. She damn sure wasn't expecting me either, but since I saw her first, I had time to get over the initial shock without it showing on my face. This should serve as a warning that she never knew when or where I was going to pop up. I threw a knowing smile her way. I got that bitch, and I couldn't wait to let Skye know.

"You sure you don't want to sit and eat, sweetie?" Mrs. Tracey asked me again, getting up to fix my plate.

"I'm sure. I have some running to do this morning. Thanks for letting me use the facilities. I'm going to tear this up when I get in the car." I laughed, bringing a chuckle from everyone except for Sajdah.

I just hoped she was enjoying her time with her parents before all this shit hit the fan. She knew just like I did that her sister was crazy as fuck. She knew all too well the dangers of crossing Selah Gordon. This was not going to end well at all.

I accepted the plate and the plastic cup of Mr. David's famous peach iced tea. She walked me to the door, and I gave her another quick hug, thanking her again before leaving.

I saw Sajdah's car parked on the corner, and I wanted to jump out and key that shit, but she would definitely know it was me that did it, and that still wouldn't be enough get-back for how I needed her set up. I hated that bitch with so much passion. My body felt like it was on fire when I was around her. I literally felt like I was burning from the inside out.

I made a bee-line straight to Skye's house to show her what I had found. I was ready to gun that bitch down in cold blood if I needed to. I would take care of her for Selah, no questions asked. I sent Skye the pics from the bathroom and refused to answer her call or text until I got to her house. We were not about to talk about that shit over the phone. You never knew who was listening in nowadays, and plotting a murder on the phone was not how the hell I was going to get caught out this bitch. Skye, of all people, should have known better.

When I pulled up, Skye was already at the door, looking like she was ready to hurt someone. How were we going to tell Selah the news without her going off the deep end?

She loved Chase, but he didn't deserve her. He would not get to hurt her like Kevin did. Not on our watch, and never in this lifetime.

"First of all, bitch, what were you doing over there? How did you get these pics?" Skye questioned as soon as I pulled up to her house. I wasn't even out the car good before she started in on me.

I couldn't tell her the real truth. She would gun me down right on the spot. It hurt a little that I wasn't able to tell her that I did this to protect myself more than Sajdah because I, too, had been riding Chase's dick and digging in his pockets for a while now. I guess in hindsight, both Sajdah and I carried that same jealousy for Selah. She always got a boss dude that really looked out for her, until he did some corny shit to get his ass killed. For them to be twins, it was like she never had any trouble snagging some arm candy, but Sajdah always had a hard time for as long as I could remember. I got hooked up with some okay dudes, but none of them ever loved up on me the ways guys did Selah. It was sickening to watch, to be truthful, and low key I was always there, if for nothing else, to see the hurt before the disposal. They say some people are just born lucky, and she was proof.

"I drove over there and asked could I use the bathroom. Fucked around and got the damn bubble guts because I was so fucking nervous. I thought I was going to have to sneak into the room, but the shit was right there in the bathroom, waiting for me like it was meant for me to find it."

I recapped for Skye everything that happened, and she gagged when I told her that Sajdah actually showed up while I was there. She laughed when I told her I had the drop on her first, but I *been* had the drop on Sajdah. That's how I'd been able to stay on top of this shit and not get caught out there in the struggle.

I wondered briefly if she would notice the missing earring since she obviously knew where she left the other one, but even if she did, it wasn't like she would ask me for it. Trust me, even though she saw me, she did not want to believe in her heart that I was on to her ass like hot grits on skin. This entire scenario was a damn mess, and my heart broke for my friend.

I watched as Skye flipped the earring in her hand, studying it like something would change. We both wanted things to be different. Too bad it wouldn't be.

I had spurts of feeling bad about the part I played in this mess. I'd had threesomes with Chase, sat on his face, unprotected sex, the whole nine. The threesome was a damn accident, but he wasn't totally innocent.

I just happened to pop up down South Street one night and saw him down there, entertaining some chicken head outside of Ishkabibbles, this cheesesteak joint right across the street from the Theater of the Living Arts. Hands down, the best steak sandwiches in the southern area of Philadelphia. I played it cool, following behind him as they made their way to his car. I had no fucking clue where Selah was and what he was telling her to get away with this kind of shit, but I always caught his simple ass doing something. I stalked and followed him so much, you would think he would have recognized my car by now.

It was no surprise when we ended up at his house. I let him drive in as usual, and I pulled in right behind them. I turned my car off and waited for him to open his door before I ran up and ambushed both of them. The girl didn't seem fazed in the least, and neither did he. He invited us both in and offered us drinks as we eyeballed each other across the living room. At this point, I had cum on Chase's dick at least twenty times, so he knew I wasn't about to tell Selah a damn thing.

He sat in a chair midway between us both and pulled his dick out. It landed with a heavy but soft thud on his lap. Then he just sat back and continued to sip his drink like this shit was regular.

I began to salivate immediately. I knew what that thang could do, and it was no lie to be found that I wanted it every chance I got. Homegirl beat me to it, though, and took that shit all the way to the head without gagging. I knew I should have just left at that moment, but something in me wouldn't let this fool think he won. I kindly undressed and tipped my way over to them.

Taking his now-rock-hard dick out of her mouth, I straddled him with my back to him and stuffed him inside my box. Homegirl didn't miss a beat. She took her time sucking his balls and my clit, making sure to service us both. That shit got so damn intense in there as I swirled around on him and continued to ride as she ate my ass. This bitch was wild, and I wasn't mad about it.

I didn't know he we all ended up down on the floor, but she eventually made herself comfortable on his face as she showed special attention to my nipples. We all rocked and moaned on the same beat until an orgasm hit us in waves that left us all stretched out.

I got dressed without saying a word and had never spoken of it since. So, yeah, I was even more guilty than Sajdah, but I wasn't about to get caught up in the process.

"Let's think on this for the weekend. We need to be sensitive to the situation. We can't bombard her with this. We have to treat this delicately. I know her mom is planning a dinner for their dad. She was telling me about it when I saw her at work the other day. Maybe we could talk with her about it?"

"Bitch, no!" I objected immediately. Had Skye lost her damn mind? "If we have to off her fucking daughter, she can't know beforehand that we had something to do with it. We absolutely are not talking to Mrs. Tracey about this." I looked at her like she had three heads. Skye could be so airheaded at times. It was sickening. I swear I was the brains of the entire operation. This bitch was trying to get us all murdered.

"You're right. I'm buggin'," Skye agreed. "Let's just wait until Monday. We need to play this correctly, but she has to know as soon as possible. I'll keep the earring for now."

I gave Skye a quick hug and left so that I could process this shit. I was ready to take Chase out, but Sajdah would be a tough one. Selah adored her sister. This shit was going to break her fucking heart. We just needed her to know that we had her back regardless. Maybe no one had to die and we could just keep shit flowing the way it was. I, for one, damn sure wasn't going to spill any of this good tea. Everything I did and knew would go with me to the grave if Sajdah wasn't going to take the fall. Maybe this was just all a big misunderstanding.

By the time I got home, Skye had texted to tell me that she set up a lunch date with Selah for Tuesday. We were just going to put that shit on the table and let the chips fall where they may. However Selah wanted to rock out, that's what the hell it was going to be. Tuesday couldn't get there fast enough. This shit was exhausting me.

Skye

Now or Never

I dressed in all black like I was preparing for a funeral. I could not believe the shit that Vice brought to me had some weight behind it. Not that I didn't believe Vice with that blurry-ass picture from months ago, but a part of me was really hoping it just wasn't true. How could she do her own flesh and blood like that? There was too much available dick in the city for her to chase the same one her sister already staked claim to. Ugh, this shit had me on fire, but I knew I would have to maintain some sort of control once we broke the news to our friend. This was not going to be pretty, but it was necessary.

Even though I knew it wasn't, hopefully it was just a misunderstanding. All the clues were right in our face, and nothing like the half-ass info from that shit with Kevin a few years back. Vice had us do this man in, and it really wasn't that serious. I learned from that day on to make sure shit was rock solid before moving forward.

Kevin was just like any other man, a fucking whore, but I really did feel like he loved Selah and was just trying to break some shit off so that he could get right with her. He probably wasn't expecting their relationship to blossom that quickly, and once he realized she was the one, he had to tie up some loose ends to really make it official. Now, keep in mind, we were on the outside looking in, and all of these thoughts were in hindsight, but when shit looked strange to us, we jumped right in feet first.

I worked in the same building as Selah and Kevin, so it was hard for me to not see him on a consistent basis. He was a flirt. All the girls liked him, and it wasn't lost on me when I would see him sneaking to the back bathrooms with some random, then come out looking disheveled afterward. That was where all of us went to get our lunchtime ride in on the job and not get caught. You didn't say shit; I wouldn't say shit. Nobody did, because if one got caught, we all went down in the fire. It was an unspoken loyalty that us freaks kept to ourselves. With this type shit, one hand washes the other. We were not supposed to be having sex at work, but sometimes you couldn't wait until the end of the day to scratch that itch.

One day, a few weeks after he and Selah went to the DMX concert at the TLA, I saw him arguing with one of the chickens in the building while I was at the coffee cart. I couldn't really hear what they were saying, but I zoomed that good iPhone camera in all the way to get that nice up-close video that I needed for evidence. It looked like she was mad they couldn't fuck anymore, but who really knew. This happened consecutively for about two weeks, each time a different girl. Now, what wasn't about to happen was that knucklehead playing in my girl's face with those bitches. One day at the cart, that argument got real loud, and the chick threatened to let Selah know what was really going on.

Pause. There wouldn't be an ambush on my sister-friend. I kindly slid out of line and made my way to Selah's office to see if she could step out. The way the building was set up, you could see all the way to the ground floor from the balcony, and sure enough, we could see Kevin's simply stupid ass still arguing with the girl. Selah looked hurt, but she held it together as she went back to work, letting me know she would deal with him later.

I made the mistake of sending the video to Vice. Why the fuck did I do that? She went and hunted the damn girl down and tried to kill her.

That night was when I found out how crazy Selah really was. She had me meet her out at Bartram Village, where the girl, Shanna, lived. I didn't ask questions. I just showed up. By the time I got there, they already had this fool tied up in a fucking chair in her living room. This was nothing like my best friend, so I knew these chicks from the projects set it up. This entire thing was getting out of control quickly. I just wanted her to see what was going on. I didn't want her to hurt the damn boy. Break up with him, yes. Kill him? Hell the fuck no! No dick was worth time behind bars.

Everything was moving entirely too fast for me. Kevin was pleading with her to listen to him, Vice was yelling at her to fuck him up, and the other two girls were rooting her on. I tried to talk some sense into her, but she was too far gone. I didn't even know where the gun came from, because Selah definitely didn't own one. I'll just say this: they never found his body. That shit haunted me for months, and I still slightly regret it.

I hit Selah up with a text on Sunday afternoon, letting her know that I missed her and we should do lunch on Tuesday. We'd both been kind of missing in action with our new loves being the center of our attention, and last we spoke, Chase had gotten her the cutest puppy I'd ever seen and had taken her shopping to get things for her new room. A few of his friends had come to put the stuff together for her, and she sounded so excited as she put me on Face Time to show me her new space. She made plans to invite us over to see the house once she really got settled.

She was so happy, but it was all so fake. Unfortunately, I could not let her live a lie. I just wasn't that type of friend, and I always wanted what was best for her and Vice's crazy ass—which was why we had to handle this shit delicately. I did not want a repeat of the Kevin confusion. I just couldn't handle it again. Kevin didn't deserve to die, and I didn't think Chase did either. I just felt like Selah was not the one for him.

I was a fucking mess by the time Tuesday rolled around. I could barely concentrate at work, and all I really did was watch the clock until it was time to meet her outside. Vice was rarely on time, but she was sitting in the courtyard, waiting on me by the time I got down there ready to rock and roll. She'd been acting a little funny lately, too, but that was an issue I'd address at a later date. Nowadays, I really only had the mental capacity to deal with one drama at a time. We had just enough time to discuss and agree that I would present Selah with the evidence, and then we would just play it by ear.

"Laaaaadiiiiies," Selah sang out as she approached us. We both stood to embrace her, and I held onto her a little longer because I knew her life was about to change.

We all took a seat, but neither Vice nor I had an appetite. She was tearing her food up until she noticed we weren't eating.

"What's wrong with y'all bitches?"

Vice turned her head as I set the earring and the printed pics in front of her—the blurry pic of Chase's car at the chicken joint, the bathroom pics of the matching bra and earring lying on the floor, the pics of them downtown at the jewelry store, and basically all of the data that Vice had collected. The evidence that she needed to make a decision on how she was going to move forward. Her face said it all. She knew exactly what she was looking at.

"So, you mean to tell me that shit belonged to my sister?" It was barely a whisper, but we heard it loud and clear. The sound of heartbreak could be heard over any other noise in the world. It was a distinct sound that you would never forget.

I hurt so deep for my friend at this moment, but I wanted her to remain as calm as possible so that we could maintain rationale in this matter.

"I didn't want to believe it either, Selah. I'm sorry you had to find out this way," Vice offered as tears ran down her face. Mine followed shortly after, but Selah really held it together. That shit scared me the most.

"Let me text Cici and tell her I have to take an extended lunch break. I need to go home right quick to catch Chase before he leaves for the day."

"We're taking my car," Vice offered as she dug for her car keys and made her way over to her vehicle. I followed suit by calling my assistant to tell her to clear my calendar for the rest of the day. I couldn't allow these two firecrackers to go by themselves. The cops would be called for sure. I just hated that I had to do this in heels. We definitely didn't think this all the way through, and I briefly paused to try to gather us up. Emotions were too high right now.

"Selah, do you really want to talk to him now? Why don't we go after work so that you have a minute to simmer down? I don't want this to end up bad for you."

"It's already bad, Skye. Now is the perfect time to go," she said with a slight smile on her face. That's when I knew the crazy had kicked in.

I feared for my fucking life at that very moment. Vice went ahead and started the car and waited patiently for us to get in. This was probably our worst idea to date, but I had to ride with my girls and just pray that we all kept our heads this time.

Selah plugged her home address in the GPS. It was dead silent as we pulled out onto the road. I wondered what she was thinking. She probably didn't want to

believe it, the same way she didn't want to believe that
Kev shit when it first hit the street. This was supposed to
be her fairy tale. This was not supposed to be happening
right now.

When we got to her house, we saw Chase's car sitting
in the driveway. A small part of me was hoping he had
already left so that we had more time to process this shit,
but it was looking like we were going to face this demon
right the fuck now. A big part of me was hoping he just
got a ride today and didn't need his car. I was wishing
so bad for this man to not be home that I was starting to
hyperventilate.

Selah typed in her code on the keypad, and I swear it
sounded like we had sasquatch feet as we stepped inside.
That shit was gorgeous. This was both Vice's and my
first time there, and I could see why she was in love. We
weren't in there long before her little puppy rounded the
corner and greeted us at the door.

"Where's your daddy?" Selah questioned as she scooped
the dog from the floor and put her down in a gated area
just off the kitchen.

Everything appeared to be in place until we saw the
pair of shoes by the step. I thought they were Selah's and
was going to compliment her on them until I saw the look
on her face. They were not hers, and it was possible the
bitch was still in the house.

Selah turned and went into the living room, where
she slid a portrait to the side that revealed a safe. She
punched in a few numbers, and amongst several stacks of
money sat a nice shiny handgun. We were floored.

Why were we back on this damn road? He didn't have
to die. All we had to do was pack her stuff. I needed her to
see that as an option before she did something she would
regret later.

"Selah, let's think this through."

I tried to talk reason into her head before she did something stupid, but she didn't miss a beat as she reached in and loaded bullet after bullet into the chamber, afterward attaching a silencer. This bitch was definitely in her right state of mind. She knew if she had to shoot, she wouldn't want to alert the neighbors. Those county cops were bored and would be there in no time. Why didn't I just mind my damn business this time around?

"I'm thinking," she said with a smile. "I'm just going to check the upstairs." At that point, she had mentally checked out.

We followed her up the stairs slowly, and I prayed the entire time that the shoes belonged to a housekeeper or some shit. We were right on the bedroom door, just standing there. You could smell the sex in the hallway as it wrapped around us like a blanket. The sounds that were coming from under and through the door were undeniable. He was fucking Selah's sister.

It all happened in slow motion. She leaned in and turned the knob, opening the door slowly. We stood there for at least a minute before they realized we were present. She was enjoying the ride as he held a fistful of her hair. Both of their eyes were shut tight, and there was clearly no condom in sight. I couldn't un-see it if I wanted to. This shit broke my heart.

I wasn't sure what made Sajdah open her eyes, but the look on her face as the sounds coming from her mouth changed from pleasure to horror was unforgettable. She was trying to get off of him, and he gripped her waist to hold her down. He was damn sure about to cum, and once he opened his eyes and saw us standing there, he practically threw her off of him, his ejaculation shooting out on her back and down his legs as he tried to stand up on wobbly legs. This was horrible. I put my head in my hands for a quick second, and that's when I heard the shot.

Chase

Let Me Explain

It finally looked like I was getting somewhere with Selah. I felt horrible that I was constantly leaving her in the house. Even though I tried to take her with me on a few trips, it was hard to conduct business with wifey on my hip. She wasn't on board with this shit, and I wasn't about to drag her in it unwillingly, so, unfortunately, I had to leave her home most times. This chick I used to fuck back in the day, but was still cool with, suggested I get her a puppy.

"That bitch need something to keep her occupied," were her exact words. After she suggested the dog, I gave her the money immediately to go get it. I didn't necessarily like animals, but if this would get her off my top for a while, I was all the way in.

She brought the puppy back to me with the box and elastic bow, giving me directions on how to package her before going in. I hurried home after letting her suck my dick. She still gave the best head, and I just couldn't pass up on it. What could I say? It was the dog in me.

Selah was distraught when I got there, and I was almost certain that she was going to leave me. I was sick just thinking about it. I wasn't ready to let her go just yet. We somehow pulled it together, and I was somewhat re-lieved. Even though I knew I had shit to do, I put Demon on the block as I did the right thing and put my time in with my lady over the weekend. I even had Demon (who she knew as Clifford) and another guy that I trusted from the squad slide through and help me put together all the shit that had come and that we got while we were out. My baby was happy, and I knew then that I would do whatever it took to step away from the game and treat her the way she needed to be treated.

By Monday, I was back trapping, but I wasn't out as late, and I didn't attack her with sex as soon as I walked in. I couldn't help it. Selah was bad as shit, and she made my dick hard. The body on her was absolutely ridiculous, and it was hard to stay off of her. She was half naked ninety percent of the time. What did she expect me to do? The pussy . . . that ish was great— tight, extra juicy, tasted delicious, very accommodating, and amazing. She knew how to give the best head, and her ride game was always on point. I promise my goal was to try to get her pregnant every time we fucked, and I made sure to push extra deep when it came time to crack that nut. I was straight trying to trap her ass.

Why the fuck did I let her sister get in my head like that? In the beginning, I didn't know who the hell was who, to be totally transparent with you. They were identical down to the freckles on their faces. I thought I was going for Selah, but come to find out, Sajdah got caught up in the mix. The dudes in my camp told me that Selah was the one I wanted. She was a tough cookie to crack, but worth it in the end. So, when I snagged her so easily, I was surprised until I realized whom I was dealing with. I wasn't all the way mad, but sis was boring as fuck. All she talked about was work and these accounts she had, and at the end of it all, I really didn't give a fuck. I was about to trash her ass like the rest, but when she offered her sister, I knew I had hit the jackpot.

"She's not going to agree to both of us dating you at the same time, so I'll step down only under the condition that I can fuck you whenever I want. It's no way she gets to keep all that good dick to herself."

This conversation was happening while she had my dick throat deep. I had no choice but to agree. That scandalous-ass bitch. I agreed, thinking that I would only have to hit her off every so often, but come to find out, twin sister was greedy as fuck.

At first, I couldn't get Selah to take the bait. She was really playing hard to get, but I was determined to catch her ass and eventually push Sajdah all the way out.

When I finally caught her at the club that night, I knew that I had finally won. She was mine. Unfortunately, so was her sister. I just couldn't shake her stalking ass. I thought she might just fall back since she saw that her sister and I was going hard, but that seemed to make her go even harder to be a part of our lives low key.

I'll admit I used her in the beginning. I needed her to tell me how to get her sister. So, yes, she set up the coffee shit in the morning and was a part of all the big occasions that happened with us. She had to see our relationship developing right before her eyes. Why didn't she just fall back? This shit had me puzzled and feeling like my back was against the wall, and like any other animal that felt threatened, I had to strike out.

I tried to break it off with her, I promise. She just would not go away. And I'll just tell you, she was a fucking freak. Selah could get nasty, too, but Sajdah . . . that one right there would have you turned out if you were not careful. She took it in every hole and loved that shit deep. She could suck a nut clean out of you and have you back up and ready in no time.

I tried to pass her off to one of my boys, but she wasn't interested in any of them. She said she felt safer with

me and agreed that if things got serious with her sister
and I, she would fall back. That was a bold-face-ass lie.
Hell, she tried to pick out her fucking ring. All the damn
alarms were right in my face. How could I be so stupid?

I'll admit that on those nights when Selah couldn't
come through, Sajdah always came to save the day. We
had to develop a greeting because I didn't know who the
hell was showing up. That was how I ended up in that shit
that night.

Finally, Selah and I were making moves to move
forward. By the time she got home from work on Monday,
I had dinner and a hot bath ready for her. I washed
her body from head to toe and massaged her with the
wax from a soy candle that Sajdah had purchased from
this Don't Paniq line that she swore by. Some chick
from Philly named Samirah helped her daughter start
the business as she learned to help her get through a
childhood anxiety disorder. Apparently, her and Sajdah
were cool, and she only ever purchased candles from
her. I noticed that Selah liked the Sweet Kisses scent
when I burned it, so I always made sure to have some on
tap. The candles were all natural soy candles that, once
melted, doubled as massage oils.

It was a struggle not to slide up in her as she lay before me, glistening from the oil. Her plump ass was calling me, and when I cupped her ass cheeks and pulled
them apart, it took the strength of Job not to put my
thumb in her pussy and test the waters. When I spread
her legs to massage her thighs, I could see how wet she
was getting.

Flipping her over, I started at her toes and worked
my way up. Her nipples were like Hershey's kisses . . . a
perfect contrast to her light skin. At the moment, they
were hard like pebbles, and the stones on her nipple
rings bounced off the sliver of moonlight that crept in
around the shades. I wanted her to invite me in, wrap her

legs around me, and let me slide in so that I could feel her walls pulsate around me.

I didn't force the issue. I let her enjoy the moment as my thumb may or may not have accidently slid across her clit as I moved my hands up to her stomach. She sucked in air quickly, letting me know that I had touched a sensitive spot. I held on to control, rolling her nipples gently between my fingers before going to her shoulders. I was on brick, ya hear me? Like, I could bust a fucking door down with my dick. That's how hard it was. I felt like at any moment, I was going to just take that shit.

Just as I was starting to unravel, she took her hand and began to massage me through my sweatpants. I wanted her to pull the shit out and put it in her mouth, but I wanted her to know that she could trust me. She obliged with my wish in my head, leaning up to take me into her mouth. I held onto her hair as I leaned back on my knees, bringing her forward with me. Once she was back comfortable, I let her hair go and found her clit, dipping my thumb in periodically to stir the pot. She was about to make me cum, but I wanted to be inside of her. I had to keep reminding myself that I was trying to build trust by letting her be in control. I had to be patient with this one and let her take the lead.

I motioned for her to lay back and let me go. My nut was damn near at the top, so I had to work it back down before I crashed early. She threw her legs up in a wide V, inviting me in. I stepped out of my sweatpants and scooted up close to her, rubbing the head of my dick across her clit and up and down her slit until I heard a sopping sound. Baby girl was drenched, and I couldn't wait to drown in it.

I finally moved close enough to just put the head in. We were both pulsating like crazy as we tried to control our collective orgasms. My chest was so fucking tight. I eased in a little bit more, and her walls clenched and tightened around me, causing me to pull out and let the tip rest just at the opening.

"Put it back in," she begged as she tried to scoot herself onto me. "Chase, please."

I slid a little bit of it in as I still tried to maintain some control. Her moaning was driving me crazy, and I had to block her out before I popped quickly. By the time I got all of it in, she was holding onto me for dear life as she sang about her approaching orgasm in my ear. Her walls were extra slippery as she gripped me and let me go in quick pulses that were knocking me off my square and making it harder to hold my nut in. I was trying to think of anything I could that would distract me from what I was currently experiencing, but I was human at the end of the day, and I didn't think I would make it much longer.

She wrapped her body around me tight and held on as she grinded down, taking me all the way in. I could feel the juices from her pussy all over my balls because she was so wet. I had to let this nut go before I fucked around and had a damn heart attack. By the time we finally erupted, it took everything we had in us. We collapsed in a sweaty heap, instantly falling asleep afterward.

Drained was an understatement. She took my soul that night, and she knew it. All bets were off, and Sajdah had to go.

By the morning, when she woke up to go to work, I tried to get it one more time but didn't want to pressure her, as that was one of her complaints. I would definitely have to stroke one out after she left, though. She was looking damn good, even clothed, and I almost bent her over the counter and took her from the back. I had a weakness for a dime in a sundress and a cute shoe to match. I made her promise me round two later in the day before she left, and I was satisfied with that. She finally left, and I went and took advantage of the showerhead, wishing I could have her in there with me.

I ended up falling asleep, and when I woke up, Selah was at the end of the bed, completely naked. When my eyes finally adjusted, I saw that it was around noon. I had missed the entire morning. I didn't even have time to ask her what she was doing home. She had already pulled the covers off of me and had me in her mouth. I was just hype that she came back to give me some more. I didn't think that she hadn't actually come back and this woman sucking my dick at the moment was her sister.

She got me up into a nice stiff erection, climbing up afterward to straddle me, with her feet flat on the bed in a squatting position. I separated her pussy lips with one hand and stroked her clit with the pad of my thumb on the other hand, causing her to almost fall off.

"Keep your balance, babe," I encouraged her as she grinded down on me.

"What I tell you about calling me babe?" she asked as she spun around to put her back to me.

At that moment, I knew it was not the love of my life there, but her evil twin sister. I couldn't stop her if I wanted to. She was riding me backward while stroking my balls, and I was too busy trying to bust and get her out the damn house. Who told her to show her ass up there? I was scared to fucking death. How did she get in? I had deleted her code months ago. Selah wouldn't be home for a few more hours, but what if she smelled her sister's scent when she got in? How would I explain that shit?

Pulling her hair made her cum quicker, so I grabbed a fistful right at the scalp, and I used my other hand to hold her steady as I pounded into her hard as shit. Since she wanted to sneak the dick, I was going to leave her ass sore after this.

The sounds that were coming from us sounded crazy, like two wild beasts fighting for power. We were so into it that we didn't hear Selah come in. I was determined to knock the bottom out of her pussy and fuck it up for any man that came after me. She started to struggle to get off of me, and I thought she was just trying to control the situation, so I gripped her harder.

I chanced a peek at her body, and that was when I saw it. Selah, Vice, and Skye all at the door, watching me fuck her sister. Devastation had never felt like this before. The way this shit looked had to be the absolute fucking worst thing Selah had ever witnessed in her life. I fucked up this time, no doubt about it.

I threw her off of me as my nut exploded beyond my control and splattered everywhere. I jumped out of bed, embarrassed, not even believing that I got caught out there like that. I fucked up big time, and I had no idea how to come back from it.

I tried to say something, and the next thing I saw was the gun. Then everything went black. As I stood and watched my soul leave my body, my heart was broken. She would never know the truth. It would forever be her sister's story against mine. I just hoped she knew how much I really cared for her.

As that tunnel came into plain view and that light beckoned me, I walked toward it, knowing it was probably better that way. There was no living in this world if I had to live in it without her. I just hoped Sajdah got what she deserved.

Selah

#TeamChase

I killed him. Before he could react, I sent a bullet across the room and into his head. I didn't give him a chance to explain anything to me, because it didn't matter. There was no explaining me finding his dick inside of my sister. I took him out like I promised I would. I had so many questions now that he was gone, though. Why did he do this to me? How dare he leave me feeling like this—hurt, confused, angry, in disbelief, in shock, remorseful, regretful. That motherfucker played me, and so did she. That's why, out of all the emotions I had, I also felt relief. They asked for whatever happened to them. I just happened to be the person who was delivering the final blow.

Digging holes was pretty relaxing. It gave me a sense of calm that I wouldn't typically get any other way. It was my way of decompressing and allowing a situation to sink in. We had a body we needed to get rid of, so we had to dig a hole to put it in. We couldn't just leave it anywhere and risk it being found, right? That would be sloppy of us, and we definitely didn't operate like that.

We took turns digging two at a time until the hole was deep enough. I had questions about my sister, too. What the fuck was wrong with her? Why would she play me as well? Chase wasn't the only one that did me wrong, so don't think my beef was just with him. She was a snake, too. A part of me wanted to know their story. How did it happen? How did they hook up? Would it make a difference if I knew their truth?

"Dig a little deeper. I don't feel like sitting in jail because of this man's foolishness."

We dug in silence, me and my ride or die chicks since day one.

I sat and looked at my sister for a long time. She had tried to make a dash when the shot went off. Vice grabbed and floored her ass immediately. I wasn't even mad about it. I tried since we were kids to force them to get along, but unfortunately, Vice always showed more loyalty. I almost kicked her ass in the face my damn self, but I refrained. Since she was out cold, I grabbed a pair of my sweats and a T-shirt for them to dress her in.

While they worked on her, I walked over to examine Chase. There was a lot of blood and brain matter on the wall where the bullet exited from the back of his head, causing his head to explode, and he slid down upon falling back and making contact. A small amount of blood trickled down his face from the point of entry. His eyes were still open but void of any form of life. I reached over to close them. It was time for him to truly rest in peace.

"How are we getting them out?" Skye asked, shaking me from my own thoughts.

When I turned around, Sajdah was still out cold, but she was bound and gagged so that she couldn't move. I didn't even know I had duct tape available, but knowing Vice, she probably had that shit in her purse. She always came ready to rock in any situation.

"I have some industrial-sized trash bags in the kitchen. We can wrap him in that until we figure out what to do next. I'll back the car up into the garage so that the neighbors won't see us putting the bodies in. They can ride in the trunk together."

Walking away from Chase, we all sprang into action, getting him bagged up and trying our best to get the blood and gook off the wall. I remembered seeing a can of paint in the garage, so once we got him downstairs, I grabbed it to take upstairs. Vice had already gathered the stained comforter and sheets from the bed and had replaced it with fresh linen. She had also wiped down the end table and anything else that she thought might have blood on it. The floor was mopped, and everything had a place. The stain on the wall, though . . . that shit would haunt me longer than was allowed.

"Skye and I will come back tomorrow and throw a fresh coat of paint on this wall. You can't go home right now, though. You can stay with me until we figure out what to do next. You have to move like everything is regular. Turn his phone completely off, and we will wrap it with his body," Vice advised.

Vice, always ready to rock and roll.

I grabbed a few things for myself and gathered up the things I needed for my puppy, and we rolled out. Before we pulled off, I doubled back and emptied both of the safes. There wasn't any use in us all suffering. He was gone. I turned his cell phone completely off and tucked it inside of the plastic that he was wrapped in. That would be buried with him. Had to get rid of all of the evidence. Thankfully, I never contacted anyone on his team, so no one knew how to get in touch with me other than actually coming to find me physically.

For three days, his body sat in that trunk, parked in the projects like it was normal. The 46th Street high rises were accustomed to crime and strange shit happening, so no one would investigate. We parked that bitch like everything was regular and kept that shit moving.

Vice burned the entire bag that held the bloodied linen in the furnace in one of the buildings. One of the security guards had a thing for her, so he didn't question anything she was asking. She said she simply told him it was some shit she was just trying to get rid of. We thought about throwing Chase's body in there also but didn't want to get dude involved in a damn murder. Besides, I couldn't stand to burn him. He needed a proper burial under the circumstances.

Three days. We finally put him in the ground after three long-ass days, but we still had work to do. What was I going to do with Sajdah? She woke up a few times, and Vice gladly put her ass right back to sleep. This was the hardest decision I ever had to make. This was my sister. The same blood ran through our veins. We shared the same face. Could I really get through life without her? At the moment, I didn't think that I could. Unfortunately, it wasn't a guarantee that, if I let her live, she wouldn't dime me out. She couldn't be trusted. She had already proved that. I was not about to give her another chance to prove me right. I had to do what I had to do.

My girls didn't badger me to make a decision. They knew I needed time to process this shit. Sajdah had such a bright future ahead of her. Why would she go and mess this shit up for herself? Would this forever be a problem with us?

I decided to hear her out. That was the least I could do. So, once we returned Chase to the earth, we went back to have a conversation with my sister.

His aunt had no idea what was going on in her house. We hadn't so much as given Sajdah a drop of water in the last three days. I didn't give a damn what happened to her. She could die of thirst for all I cared.

By the second day, my mom had called to see if I had heard from her. Her job had called because she left early on Tuesday and hadn't been back to work since. No one had heard from her, and they were concerned. It wasn't like her to just disappear.

"No, Mommy, she's still not speaking to me. I'll try to giving her a call to see if she'll answer me. I haven't seen her since I left to move with Chase," I lied to my mom as I choked back tears. What was I supposed to do, tell her that I caught her fucking my man and now I was contemplating killing her? My mom would never forgive me, so I had to act like I didn't know a damn thing.

"Okay, honey. I'm just starting to get worried. Please let me know if you find out anything. I love you."

"I love you too, Mommy."

I broke out in tears as soon as I hung up. This shit was killing me, but unfortunately, I had to kill her.

Skye called one of her friends that owned a junkyard and had Sajdah's car removed from the employee parking lot and smashed in his yard after he dismantled it to sell the good parts. We discovered her car in the employee lot when we went back to work the next day, concluding that she must have taken an Uber or Lyft over to Chase's house so that no one could track her car there. She was one smart cookie. I'd definitely give her that.

When we got back into Chase's aunt's house, I could hear her in the basement, trying to yell for help. Unfortunately for her, no one would respond to that call in this neighborhood. They all knew it was better to mind their business.

When Skye and Vice sat her up in the chair, you could smell the aroma of her losing her bladder and bowels while we were gone. I stared at her as she cried. I had not one ounce of sympathy for her.

Skye removed the tape from her mouth and stepped back. She looked like she wished I would just kill her already.

"Selah, I'm so sorry. I'm so sorry! Please let me explain," she begged as she tried to adjust herself in the seat. It had to be uncomfortable for her, sitting in her own bodily waste, but honestly, that was the least of her worries.

"Why did you do it, Sissy? Why couldn't you just be happy for me?"

"Jealousy. You were always the popular one. I've always envied you. I just could never understand why people never chose me."

We sat in silence. I wasn't buying any of the bullshit, but I also wasn't expecting her to be so blunt about it. We'd never struggled for anything, especially not a man. We were damn near beating them back with a bat as we grew up. There was no excuse for her betrayal. Maybe she thought if she told me what I wanted to hear, I would spare her. I was beyond that point and really just wanted her to feel my pain.

"You could have had any man you wanted. Why mine?"

"He chose me first, Selah. I guess once he realized that I was more career driven, he decided to go with you."

"So, I was his second choice?" I asked in disbelief. Get the fuck outta here! There was no way I was choice two out of the two of us. She had to be lying.

"He chose me first, but once I made it clear that I wasn't an option, he went for the better choice. I told him everything he needed to know to win you. The coffee every morning, the random flowers, the chef-made dinners . . . all me. If you check my wallet, you will find his bank account information. I paid the bills. I did it all. Yet, he still chose you. He loved you, Selah. He—"

I jumped up and punched her right in the mouth, the action catching us both off guard. I had never laid hands on my sister, but she was not about to sit there and act like she was doing me a favor. I'd never needed help getting a man. She had me chopped and screwed if she thought that logic would save her.

"Selah, I love you. I'm sorry," she said as blood poured from her mouth.

I already knew what I had to do. There was no other choice. She had to go. I would just have to play the part until I couldn't anymore. I made a mental note to go back to Chase's house to grab her belongings from there, just in case someone saw her enter. I didn't want any obvious evidence of her ever being there. I could easily say the clothing was mine, but I just didn't feel like going through the motions.

"I'm sorry, too." Reaching into my bag, I pulled out the same weapon that I had used a few days ago to kill Chase. As painful as this was for me, there really wasn't any other option. I would help my parents get through this the best way that I could, but when someone betrayed my trust, they were disposed of—family included. I would miss my sister and would probably regret this decision for the rest of my life. No amount of prayer could pray this sin away. I'd just have to meet her in hell at a later date to discuss it.

Taking aim, I caught eye contact with my sister one last time. A tear dropped from my eye at the same time the bullet exited the weapon. We were at close range, so upon connection, her head exploded out the back more than we expected. Her body fell over in the chair almost in slow motion, and whatever she had left in her bowels seeped out and covered her.

I wiped my tears and sprang into action as we cleaned up the mess and stuffed her into the same typed of industrial bags that we used to dispose of Chase. Skye decided that it would probably just be best to drop her into the same hole we dug for Chase since the dirt was still soft. I agreed. Knowing the two people I loved the most in this world would get a chance to rot together made me feel a little better.

As Vice poured the last of the bleach onto the bag and secured it shut with tape, I broke down again. Our mother didn't deserve this. What did I do?

We put Sajdah's body in the trunk and parked her in the 46th Street high rise, the same as we did Chase until it was time to move. I stayed another night with Vice, and in the morning, we swung past the condo to do a last-minute cleanup. The three of us painted the wall in the bedroom, and it looked like nothing had ever occurred there.

I took the time to gather all of my things and the outfit that Sadjah had left there when we busted in on them. As I inspected her purse, I found the info for the bank, just as she said I would. Her phone had already died, so I took a hammer and smashed it into a million pieces, planning to put it in the ground with her when we buried her.

Skye took my clothing to her house until later, and I went to the bank to check into this account situation using my sister's ID, of course, since the bank info was in both of their names.

Listen, I was not prepared for what the bank teller was about to reveal. This man had damn near twenty million dollars in his account! Drug money! Like, where they do that at? I sat with the banker to close the account, having them put the money in my real name so that I could cash the check. I gave them some story about the money being a gift that I had been planning to give to my loving sister after she graduated. They ate that shit up at the bank. Because I banked there as well, they were able to deposit the check in my account for free. Sadjah had major bank in her account as well, but I left that there for my parents to handle upon them learning of her demise.

I got to work a little bit later than expected, and when I arrived, everyone looked so sad. I had no idea what was going on until Cici pulled me to the side to talk to me.

"Have you seen the news?" Cici asked in a hushed tone as we walked toward the break room.

"No. I woke up late this morning, so I was rushing. What happened?"

Just as we tuned in, I saw on the news a million cops surrounding the car that we had Sajdah's body hidden in. I was instantly sick to my stomach. The trunk was open, and you could clearly see what looked like a body wrapped in a trash bag on the inside. I played it cool as I listened to the story to hear any names.

"Your mom has been calling here all morning, and they say it's your sister. The security guard was doing his rounds and found a child asleep in the car. When he went to get the child out, he popped the trunk to see what else was in the car and discovered the body. This shit is—"

I totally started to freak out as I ran out of the room to grab my phone out of my purse. I had so many missed calls from my mom, Vice, and Skye. I was sick and having a hard time keeping my breakfast down.

"Mom, what happened?" I asked as I gathered my stuff up to leave. I could hear my boss telling me to leave, but I just waved her off as I ran out of the building. I was shaking like crazy. What if they found out we did it?

I stayed on the phone with my mom the entire time, texting the girls to tell them to meet me at my parents' house. This was definitely not the fucking plan. What if we got caught this time?

When I pulled up to the house finally, I jumped out of the car and ran right into my parents' arms. My mom was a mess, and my dad wasn't much better. They were so hurt and confused. Who would want to hurt their daughter?

I avoided eye contact because the guilt was eating me alive. We were able to get my mom laid down after a while, and Vice and Skye stayed home with her as my dad and I went down to identify the body.

I felt like my heart was going to jump out of my damn chest. I didn't know what we were going to see when we got there. I had seen plenty of dead bodies, but it was different when it was your flesh and blood lying on the table.

When we got to the morgue and they led us to the room, all I could smell was a strong amount of bleach with underlying feces. As we got closer, I had to lean into my dad to keep from fainting. Her body was so bloated. She didn't even look like herself. The things that made us the same were absent from her features. This would definitely be a closed casket. The bleach had already started eating at her skin and forming holes. Her eyes were bulging out from her face.

I felt myself about to vomit, so I ran out of the room, all dramatic. Of course my dad thought it was because of my sister's fate, but he didn't know I was the reason why she was there. All of this was a damn mess.

When we got back home, my mom was asleep, and my friends were waiting for me. My dad thanked them for staying with my mom, and he made his way upstairs to go be with her. There was a heaviness in the house that was so suffocating. I knew I had to lay down and get comfortable in it, though, since it was my fault.

"There's nothing to worry about." Vice spoke to me barely above a whisper. "The car that she was found in was just a junk car from my friend's lot. No names are attached to it. I made sure everything was bleached. We're good."

That was good news to hear. At least we wouldn't have to worry about the law coming for us, causing my parents more pain.

They got up to get ready to leave, hugging me so tight. Thank God I had them. I locked the door and went up to peek in on my parents. They were both asleep, so I went into my old room to try to get myself together.

While I lay there, staring at the ceiling, I questioned what kind of person I really was. There was no doubt the karma that would come from this would set me back into the ice ages.

It would be weird without my sister there. I got up and went into her room, just taking in her space. I fingered the perfume bottles she had on her dresser and thumbed through the textbooks she had left on her bed. My womb-mate was gone. That shit was unbelievable.

I went back to my bed and checked my phone again, seeing a text from an unknown number.

I know what you did. I'll get you when the time is right.

That shit sent a chill through my spine. I didn't even bother to respond. That was clearly one of Chase's men. When drug dealers of that caliber die, you don't report that shit; you pick up the pieces and keep it moving. They probably were wondering why they hadn't heard from him in a few days, and when they went to his house to check and saw all my shit gone, it was obvious what had transpired.

A part of me wanted to die. What did I have left to live for? The other part of me knew I wasn't going out without a fight. So, here's to life looking over my damn back.

Epilogue

Sajdah's memorial was beautiful. We used the photo from her graduation as the centerpiece. She was cremated due to the condition of her body. The wails of sorrow that poured out of my mother were like the sharpest knives in the world stabbing me all over my body. I accepted this as my punishment and didn't complain. I deserved all of this.

After the service, I took her urn and held my mom's hand as we walked out. We were having a little something at the house for family and friends, and then we would begin to try to start living again.

A news reporter had come to talk to us about the gruesome murder, and I could barely hold it together as I wore a T-shirt with my sister's graduation pic on it and a baseball cap that read #ForeverSajdah across the front. I performed as the news camera followed me around the neighborhood, videotaping me stapling reward posters on telephone poles for the person that found my sister's killer. We were offering $20K for the tips that led to the person. The money came from my account.

My mother handled the closing of Sajdah's accounts, depositing damn near a million dollars into a family account. My mom had us both insured, so her policy was more than enough to cover her wake and to pay off any expenses that Sajdah had, leaving a nice chunk of money left over.

So many people came out to show my sister love. I was shocked at the number of people that came through. She was well loved at her job and had even more friends than I even knew about. My sister was definitely loved.

By this time, I had gotten all of my belongings and my puppy from Skye and Vice's house and had officially moved back in with my mom and dad. I doubled back to Chase's to remove all data from the security system, just in case the law got the bright idea to check there. I was never leaving again. It would take a special kind of man to get me to open back up again.

I didn't tell Skye and Vice about the mysterious text that I received. I just deleted it. It was easier that way.

Pretty soon, I started to fall back into a routine. I went to work, went back to school, came home, repeat. I didn't give anyone more than what was required, and even hanging out with my girls was few and far between. They came to check on me and my parents but understood my plight. I cut them both checks for a hundred thousand each. With the amount of money I had at hand, I didn't have to work, but I needed to keep myself occupied.

A few months had gone by, and the nightmares were slowly backing off. I got up to take a shower so that I could be ready for the morning. I had been speaking with some bankers about opening a boutique, and we were set to meet in the morning.

After moisturizing my body, I threw on some night clothes and lay in the bed. I turned the light out and lay in the dark, willing sleep to come sooner than later. Just as I was dozing off, my phone vibrated against my pillow.

When I looked at the screen, the message was from Chase's number, and it simply read: tick tock. I was shook. Didn't we bury Chase's phone with him? Someone was playing a cruel trick. What could I do?

I texted Vice and Skye to let them know we had to meet up tomorrow. Apparently, someone was coming for us, and we needed to be prepared.

Vice

When Play Time is Over

I must say, I didn't think she was going to kill his ass. Better him than me. While digging that damn hole, so many things ran through my mind. Truth be told, I was a fucking slime ball. I should have just stayed in my damn lane. I was even more of a slime ball once I found out how much money this bitch came up on. Twenty million fucking dollars? Oh, she hit that good lick, and although she broke us all off properly, I felt like we should have gotten more. I mean, the $100K was a nice gesture, but the bitch could have given me a smooth million. She wasn't the only one that didn't want to work anymore.

There was a small sense of relief once we put him in the hole. That solidified that he wasn't coming back, but I made sure to grab that phone out of the plastic while Skye was busy pulling Selah out of the grave. I wasn't sure at the moment what I was going to use the phone for, and imagine my surprise when I found out it was still on after all those months.

I sent the text really quick, then turned it back off. That Find My iPhone tracer was real, and it was no doubt in my mind that people were still looking for him. His parents came to Philly once to talk to Selah, and we never saw them again. I had no clue what even came from that conversation, and I didn't ask. It wasn't my business.

Needless to say, I blew through that money like it was $5 in food stamps. Ya girl was living high on the hog, even though both Skye and Selah kept telling me to invest the money somehow. A part of me felt like she may have even given Skye more than she gave me. All I knew was they both slowly started to fall off, and we didn't hang as much as we used to. Selah was busy with depression, and Skye had managed to get herself engaged and pregnant by her boyfriend. That basically left me out there on the ho stroll alone, and I was not happy about it.

When I approached Selah about my funding situation, she basically brushed me off. This bitch was sitting on millions. Surely she could afford to bless me one more time. After all I did for her, she owed me. She, on the other hand, felt differently about it. All she wanted to talk about was investments and business. I was just trying to grab a new bag and ball out at King of Prussia Mall. This entire thing was getting to be too much.

So, I sent the text, just to see if I would get a reaction. I turned Chase's phone off right away, so I wasn't sure if she texted the number back, but I knew for sure she was spooked out when she sent the group text to me and Skye, saying we needed to talk.

I hated to extort my dear friend. At one point, I loved her like a sister. Unfortunately, recent circumstances changed that for us, and I had to do what I had to do.

Let the games begin. . . .

The End . . . kind of . . .

For Discussion

1. Who was your least favorite character and why?
2. Which character did you like the most?
3. Is Vice and Skye's friendship a true example of how real friendships are in our current climate?
4. Do you feel that Chase's feelings toward Selah were genuine?
5. What were your thoughts upon reading the opening chapter?
6. Do you think Selah killed Chase on purpose? Or was she just caught up in the moment?
7. How do you feel about Vice now that you know her part in the double cross, versus how you felt about her in the beginning?
8. From past movies like New Jack City, Dead Presidents, and other hood tales, oftentimes, when a dealer messed up money and had to die, they took the entire family out. This proved true in some real life situations as well. Do you think Chase overreacted in the scene where he killed OG and his family?
9. Chase's life was set up for him to work in the family business. He never knew what struggle felt like, unlike his roommate, who came from the environment he pretended he knew about. Why do you feel he chose the drug dealer life as opposed to stepping into a safer lifestyle that he didn't have to work for?

10. Why do you think Vice flipped the way she did on Selah? Was she just as guilty, or guiltier than Chase in this situation?

11. Who do you think was more of a friend to Selah overall? Skye, Vice, or Sajdah?

12. If you were in Selah's shoes, would you have killed your sister? Did Sajdah deserve to die? Did Selah overreact?

13. Put yourself in Sajdah's shoes. As Selah's twin, what could she have done differently to save her own life? Did she even have the option to negotiate?

14. Do you think Sadjah fell in love with Chase at some point? Or did she just not want her sister to be happy with him?

15. Jealousy is a sickness that can ruin just about any type of relationship, and clearly, Sadjah was jealous of her sister. Is this considered "normal" behavior for siblings?

16. Come to find out Vice wasn't as good of a friend as we thought she was. What should her punishment be for betraying Selah the way she did?

17. The story ended with Selah getting a text from Chase's phone, which she thought for sure was buried with him. Who do you think she thinks has the phone?

18. Now that her twin sister is dead, how do you think Selah should move forward?

A Sneak Peek . . .

The Double Cross 2

Selah

And Then There Were Two

Friends . . . how many of us have them? Such a simple question that should be easy to answer but has so many stipulations that you have to really think about that shit for a while before you're confident you answered it correctly. I'm talking about true friendship, ten-toes-to-the-ground, standing-side-by-side, we-in-this-together friendship. The ones you never have to have doubts about because you know where their loyalty lies, and it ain't a lie. They have your best interests at heart over their own every single time. The ones that you can have around your man and not think sly thoughts because they wouldn't dare cross that line. The ones you have around your parents and they feel at home because your home is their home and vice versa. Your girls. You tell them all your bullshit, and they never judge you because they did shit just as fucked up, or worse. Your secret keepers. Your friends.

Well, let me tell you about friendship. You have to be careful with that shit. You have to make sure that the same level of friendship that's in your head is the same in the other person or people's head too. Make sure that shit is consistent across the board. You'll be out here talking that best friend crap, ready to pull the trigger and do time in the clink for they ass, and low key they don't even fuck with you like that. The same bitch you riding for will sell you out like $50 for $100 on an EBT card with her food-stamp ass. What's even crazier is everybody knows this but you. This is your best fucking friend. The one you give your last to. The one you stop all conversation about because can't nobody tell you no bad shit about your main bitch. The one that does you the dirtiest. The one that you least suspect.

You'll come to find out that the same one you stand for is the same one you'll eventually have to dig a hole for. When you stay ready, much doesn't surprise you. However, it will still hurt like hell, and that's when you have to think rationally. Sometimes, without a shadow of a doubt, you have to put them down first, or they will come get you for sure. Know it, own it, claim it, and act appropriately when the time comes. Now is not the time to hesitate. Shoot that bitch dead in the head and deal with the body later. And for the record, staying ready is a learned behavior that's in direct correlation with distrust. These hoes ain't loyal, period.

"Dig just a little deeper. I gotta be sure this ho doesn't pop back up on us. We don't need a repeat of what happened before," I said to my girl Skye as we dug a fresh grave not too far from where we put Chase in the ground just a year before. It took everything in me not to dig his dumb ass up and shoot him again. You would think it got easier, but each time was harder than the last. You learn a lot about a person once they're gone, but you have to decipher through the bullshit to find the truth. Everybody always want to tell you what someone said about you when they mad, but you can miss me with the bullshit. If you didn't feel inclined to clue me in on the spot, don't try to backtrack that shit months later. You just as shady as the bitch that started the conversation.

Chase hit me close to the heart, but this one hit dead center like a bullseye. I never thought the day would come that I'd have to put down one of my own again, but it just goes to show that trust is earned, and even when you think you can trust them, you can't. I hate that the people I loved the most kept proving me wrong.

We dug in silence a little more, and then I boosted Skye out of the hole first, her reaching down afterward to pull me up. The first thing I did was make sure both phones that needed to be discarded were in the hole first. Not that I didn't trust Skye, but I just needed to make sure for my own sanity this time that Chase's phone was gone. This time, I had to make sure Vice's phone was gone too. Jealousy will have you doing some crazy shit, and I had to protect myself at all costs by every means necessary.

We popped the hood on the trunk and dragged her body out with a hard thud as it hit the ground. She definitely wasn't handled with care like Chase was, as I carelessly scraped her body across the concrete. I almost wanted to stomp on her ass again before throwing her in the dirt, but I resisted. Her being dead was far worse than anything else I could do to her now.

I started to hide her ass in the basement in Tasker Homes and let the rats eat her corpse, but the residents didn't deserve that kind of torture from having to smell a dead body for weeks on end. They weren't the type to snitch over there, so she would have just sat until there was nothing but bones left. It wasn't their fault she was a snake-ass bitch.

When we got her to the opening, we rolled her in head first, not caring how she landed at the bottom, her body hitting with a hard thud that echoed a little in the quiet of the night. Immediately, we began filling the hole again, each pile of dirt hitting harder than the last. No words of solitude. No prayers for forgiveness or a peaceful rest. No remorse. I got her before she got me. That's the way the game was played.

Once we were satisfied with the filling of the hole, I knew the hole she had placed in my heart wouldn't last long. I hated to have to do this to her, but she begged me for it. Skye knew it too. Shit, we were the last of the Mohicans. The only difference between her and Chase was no one would look for her for long. They would inquire, but she'd be a distant memory in no time.

Taking the broom we brought along with us, I evened out the leftover earth as best as I could in the dark, being sure to sweep away our boot prints as we backed our way up out of the yard and to the car, same as we'd done before. It felt almost routine at this point.

Heading to the projects to drop our dirt in the furnace was next on the list as we undressed and bagged everything up before getting into Skye's vehicle. Vice's truck had been smashed days ago at the scrap yard on Essington Avenue after it was stripped of useful pieces that could be sold for cash. I wanted to be sure that it was truly the end of that bitch's reign and she would never be heard of again.